Kitty's War

ALSO BY EIMEAR LAWLOR

Dublin's Girl

EIMEAR LAWLOR

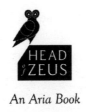

An Aria Book

First published in the UK in 2024 by Head of Zeus,
part of Bloomsbury Publishing Plc

9 7 5 3 1 2 4 6 8

A catalogue record for this book is available from the British Library.

ISBN (XTPB): 9781803284514
ISBN (E): 9781800249318

Cover design: Head of Zeus

Typeset by Siliconchips Services Ltd UK

Printed and bound in Great Britain by
CPI Group (UK) Ltd, Croydon CR0 4YY

Head of Zeus Ltd
First Floor East
5–8 Hardwick Street
London EC1R 4RG

WWW.HEADOFZEUS.COM

For Ciara

1998–2016

In 2016, our beautiful daughter Ciara took her
final breath to fly with the angels at the Kodaline concert
in Dublin. We are so grateful to the band, for penning
the song 'Angel' for her, and immortalising her memory
in music.

On a Wednesday morning in July
We dried our tears and we said goodbye
Another angel gone before her time
But she's still alive in our hearts and minds

Prologue

19 February 1939

Éamon de Valera, the Taoiseach of Ireland, stood in the studio of 2RN, Ireland's radio station. He stooped down slightly towards the microphone, positioned more suitably for a man smaller than his six foot two inches. His grey eyes travelled to the light bulb on the wall, his cue to deliver the news that the nation had been waiting to hear. When it lit up, he leaned into the microphone, glancing briefly at his pencil-written notes.

'I am speaking to you tonight without any manuscript, so I must speak to you only from notes.'

An equally tall man stood at the door, holding his breath, running the words over in his head. He had heard them at the cabinet meeting the previous week in Dáil Éireann.

The Taoiseach continued. 'You know from the news bulletins that the great European powers are again at war. A short time ago in Munich, there was hope, but that hope is gone, and it will again plunge the people of Europe into the misery and anguish of war.'

He pushed his round metal glasses up his thin nose, glanced one more time at his notes, and cleared his throat.

'You, the people of Ireland, have been listening and reading about the threat of war in Europe, and noting this, the Irish government decided the policy early last week and now I announce to you, and the world, that Ireland has resolved the aim of our neutral policy is to keep our people out of the war.'

The man at the door closed his eyes, imagining the collective sigh of relief around the island of Ireland.

'With our history and our recent experience of the last war and with a part of our country unjustly severed from us, we felt that no other decision and no other policy was possible.'

De Valera brushed the sweat off his palms on his jacket as he put the notes in his breast pocket. His impassive expression didn't betray him. He may have been unsure if he had done the right thing.

The light on the wall buzzed a little before it went off, and the room was silent. The two men looked at each other.

'You've made the right decision, sir,' said Frank Aiken, minister for defence. 'We're just shy of twenty years since the Civil War, and families are still torn apart.'

The Civil War began in 1922 and lasted less than a year, but it had divided men who had fought together in the War of Independence the previous two years. Men had been torn apart by the government's decision to leave six counties in the north of Ireland with the British Empire. It was, some believed, the price Ireland had to pay to gain independence.

'I know the British will regret relinquishing our seaports back to us in the last act of independence. They will see that giving them back to us only last year was a mistake, especially as they were on the brink of war. Those three ports are invaluable in their strategic importance on the Atlantic coast and as a gateway to Europe. But, Frank,' his brow furrowed then relaxed, 'they may keep Germany and Britain from invading us and bringing us into war.'

Frank tapped his foot on the floor, leaned into the table and stubbed his cigarette into the ashtray. 'Dev, we'll have to stop those IRA lads from thinking they can do a deal with Germany to help them invade the North for a united Ireland. We still have to comply with Britain.'

Ireland was still a member of the Commonwealth; it was still a dominion of the British Empire, making it answerable to that empire.

De Valera hoped this would be enough to keep Germany from Irish shores.

I

January 1941

Two years had passed since the announcement in February 1939 that Ireland would be staying out of the war, and the events on that day changed my life. The train shuddered to an unexpected halt, I sat very still, hoping like the other passengers that the Germans would drop their bombs elsewhere and we would arrive intact at the port of Fishguard in Wales. The carriage filled with the shuffle of stretching arms and legs and the murmur of weary sighs.

Within minutes, the train shuddered back into motion, resuming its journey. The compartment quietened as the steady cadence of the wheels on the tracks lulled us into serenity, much like a lullaby settling restless minds.

I inched the blackout curtain aside. My breath spread across the icy glass, and I wiped it clean with my glove. A translucent winter sun rose as the waning moon descended, the first strains of daylight streaking across the dark, grey sky, meeting the fields that I guessed fell away into the valleys of Wales.

I had only been in London two months when Chamberlain had declared war, and though many Irish men and women had clambered aboard trains to Liverpool, then Fishguard for the steamer home to Ireland, I had stayed. But at the beginning of 1941, I left too.

'Do you think we're near Fishguard?' whispered a woman sitting opposite me. She was barely in her early twenties, not much younger than me. In the dim lighting, I could see the shadows of tiredness and fear etched on her face, her blue eyes bloodshot. She held a pink blanket tight to her chest. It moved and whimpered, and the woman rocked the baby gently, softly singing 'Silent Night'.

I closed my eyes, lost for a moment in the song, remembering the Christmas mornings of years past, sitting in my kitchen, the candlelight flickering on the wall. But my mother was not soothing me with words, she was quieting me with her fists.

Pushing the memory away like an unwanted guest, I looked down beside me to see three pairs of blue eyes staring at me, three boys hardly out of nappies. They sat beside the woman, wedged together, arms and legs entwined so they wouldn't fall onto the floor.

One of them tugged my elbow and whispered, 'Are there going to be any bombs?'

'I hope not,' I said.

Satisfied with my answer, he put his arm back around one of the others.

'I'm Olivia,' the woman said, offering me a hand as delicate as her voice.

I smiled politely. 'And these little ones?' I asked.

'Oh, these are my sister's boys,' she replied, ruffling the curly red hair of the one nearest her and leaning closer to me. 'Their daddy has gone to war, and their mammy is afraid of the bombs. She said she would work until Easter and follow me back home to Ireland.'

She pulled part of the blanket back to reveal the top of the baby's head. 'And this is Róisín. She came a bit early.'

Olivia adjusted the bundle in her arms, the pink blanket rustling as the baby stirred. Her eyes, widened and alert, were fixed on me, her lips parted as if preparing to catch whatever words I might release.

'I'm heading back to Kilkenny,' I muttered, my voice tinged with fatigue. 'My mother's passed.'

There was a soft intake of breath, and Olivia's hand flew to cover her lips. 'Oh, God love you,' she said, a hushed tone of empathy colouring her words. 'I didn't mean to upset you. Sorry, I know how you must be in pain.'

'It's no trouble, and thanks, it's not painful.' I said softly, my eyes downcast, my fists clenched in my lap, remembering the pain of the deafening silence when my baby was born. The child I had carried for nine months, loved and yearned to meet, had been torn from my arms by the nuns before it could draw its first breath. I turned away from Olivia to hide my tears, I never even saw my child's face.

'Impure women bear impure infants,' the nun had said as I screamed for my child.

And like a burst dam, memories of the home for unwed mothers gushed forth, bringing with them my mother's letter in her native German. That language sent shivers down my spine. The last time I had encountered it was in her vitriolic letter, accusing me of being responsible for my father's death. It was as if her pen had jabbed into my gut, precipitating my early labour.

The German language lingered in my mind as a grim memento of the sorrow and anguish that had been inflicted. I had vowed then to keep those memories caged, as trapped as I'd felt hearing my father's screams from the burning barn back in 1927.

The tension radiated white beneath the blue veins in my knuckles, as I thought about the confrontation with my past that would come once I reached home – how, like from Pandora's box, all the demons would escape.

A long sigh escaped my lips. I opened my handbag and took out James's letter. A part of me wished I had never read it. I hoped the girls in the Underground taking shelter from the bombs were wrong. The whispers of the runaway girls in the Underground lingered in my mind, stories of nuns sending the guards to their family homes after they escaped the clutches of the mother and baby homes. I had dismissively brushed off these stories as nonsense.

Yet what if they were true? Did they still want the hundred pounds for a dead baby?

I held on to a thin shred of hope that they wouldn't expect payment for my baby, who'd never taken a breath. Surely, they would have some decency. With a heavy heart, I turned away from the memory and looked out of the train window, the landscape a blur of passing fields and trees.

I could not avoid the inevitable. I reread the envelope, 'Passed by Censor EXAMINER 3810' stamped in red ink, beside the two penny stamp. James helped on our farm and was a friend to me and Anthony.

January 1941

Kitty,
Your mother has died. The funeral was on 28th December.
But you have to come. Anthony is seriously unwell.
James

I shoved the letter back to the bottom of my bag, the word 'mother' burning me. I wished I could have ignored it, but my brother was unwell. Anthony had been only seven when Daddy died and had caught bronchitis shortly afterwards. When he should have been in bed, Mammy had forced him to help James on the farm.

'Mrs Flinn, he should be in the fever hospital!' James had said to her.

She had snapped at him. 'You shouldn't be pampering him – time he was out earning his keep.'

I was Anthony's only family now, but James had thought of us as his children. And in a way, he had been more than family to us both. He was the only person who never bowed to our mother's delirious ways, protecting us in any way he could, and like a shining light in a dark storm, he would come into the kitchen when she went into one of her rages, calming her, promising to take us to his cottage.

The smallest boy shifted on the seat, and one of his brothers fell onto the carriage floor and started to wail, bringing my thoughts back to the present.

'Would you hold Róisín for me?' Olivia handed me the pink blanket before I could reply and picked up the boy, checking him for bruises. She was flushed from the extra burden of minding her sisters' boys.

Hesitantly, I took the baby and stared down at her, unable to blink or breathe. She had a thin, wispy tuft of ash-blonde hair tied in a pink ribbon. Her almond eyes brimmed with tears. Her mouth puckered, then her lips opened, ready to wail.

Olivia tucked the boy in with his brothers, cleaning his nose with a hanky.

I handed Róisín back. 'I think she's hungry.'

'Thank you,' she said, cradling Róisín in the nook of her elbow. She deftly loosened her blouse and put Róisín's head inside, the baby searching in the darkness for the warm breast. After a few seconds, she stopped whimpering.

I shivered. It wasn't that an act so natural repulsed me; it was just so intimate, so raw, so real. Looking out of the window, I clasped my fists tight, my nails sticking into my palms. Sometimes physical pain could squash the memories in my heart.

'Don't you just love the smell of babies?' Olivia's words were muffled as she nuzzled her daughter's neck. 'I hope one day she will have a brother or sister. Do you have siblings?'

'It was only me and my older brother,' I said. 'We're eleven months apart.'

'Irish twins!' Olivia said.

The carriage started to wake. The passengers stood, only too eager to get on board the steamer after a long, uncomfortable journey. A boy and a girl sat in the aisle, flicking cards, each hoping to outwit the other. 'Snap!' the boy said, and gathered up the cards.

I flicked specks of dust from the tips of my blue gloves. They matched my coat.

Olivia blessed herself. 'I prayed there would be no bombs

on the line. Thanks be to God, we're going home to a good Catholic country.'

'I hope you're right,' I said, not wanting to dispel her innocent belief that prayers would stop the Germans from dropping a bomb on our train.

'When bombs started every night, my Tommy said he couldn't bear for us to be in London.' She held Róisín tighter. 'He insisted we go back to Ireland, even though he said that he would be half a man without his family,' she continued, her voice lowering. 'I think the final straw was when an ARP warden suggested we get a wee gas mask for baby Róisín.'

She pushed a strand of chestnut-brown hair behind her ear. Her face was strained with obvious fear for her husband, but this couldn't hide her pretty, elf-like features.

She looked at her nephews, their wide eyes brimming with fear. 'When the air raid sirens blasted, I went to Clapham Common Underground. I hated it there, it was so crowded and smelly. Eventually, I agreed with Tommy. I just couldn't take it any more.'

A single tear fell. 'I don't know how I'll manage without him, though. But I'm glad to be going home to Waterford. You must be glad to be leaving London as well.'

I forced a smile. I had made a life in London. When the air raid sirens echoed in the streets, my friend Eve and I had slipped on our black Air Raid Precautions armbands and helped guide people to the Underground for shelter. Now I thought of her waving goodbye to me earlier today at Paddington Station. We had hugged, and I'd reminded her to post our applications to be nurses. There were daily reminders on posters and on *Pathé News* at the picture houses, telling women to apply to the Ministry of Labour or any training hospital. I had gladly done so.

The train slowed to a stop as we arrived in Fishguard. We all disembarked and I fell into step with the crowd as we moved towards the *St Patrick* steamer. A huge green, white and gold tricolour flag hung over the side of the ship. Would the Luftwaffe see it, let alone care about our neutrality? A wave of dread washed over me like a dark tide as I tucked my British and Irish Steam Packet ticket inside my coat.

Ahead of me, Olivia pushed a pram, looking like a child herself, face white from exhaustion. One boy sat beside Róisín, and the two others struggled with a case. The younger boy's tears flowed down his dirty face like rivulets in mud, and his lower lip quivered.

I pushed my way through the crowd. 'Here, let me help you.' I pulled the battered suitcase off the ground and gave the boys my smaller case.

'Thank you,' Olivia whispered, colour rising in her pale cheeks. She pulled her cardigan tight. Smiling at the boys, her voice barely a whisper, she said, 'I'm looking forward to setting foot on Irish soil.' Her brow creased with worry again. 'You must have heard what happened to the *Isolda*?'

I nodded. The sinking of the SS *Isolda* steamer had been in last month's newspapers. Six lives lost for what? And just before Christmas.

'I'm in such a state,' Olivia said, looking down at her skirt. Her gaze shifted to me. 'And look at you in your lovely blue coat.'

Her hand flew to her chest. 'I'm sorry, Kitty. With all this chaos, I forgot you're on your way to your mother's funeral.'

The wind rose, her words lost in the Irish Sea.

2

On the steamer, Róisín and the boys melted in with the other passengers. Thick mooring chains groaned as they were pulled in, preparing us for departure, and children cheered and ran to the side of the steamer, waving goodbye to a near-empty dock. A lone docker lifted his black cap and waved back. A horn blasted, its deafening boom reverberating through the deck, and the children cheered again as a cloud of steam belched from a chimney and the steamer moved into the Irish Sea.

'Get away from there!' shouted a man in a navy jacket, running towards the children. 'You'll fall over!'

He grabbed one boy, but the rest escaped from his clutches like slippery eels on their way home to the Sargasso Sea, running to the other side of the ship, whooping and clapping. Many of them were probably on a ship for the first time, bombs and fathers momentarily forgotten, oblivious to the palpably uneasy faces and watchful eyes of their mothers, wringing their icy hands.

'Excuse me, miss!' A strong hand pulled my elbow. A

large seaman, his black beard mottled with grey bristles, his eyes hard, spoke kindly. 'The ladies are moving down below. The wind is brewing up a storm and it'll be safer inside. Ye don't want to get blown out to sea!'

But would it really be safer? What if we hit a mine or were torpedoed? Wouldn't we be safer on deck, ready to get into a lifeboat? I looked out to the angry sea, the waves rising like wild sea horses crashing into the ship.

I nodded, with no energy for an argument. 'I'll go down in a minute.'

He nodded and shuffled off, his attention gone to the children sliding on the deck.

The shoreline of Wales faded as the *St Patrick* rose and fell, thrashing through the waves, leaving behind a path of white foam and squawking seagulls. I held on to the rail for hours.

I released my grip when a scream pierced the air.

'Help, somebody help!'

Turning, I saw the boy who had been playing cards on the train lying on the other side of the deck beside a lifeboat, his sister trying to pull him up. As the steamer lurched again, his sister slipped. A woman ran to their side screeching, her hat long gone, followed by the crewman that had spoken to me.

Moving to join them, I saw that the boy lay still, eyes closed, blood trickling from his left temple.

'Is there a doctor here?' the crewman asked.

The gathering crowd looked expectantly at each other.

'A nurse, maybe?'

I inhaled and stepped forward. Maybe my week of first-aid training at Charing Cross Hospital hadn't been in vain.

I knelt beside the boy. 'I have training,' I said and bent down. I cradled his head in one hand and cleaned the wound with my handkerchief. It was no more than a graze.

He opened his eyes. 'Howya, gorgeous?' he said, laughing with a wide toothless grin.

His mother stepped forward. 'You behave yourself, John Brogan!' She pulled him up and swiftly grabbed the girl, dragging them into the belly of the ship.

The crowd dispersed, leaving me with a knot in my stomach that was getting tighter with every passing hour, my anxiety rising with the waves as I thought about home – if we would make it safely and whether I cared. Would drowning at sea be any worse than facing the ghosts of my past?

I slipped as the steamer rose.

'Jesus, love, you could fall over the side!' a man said in a clipped accent that I couldn't place.

My coat billowed open as I slipped and shivered in the icy wind. 'I'm fine.' As I straightened my coat, my hat was ripped from my head and tossed out to sea. My hair pulled loose, its natural curls escaping, long strawberry-blonde twirls flowing around my shoulders. Behind me, music and the laughter rippled through the sea air, filtering from the ship's belly where a man sang 'Molly Malone' while other passengers shared stories – and no doubt whiskey.

'Are you all right?' the man with the clipped accent asked. 'You've gone green.'

I nodded, though my stomach retched, acid rising, burning my throat, and I was thankful I hadn't eaten in hours.

'Here, I think you need to sit down, and maybe have a

drink of something.' He pulled a small silver flask out of his trouser pocket. 'Drop of good stuff?'

I shook my head.

His forehead crinkled, his face red from too many drops of the *good stuff*. 'A good Irish Catholic girl.' He smirked under his copious black hair.

I was neither.

He shrugged, and left me alone on the deck with my thoughts.

An hour later, through the thin mist, the coastline of County Wexford emerged, and the knot in my stomach tightened as I watched the frothy white sea horses race towards the rugged cliffs of Ireland. I tried to stop the echoes of my mother from creeping closer, but the ghostly fingers of my memories of her were clawing their way into my mind. No matter how deep a breath I took, I couldn't seem to take in enough air, like I was constantly winded from a punch, and as the shore got nearer, my stomach heaved with the rocking waves. I grabbed the rail as the acid from my stomach filled the back of my throat. I leaned over and vomited.

3

At Wexford, the steamer haemorrhaged passengers as status became invisible, first class mixing with third, everyone relieved we had made it safely across the Irish Sea. With quick steps, we walked down the swaying gangway, which groaned in protest at the onslaught of weight. Parents held on tight to their bags in one hand and children in the other.

'Have your identity cards and travel permits ready!' shouted a broad man in a black uniform, his beard keeping his face warm. We moved slowly as the cards were inspected, but as I neared him, I read a poster on the wall behind him that sent a chill through me.

NOTICE TO MARINERS
RIVER SUIR
As of Wednesday, 31st October 1940, all vessels entering the port of Wexford must stop at Dunmore East Pilot Station for examination.

Any vessel disobeying this order will be fired on by the military at Duncannon Fort.

R. Farrell

Squeezed between a man reeking of vomit and whiskey, and four whimpering children hanging on to their mother's pram, I ran my fingers around the paper edge of my identity card. My eyes traced the cursive letters of my name, each curve so familiar in an uncertain world.

Kathleen Flinn
ISSUE DATE: 4th July 1939

Behind the ticket inspector stood a man in a navy pinstripe suit, his eyes shifting over the passengers, a fedora hanging low on his face. As I neared, I could see that his chin was dimpled with pockmarks, probably from measles. I shuddered. They looked like a long red scar.

Without looking at me, the ticket inspector held out a hand, his fingernails dirty. 'Identity card?' His voice was annoyed, as if it was my fault the line was so slow.

He read it slowly, 'Kathleen Flinn.' His forehead crinkled; his eyebrows, as black as his hair, rose up, joining like a centipede. 'Is this yours?' he asked, lifting my card.

I nodded.

'Miss, your travel permit?' he said.

'I didn't have time to get one; my mother died suddenly.'

He looked up through thick round glasses, his black pupils large like he'd had a fright. He shifted his weight, looking over my head at the long queue behind me, and sighed. 'You are supposed to have a travel permit now to travel to Ireland.'

I showed him James's letter, and he pushed his cap up on top of his head. 'I'm sorry for your loss,' he said with regretful eyes.

Behind him the man in the pinstripe suit leaned forward, reading my telegram, and lifted his head a little to look at me, the shadow of his hat falling to below his nose. He took my identity card and whispered in the ticket inspector's ear. He nodded while keeping his eyes on me and handed me my card, waving me on towards the dockside, his freckled hands so large that they didn't look like they belonged to someone of his height. The wind whipped his hat off, and he grabbed it before it blew away. His bright hair was clipped tight and his face flushed angrily from the icy wind; he looked like he wished he was somewhere else.

My fingers curled tight around the handle of the suitcase as I scanned the dockside. Ropes dangled over the wall down to the sea into empty moorings, the fishermen gone to throw their nets for their daily catch. The crowd had quickly thinned as passengers got into cars or horse and traps.

Soon I was alone. Then the reality of what I had done sank in. I just wanted to sort Anthony out so I could return to London. I groaned, thinking of the inspector's mention of a travel permit. I would need one to return.

Behind me the ship's horn blasted, belching steam into the sky. I gripped my case tighter, watching as the gangway was hoisted back onto the ship, and looked at my watch, wondering where James was.

'Kathleen, over here!' a man shouted behind me.

James. He stood beside the horse and trap, waving his wooden shillelagh in the air. Soon he was wrapping his muscular arms around me. A familiar wave of warmth swept through me as I inhaled the scent of his Sweet Afton mixed with Pearl soap – the smell of a friend. His beard tickled my face.

'It's so good to see you!' he said and pushed me back. 'Let's get ye home and fed. You're skin and bones.' He threw my suitcase into the back of the trap. 'It's very light, Kathleen. Ye'll need more than a few light sweaters.'

'Kitty, James. Call me Kitty,' I said, brushing away the name my mother called me. Daddy had called me Kitty.

'And that coat won't offer you much warmth. It's been the coldest January for a long time. Hopefully next week will bring some warmer weather.' He looked at me with his soft blue eyes, now a watery grey, his once thick beard thinned with age.

'What's wrong with Anthony?' I asked.

'I thought he'd got consumption.'

'Consumption? TB – but that's fatal.' I pushed the blanket from my legs. 'Did you not get him to the doctor?'

'Dr Hurley said it wasn't TB, but he's still not right, Kitty. It's the bronchitis he had as a child.' He flicked the reins. 'You need to talk to him; he's in all sorts of trouble. He'll listen to you. I'm really worried for him, but you'll make him see sense.' He stretched his back and I could see how he had aged, he winced as if in pain.

He was silent for a few minutes then spoke again. 'He's not well.' He stopped for a minute as if searching for words. 'It's something more,' he turned to look at me, a smile softening the lines on his face. 'Now you're home and settled, Kitty, he'll improve, I know things will get better.'

Now was not the time to tell him I had to return to London. I couldn't stay here – I had a life in London, there were promises I had made to Eve. There was nothing for me here. A claw of anxiety dug into my chest.

I blinked back tears, nodding silently.

James squeezed my shoulder. 'Don't you worry none. We'll figure something out. Your brother's a fighter. With you back, he'll be right as rain in no time.'

I tried to return his reassuring smile, but it came out as more of a pained grimace. In truth, I was terrified. Terrified of what Anthony's illness could mean, not just for him, but for us both. Would I return to London? Pursue my dreams? Or was my fate sealed to this place, destined to care for my ailing brother? The weight of it all threatened to crush me.

James flicked the reins and the horse started to canter, jostling the trap along the bumpy road. 'Kitty, it really is good to see you. Anthony missed you.' He put his hand on mine and squeezed it.

James reached for a red tartan blanket and offered it to me. I stiffened.

'Wrap it around your legs. It's damp one today.'

It was my mother's. Another reminder of the memories I had to face. I wished I had not read James's telegram. If I had waited, Eve and I might have already started nursing training – a few weeks wouldn't have made a difference.

James had been the one constant in my life after my father died. He had bandaged my knees when I fell from the apple tree, and given me the warmth that my mother should have. My poor father had suffered from my mother's words as well. Every night she would go into one of her rages, screeching at him that she was going to kill herself. Anthony and I would lie in our beds with our hands over our ears, listening to the nightly vitriol coming through the bedroom floorboards.

'You'll be sorry. I'll throw myself into the river! You'll be sorry when my body is dragged from the Nore.'

Lying under the eiderdown, listening, I'd imagine Daddy below, sitting in his armchair, staring into the fire, silent. Her words rising: *river, your fault.* Then she'd leave the room, slamming the door, and her steps would go halfway up the stairs before she would turn around, stamp back into the kitchen and start screeching at Daddy again.

In the mornings, James would often find me crying under the apple tree. He'd sit beside me, put his arm around my shoulders. 'Kitty, was she in one of her rages again?'

'Why doesn't he shout back, or throw her out?' I had asked once.

I remembered his answer as if it had been given the day before: 'Your father is such a gentleman. He loved the woman he married and believes her when she says she is sorry. He said in his marriage vows he would honour your mother, and he is a good man, finding it hard to believe people like her exist, especially a woman. Your father is like my younger brother.'

I was brought back to the present as James said, 'Hold tight, Kitty, might be bumpy, but horses are clever creatures. They know their way with little light.' He flicked the reins, the usual slick sound of leather dulled in the thick fog, more like the gentle flick of a towel.

'We'll be home in Kilkenny in a few hours.' He flicked

the reins again and the horse's hooves slapped faster on the stony path. 'Tell me about London. You must have been so frightened. I'm so glad you're home to safety.'

'No, it wasn't too bad, James. It was…' Could I tell him how terrified I'd been when the air raid siren wailed and I ran from the house as plaster fell from the buildings around me onto the streets, as I clutched Eve's hand, neither of us stopping until we reached Camden Town Tube station? We'd joined hundreds of other Londoners filing down the steps to the Underground for safety. When Eve and I saw the newspaper advertising Morrison bomb shelters, it offered us little hope. What protection could a little metal cage in your kitchen give you when a Luftwaffe bomb fell? So we'd chosen the Underground for our air raid shelter.

'But I'm glad there's no war here,' I said.

James flicked the reins. The horse trotted faster. 'Well, I hope not. They said the bombs were a mistake.'

I sat up quickly, the blanket falling. 'What bombs were a mistake?'

'A while back, three women were killed in Knockroe, near Borris in County Carlow.' James blessed himself. 'Two sisters and a friend. The house flattened.'

'James, are we being invaded?' I said, fear in my voice as I searched the sky, but all I saw were black clouds rolling across the sky, heavy with approaching rain.

'No, not at all. What would Germany want with us? It was just a mistake, they mistook our coast for Wales.' He patted my knee. 'Nothing to worry about, Kitty, no Germans on our soil.'

Sitting back, I said a little prayer that James was right.

Soon we were approaching Bennettsbridge, the townland before Kilkenny.

As we neared the bridge, we saw a car pulled up onto the ditch and James chuckled. 'Cars left by the roadside are hardly a rarity these days, what with the petrol rationing. Only priests, doctors and the Garda Síochána have one these days.' His voice trailed off abruptly and his eyes narrowed.

'Ah, it's the Gardaí,' he muttered, as a man clad in a dark blue tunic and a peaked cap raised his hand, signalling for us to halt. James nodded past Garda Hogan to a man wearing a brown jacket and black slacks the colour of his shiny shoes. 'That's one of the Special Branch guards. Wonder what they want,' he muttered.

He twisted the reins around his hand, the horse slowed to a stop.

'Morning, James. How are you?' said Garda Hogan.

'Garda Hogan, good to see you. Anything wrong?' James glanced at the young man standing behind him.

'Nothing to concern you. We've got some troublemakers roaming about, so we're just carrying out checks.'

I surreptitiously glanced at the man next to him. He was studying us intently. My pulse quickened while James continued his exchange with Garda Hogan. The man in the brown jacket walked over to me, removing his trilby to reveal a tightly cropped, shiny haircut. It was Sam Daly, his once curly black hair gone.

'Morning, Kitty,' he said. The refined cadence of his words showed no trace of the Kilkenny accent.

'Hello, Sam. It's been years,' I said, forcing a smile. 'You've changed.' My eyes traced the contours of his once youthful face, now chiselled into that of a man with confidence, defined by an angular jawline. Broad shoulders framed his tall stature, a transformation that made the boy I knew seem like a distant figment of my imagination.

The dissonance between my memories and the man standing before me pressed heavily upon me, reminding me how different our lives had become since those carefree days beside the river. I felt a twinge of fear, irrational but palpable, that somehow the nuns might have sent him to find me. I dismissed the thought almost as quickly as it had appeared, but a sliver of doubt lingered. Surely they have forgotten about me?

His eyes flicked momentarily to my suitcase, before moving back to me. 'How's Anthony? Is he well?'

His probing gaze made me feel like a suspect under scrutiny.

'He's fine, Sam, doing very well,' I lied, averting my eyes.

'You're all set, James. Nothing to concern yourself about,' said Garda Hogan, giving our horse a gentle tap to move along.

Sam's eyes met mine briefly, his nod almost imperceptible, as if acknowledging a secret we both kept. A shiver coursed through me, leaving me unsettled as we moved away from the bridge, and from the past that had so unexpectedly re-emerged.

James looked over at me. 'We'll be home in a little while, and before you know it, it will be spring and the place will take on a new life. You can nearly smell it coming.'

He was right. The air was fresh and clear. The hedgerows were covered in spiderwebs and white with frost, like a bridal lace had been thrown over them. Soon we crossed the bridge across the Nore, its waters flowing high up the banks.

As we made our way towards Kilkenny, I glanced back at the bridge where Sam had stood. He was gone, but scrawled in black ink across the bridge was *Heil Hitler, Up the IRA, Up the Nazis*, and a crude swastika.

'James, why would someone write that here?'

'It's a protest after Dev Valera arrested all those IRA lads last year and sent them to an internment camp in County Kildare. Some were making a deal with the devil by helping Germany to come here, thinking if we helped them get to the North, Hitler would get the six counties back for us.'

He shook the reins, his face like thunder. 'And Dev had them arrested after they stole a load of ammunition in Dublin in the Phoenix Park warehouse just before Christmas in '39.'

He slowed the horse and turned to me, his face serious. 'Kitty, Anthony was lucky he wasn't arrested, running around with those lads from Castlecomer. I told him not to get involved with them – nothing but trouble those communists. I don't know what he was thinking when he went to Spain with them to fight against Franco. Anthony said it was for socialism, for those who have no voice, but some don't draw the lines between the IRA and socialism. Dev Valera and the Church hate the communists as much as the IRA and draw little comparison. So, he was lucky he wasn't put in prison when he came back from Spain.'

My stomach churned at the memory of Anthony limping into our yard back in '37, his body swathed in bandages and supported by a crutch. Until the year before, I'd never even heard of the Spanish Civil War. But then the priests started urging us from their Sunday pulpits to go fight for Franco, claiming it was a battle for Catholicism. Anthony, in stark contrast, had gone to fight against him.

James caught my eye. 'I know he shouldn't have gone. Anthony believes in men being equal, and always fights for the underdog.' He put both reins in one hand and rubbed his beard. 'Physical wounds eventually heal, but it's what's happened to his mind that concerns me now.'

The horse faltered for a moment; James quickly tugged on the reins to steady it.

As we rode towards Kilkenny Castle, the horse seemed to sense that he would be home in minutes. The streets were quiet and untouched by war. We soon passed St John's church and headed for Ballyfoyle. My stomach knotted up as we twisted and turned through familiar hedges and roads. When we rounded the corner, I could see my home.

My tears had fallen with the rain on the day of our father's funeral, when our mother smiled and said, 'It's just the three of us.' Now, as we passed through the yard, the house looked even more desolate – damp rising above the porch roof, yellowed newspaper blocking the windows, grass growing at the front door. I wanted to burn it down.

4

My shoulders tensed as I pushed the door open, my mother's ghost meeting me as I stepped across the threshold. I wanted to walk straight back outside and return to England. Now I was standing in the low-ceilinged kitchen, struggling to catch a breath, suffocating in my past. The musty, damp air, mixed with paraffin from the Tilley lamps, clung to the back of my throat.

Bessie ran barking through the back door across the kitchen, yelping, slipping on the tiles and jumping up, putting her paws on my shoulders, licking my face. Her four white paws made her look like she was wearing socks pulled up on her black fur.

Immediately, James busied himself, pulling back the net curtains, torn and tattered, and moving piles of newspapers and books stacked haphazardly on the windowsill. A shaft of light fell across the kitchen tiles.

'Is Anthony here?' I asked.

James didn't answer. He gathered the empty teacups and an ashtray laden with half-finished cigarettes from the kitchen table, revealing bits of the gingham tablecloth. He dipped his fingers into a tin pail beside the sink.

'He's not long gone; the milk is still warm,' he said, wiping his hand on his trousers. He turned on the wireless; nothing happened. 'It's not working. I only got the battery charged last week,' he muttered, bending down and turning the black knob. He stood after a minute, giving up, and turned to face me with a serious expression.

'Sit down for a minute, Kitty. We need to talk.' He pulled a kitchen chair out for me.

I rubbed my arms, my breath white, sending a shiver through my bones. 'This sounds serious.'

He sat opposite me and folded his hands, lowering his eyes as if making a confession. 'As I said, Anthony... he hasn't been thinking straight. He gets into all sorts of things.'

The room was silent, save for Bessie's thumping tail on the rug. I looked at her and she raised her head, wagging her tail quicker, waiting for her ears to be ruffled. But she lowered it when I turned to James. The shadows on his face accentuated his age. I hadn't noticed how white his hair was when I met him in Rosslare.

He sighed. 'Listen carefully to me. It's important to tell Anthony to be careful. There are people out to get him and his kind.'

'Because of what happened all those years ago? Don't tell me he's still hanging around with that crowd of communists, dissenters – whatever the Church called them.' Suddenly a thought stuck me like a thunderbolt in a cloudless sky. My heart froze for a minute.

'He's not involved with the IRA lads?'

'No, he's not involved with any of them at all.' James rubbed his beard, shaking his head. 'Kitty, there are some things you may have seen in London that you wouldn't see here.' He looked me directly in the eye, his once clear blue eyes now watery with age, and frowned as if searching for words. 'Just… just tell him to be careful. He could get arrested.'

'Arrested! Why? Who? Is it because of me?' The question emerged from my throat, which felt as if it were being constricted by a nun's skeletal grip, and I shivered.

James shook his head vehemently, stroking his beard. 'Why would you think it is anything to do with you?'

I began nervously twisting the hem of my coat. I sat, lost in the distant memories that haunted my soul. James, seated across the kitchen table, watched me with a mix of concern and curiosity. The air was thick with unspoken words, heavy with secrets I was yet to reveal.

'James,' I began, my voice barely above a whisper, 'there's something I need to tell you.' My eyes, brimming with unshed tears, met his. In them, he must have seen a deep well of shame and regret.

'In 1938,' I continued, my voice growing steadier with each word, 'Mammy arranged with Father Fitzpatrick for me to go to St Margaret's, in County Laois, a home for unwed mothers. His own sister was a nun there, Sister Assumpta. My baby was born just a day apart from that of my friend, Eve.' James watched me silently. 'My baby never lived. We fled those walls, those nuns, seeking a new life in London.' My hands trembled as I spoke of the past, of dreams shattered and innocence stolen.

James leaned in, his expression one of understanding. He

knew the pain of leaving behind a life, the ache of memories that clung like shadows.

I struggled to voice the deeper truth. 'Seamus McGinty, from Castlecomer,' I said, the name tasting bitter on my tongue, 'he was the father. I thought... I believed it was love.' I closed my eyes, a single tear escaping down my cheek.

James reached out, covering my hand with his. He didn't speak, but his presence was a silent balm to my wounded spirit.

My breath hitched as I recounted those moonlit nights, the promises whispered under a starry sky, and the crushing realisation of betrayal. 'He said we'd go to America, but he left me, James, went on his own. Left me to face the scorn of my family and the cold judgement of the nuns.'

In the quiet of the kitchen, I shared the pain of my past, the loss of my child, and the harsh words that still echoed in my ears. 'The night I left, as I got into Father Fitzpatrick's car, my own mother called me a whore,' I said, my voice barely audible, still feeling the sting of her words.

James listened, his face creased for the pain I had endured.

My breath came in short gasps as I tried and failed to contain my emotions. 'James, I'm so ashamed – I've let everyone down. Anthony would be so devastated if he knew what I had done, the shame of it weighing heavy on his good name, and my father's name.'

James reached across the table, his touch gentle yet firm, anchoring me in the present amidst the turmoil of my past.

'Kitty,' he said softly, 'you did nothing wrong.' His eyes, filled with empathy, met mine, offering a refuge from the storm of my memories.

Warmth spread through me, a contrast to the cold dread

that had gripped my heart. 'Thank you, James,' I murmured, my voice thick with emotion.

He squeezed my hand. 'Your secret is safe with me, always. I'll always be here for you and Anthony – remember that. Always.'

We sat in silence for a moment, the comforting presence of each other filling the room before James spoke again, 'Kitty the nuns aren't looking for you. It's worse – it's Anthony.' He walked over to the window and stared out at the fields. 'But now you're home, you'll make him see sense.' He smacked his lips as if thinking.

'What do you mean, I'll make him see sense? I don't understand. How can I help him?'

But he didn't reply. He just looked out the kitchen window at the hills and glens of Ballyfoyle.

'What's wrong with Anthony?' As I spoke, my mind grappled with the idea that I was not capable of helping him.

'He's very weak,' James said, sighing. 'His mental state has been affected by his time in the Spanish War. He does and says things that are strange.'

'Like what?' I asked, curious.

The room was momentarily filled with the distinctive sound of the cuckoo clock. Its chimes echoed, marking six o'clock, and James clasped his hands and bowed his head in prayer.

When he finished murmuring the Angelus, his eyes, usually a bright blue, seemed clouded as they met mine, a shadow of worry flickering within them.

'He's skin and bone, Kitty. He really needs your help. But keep him comfortable and make sure he is properly fed,' James advised, 'and he'll come around soon enough.'

The weight of James's words bore down on me like a leaden sky, intensifying the turmoil already stirring. How could I bear the responsibility of another when my own heart was so frayed at the edges?

When James left, my tears flowed, and as I looked around the kitchen, despair crept over me; sorrow like a thick blanket of fog that rises from the river, bringing with it that uneasy feeling you get when everything is shrouded, reduced to mere shadows and shapes.

5

Later, I stood at the back door looking over the hills, waiting
for Anthony, wondering if he would return at all. I knew I
would find it hard to sleep with the full moon and could
hold off my nightmares by staying awake. Old wives' tales
told of lunatics and werewolves howling at the moon. Light
snow dusted the ground. The night was only broken by the
occasional bleat of a lonely sheep echoing through the air.

My hands wrapped around a warm mug, I listened to
nothing but silence under the inky sky dotted with stars, the
moon flooding the countryside, catching the bright, crisp
frost on the fields. My white breath floated in the air. It
was nearly midnight, the hills and fields brightly bathed in
moonlight, a black-and-white photo, the ground glistening.

The bushes by the side field rustled; a fox emerged and
stopped about three feet away from me. Foxes are clever,
rarely getting caught, stealthily stealing chickens and
lambs, a farmer's worst nightmare. His dark eyes glinted
in the moonlight. He fixed my stare; our eyes locked for

a few seconds before he ran off into the field, startled by a noise.

I stopped breathing to listen. There was a low drone in the distance – an engine. I cocked my head, my brow furrowing.

The noise got louder, but it was above me. A plane. It was the low drone of an aircraft, like the ones I'd heard in London. My heart beating fast, I searched the sky. The hum got louder. Then it stopped. Then the low drone began again, and I waited for it to crash. Nothing.

I scanned the sky in between the twinkling tea lights of stars. The trees rustled again. I shivered. After a few seconds, there was a slight distortion in the black sky, a subtle colour change. I squinted and stood on my tiptoes, as if an extra inch would make me reach hundreds of miles into the night. It was a tiny white speck, falling like a snowflake. Then a puff – a mushroom of smoke. I held my breath, my heart racing, a shake running through me. It then floated like a leaf, moving slowly side to side, and then disappeared as the clouds passed over the moon. A parachute.

I squinted to see where the plane was going to crash. Its engine revved to life, but soon the noise receded. It was gone, and I breathed a sigh of relief. If the Germans were to boot-march into Ireland, my path back to London would be irrevocably closed.

I stretched my neck as the journey finally caught up with me and the cold of the earth seeped into my feet. The hairs pricked up on my neck and I stopped breathing, listening; something unsettled me. It was just the wind whistling in the treetops. A bat swooped down, passed me, and flew up to the eaves on the coal shed. But it wasn't the bat that had unsettled me; it was something else.

Any tiredness was gone. The sound came from the orchard at the end of the garden. I searched the trees.

'Anthony!' I called. No reply.

In the moonlight, I quickly navigated my way to the orchard. In between the trees, a figure moved. It was ghostly white, with long stringy hair and layers of clothes. It wasn't a man. It was a banshee; the legend said her appearance was an omen of death. I waited for her to scream. Her keening.

Caoineadh, it was called, a warning that a death was imminent, a long wailing cry. I had come home too late. Was Anthony dead? My legs trembled; tears burbled at the back of my throat.

She moved silently between the trees, her skirt billowing behind her, flitting in and out of sight. I held my breath and cautiously moved through the moonlit orchard, stifling the pain as overgrown bushes scratched my ankles. I scanned in between the shadows of the trees.

My mother's ghost.

I inhaled, chatter running through my mind, telling myself I should fear the living, not the dead. Ghosts are just emotions attached to memories.

I left my cup on the stone wall by the orchard and followed the ghost. She bent, picking up twigs and putting them into a sack on her back, and then turned to stare directly at me.

I exhaled. It was only old Mrs Doyle. Her grey face stared at me, gnarled from her harsh life of walking the hills, no matter the weather: hail, rain or sunshine. The poor woman's husband and child had disappeared one Halloween night long before I was born, but she still wandered the hills at night, looking for them, wailing like a banshee. She was a *fáith*, a healer woman. She used herbs and words to cure others, but could never cure herself.

Her eyes held mine as she gave me a slight nod and pulled her bag tight on her back. Twigs stuck out of the bag like children's arms reaching up to the sky for help. We stood for several minutes in silence, the mist of our breath melting in the chilly air.

I felt sorry for her. She couldn't let the past go. She clung to the hope her husband and son would come back.

Cold seeped through the soles of my shoes, up my bones. Shivering from cold, and the sight of Mrs Doyle, I ran into the house, pulling the door tight. Mrs Doyle unsettled me, but the sight in the kitchen unsettled me more. Anthony, gaunt and frail, stood by the fire, his weight supported by a walking stick fashioned from an ash tree. Even though James had warned me, the reality was more harrowing. His once robust frame had withered away, and his hair, now shoulder-length, was tangled and muddied.

He didn't look at me. 'Kitty, you're home.' His voice was hoarse and hollow. This was a shadow of my brother. His coat hung loosely from his once broad shoulders, his cheeks hollow.

'Anthony!' I ran to him as he turned to face me. 'I didn't realise you still used a walking stick.'

'I don't really, just when I haven't slept, my legs get tired.'

I stepped back and looked at him from head to toe. His once handsome countenance had faded, replaced by unkempt, mottled stubble.

Moving towards him, I embraced him gently, afraid I was going to break him. He didn't hug me back but pushed me away. He had aged; he looked older than his twenty-one years. He looked more like an arthritic uncle.

My heart broke for my handsome brother, the mirror image of my father, with the same blond hair and wide blue eyes, and black eyelashes that could sweep away all the troubles in the world. Now these eyes were full of their own troubles.

'You need to eat,' I said. I took the bread and cut a thin slice, slathering it in butter, before quartering it into squares.

He ate with care, as if every mouthful hurt. His mouth looked painful, dried blisters around his cracked lips.

'Does it hurt?' I asked, watching him over the rim of my teacup.

He was silent for a minute. 'Everywhere. Every bone hurts. In the frost it's worse, and the mouth sores get bad.'

'James thought you had consumption. And he also…' I stopped for a second to prepare the weighty words. 'He said that you might be arrested. What for?'

His reaction was not what I expected. He stood quickly, the stick scraping on the tiles. 'Nothing.' His demeanour changed, his face tense. 'Don't mind James. He talks nonsense sometimes.' He rubbed his leg and caught me staring at the stick.

I bit my lip and forced a smile. My throat tightened. Stubborn as he was, Anthony had the gentlest heart I knew. These were not his words.

'Together we'll get through this,' I said, gripping his hand with reassurance. 'That's what family's for, right?' My eyes drifted to the window.

A muffled thud resonated from somewhere in the yard. A shadow of unease crossed his face.

I glanced at Anthony seated at the table, his frail fingers clutching a bread knife as though it were weighted with lead. Could I really be of any help?

Wondering who would call at this late hour, I looked out the window expecting maybe to see James ambling up the path. But the yard was empty, the moonlight swathing the buildings in hues of grey, all still save for the swaying apple tree branches and the gate leaning askew.

A chill crept down my spine. A thud came again, louder this time. My breath caught in my throat as a figure stepped out from behind the tree. Tall and broad-shouldered, with a familiar gait – it was Sam Daly. What was he doing here now? My hands trembled as I stepped away from the window.

Anthony gazed at me with concern. 'What is it, Kitty?'

I swallowed hard. 'Nothing. Just the wind.' I would not worry him unnecessarily. Some burdens I must bear alone.

What was Sam doing here? I stayed at the corner of the window watching him from the shadows. In an instant he was gone. Maybe I had imagined his presence. I looked back at Anthony and shook my head, trying to clear the image from my mind. He was now coughing violently into a handkerchief.

'Are you all right?' I rushed to his side. The handkerchief came away stained red. My heart dropped.

Anthony nodded weakly. 'I'm fine, just a tickle in my throat.' But the pallor of his skin told a different story.

I bit my lip, anxiety rising within me. I thought of the

few pennies I had for my return ticket. Could I just leave Anthony now and go back to my life?

'I'm stronger than I look.'

He broke into another fit of coughing. As I rubbed his back, my resolve hardened.

'I'll get you better, and before you know it everything will be all right,' I said as I watched him take off his pullover and shirt, and I shivered at the sight of his ribs. He left me to hang his clothes on a chair in front of the fire. The damp rose from them like ghosts.

'Anthony, we'll get you to bed and talk tomorrow,' I said, taking the cups to the sink. I'd wash them in the morning.

He got his stick, and when I heard the tapping on the floorboards in his room I raked the fire like Eve had done in our little room in London. Drawing a cross in the ashes with the tongs: I rake this fire in the name of the Father, Son and Holy Ghost. I think it had been a comfort to us both as we sat staring into the embers in silence, hoping we would make it through the night.

As I passed the chair, I picked up his jacket, which had been flung aside, and paper fluttered to the ground. Thinking it was just a note, I lifted it to the now fading Tilley light, my mouth going dry as I read it.

The Link Magazine

PERSONAL

Tony, 21, tall, likes poetry, reading.
Refined, would like to hear from a sincere mature man.
Likes musicals.

Likes musicals.

My head spun. *Christ, is it Anthony's?* Men get arrested for meeting other men. In London, Eve had shown me a cabaret where men met others like them. *Homosexuals,* she'd called them and had told me many men in Dublin were sent to Kilmainham Gaol for such activities; that they used to hang men for being homosexual. I could only hope this paper wasn't his.

6

The following morning, the scratchy veil of fatigue irritated my eyes, and my mind was fogged. I lay in bed, part awake and part asleep, with trails of Mother's voice penetrating my dreams – or was it Mrs Doyle screaming for her child? Or me, screaming for my child.

I sat up and shoved the dreams away, hoping they might dissipate with the rising sun. Thankfully the tendrils of the nightmare slipped from my memory. Inhaling slowly and steadying my hands, I buttoned my blouse and mentally made a list of things to do.

As I entered the kitchen, Anthony was already sitting at the table, and I wondered if he had gone to bed at all. I braced myself to confront him about what James had meant, and about that magazine cutting. But he looked so frail and tired... it would wait.

'Anthony, you need to eat, wash yourself and get into clean clothes.' Despair crept into my bones at the yellow hue of his face, and I busied myself filling the kettle for tea. But before I could set the kettle on the stove, a forceful knock echoed through the kitchen, the peeling paint and worn wooden table absorbing the sound.

Anthony's eyes darted to the door. He cautiously moved aside the faded curtain, peered into the yard, then put his fingers to his lips, demanding immediate silence.

'It's—it's Father Fitzpatrick, Kitty,' he stammered, his childhood stutter resurfacing in moments of stress, his face drained of colour. 'Don—don't let him in.' He retreated from the window. 'I can't face anyone right now, least of all the priest.'

There was another rap on the door. 'Kathleen, are you home? It's only me, Father Fitzpatrick.'

'Kitty, tell him to go.'

As I looked into Anthony's anxious eyes, a flurry of thoughts rushed through my mind. Christ is the priest's visit connected to what James had cryptically alluded to? Or was it something even more ominous? A prickling sensation crawled up my spine at the thought that the nuns from St Margaret's might have sent him to collect the money I owed them. The room felt smaller, as if the walls were closing in, and my stomach knotted in dread.

'Kitty, please.' Anthony's voice quivered, snapping me back to the moment.

It was rare to see him so undone, and the weight of his plea added to the swirling emotions within me. I was caught in a vice of competing fears and obligations, torn between the brother who clearly needed me in some undisclosed way and the looming shadows of my own past. Every knock on that door seemed to reverberate through the core of my being, amplifying the sense of impending doom that neither of us could escape.

Behind me the door to the hall creaked quietly shut, and I spun around. Anthony was gone.

The window rattled. Father Fitzpatrick looked through, his round face cupped in his hands. He knocked on the door again, turned the old brass handle and stepped into the kitchen.

He had aged. The skin on his face was cracked like dry earth in the summertime, covered with pockets of sunburned pink flesh that was almost transparent. He had a thick nose that had been broken once years ago and healed crookedly. He was as rotund as ever, his chin meeting his neck.

This was the man who'd changed the course of my life. His black Morris Fourteen sat in the middle of the yard – the same car I'd sat in two years ago as we drove in silence – he'd left the door open.

He didn't offer me his hand, just kept his fingers clasped, resting on the top of his stomach.

'Kathleen.' He softened his voice. 'I'm not here to judge you.'

I looked past his ears, a trick I'd learned when I didn't want to meet my mother's eyes.

He sighed. 'This is not about you, but about Anthony. There've been break-ins on the farms around here. At Farrell's farm, milk was taken, eggs stolen, and some blankets. The Gardaí want a word with him.'

I looked over his shoulder. A man stood beside the car. He was vaguely familiar, something about his height, but I couldn't place him. I narrowed my eyes, trying to focus, but he kept his head low and his height concealed as he leaned against the car. Then he shifted and stretched his back, his hand on his hips. It was Sam Daly.

'I'm concerned about Anthony,' Father Fitzpatrick went on. 'He wanders the hills of the mountain all night, sleeping like a wild animal. It's not right.'

He shifted and looked down at his black shoes, then his eyes met mine. His cheeks slightly rose in colour. 'He has been seen swimming in the River Dinan with no clothes on, near where the children swim.'

In my surprise, I managed to swallow the truth. 'He's not here,' I said, folding my arms and keeping my voice even.

'It must have been difficult for you after you left St Margaret's.'

A steel knot turned in my stomach. 'Father, I don't have time. There's a lot to do here, so do you mind? I've got to get back to work.'

I didn't wait for a reply. I walked to the door and opened it wide. That was how my mother used to tell visitors they had outstayed their welcome. I gripped the brass handle, hoping it would lend me strength. Father Fitzpatrick would not be used to people making demands of him. Men of the cloth were more respected than the president of Ireland; some said the Church *was* the government.

I glanced out into the yard at Sam. He moved across towards me, and I looked back at Father Fitzpatrick, waiting for him to put his hand on my shoulder and say either 'You're under arrest' or 'You're going to hell'. Or both.

But he walked past me. 'Kitty, child,' he said, 'look after yourself. You're a good person, but your brother, he—he just needs to be careful.'

A cat meowed from the shed.

He grimaced. 'I dislike cats.' And he shuddered, pulling his coat tight. 'I'm more of a dog person.'

He took my hands in his and looked me straight in the eyes. 'Kitty, I won't tell them – the nuns – that you came back here.' And gave them a slight squeeze before he left.

I remained on the doormat, listening to the closing of two car doors. I inched the curtain back, watching the car drive away, the sound of its engine gradually fading into the countryside.

'I-is he gone?' Anthony stuttered.

I spun around. 'Anthony, what are ya at? Stealing and swimming in the river with no clothes on?' I looked him straight in the eyes. 'Don't lie to me. Is this what James meant when he said you could get arrested?'

Anthony slumped in the armchair in front of the fire, rubbing his leg and rocking ever so slightly, a movement both of us had found comfort in as children.

'Kitty, I'm n-not stealing anything.'

'Calm down, Anthony. Count to ten; breathe like Daddy showed you.'

The flames in the fire suddenly jumped as a wet log spat its winter sap. Many a Sunday afternoon in the barn, Daddy had sat on a log, teaching Anthony to breathe properly. I'd sit on the bale of hay, loving this intimacy, just the three of us.

'Breathe slow and take deep breaths. Count to ten, and then start over again. Then try the letters, saying them slowly with each breath.'

Anthony leaned forward, placing his head in his hands, his fingers rubbing small circles into his temples. He seemed like a worm burrowing into hard, dried mud, seeking someplace dark and safe.

As I watched his shoulders rise and fall, I spoke. 'Sam Daly was with him.'

His shoulders tensed, but he remained incredibly still as I went on. 'He's working for the guards now. Special Branch, James said.'

He jerked upright and spat into the fire, which crackled and hissed in response. His blue eyes met mine, filled with a pleading expression. 'Kitty, I'm not stealing anything!' He shook his head. 'That wasn't me. Sam Daly, he was always a sneaky bastard.'

'But we were all such good friends once. Don't you remember the summer evenings, all three of us wading ankle-deep into the stream, throwing our nets to catch minnows? And don't you remember how you and Sam formed an unbreakable bond when you became blood brothers – etching tiny slits into your thumbs and sharing your blood?'

Anthony spat on the floor. 'That's the past, Kitty, we were children. Nothing more than silly games. Kitty, why did you leave without saying goodbye?'

I straightened, placing my palms on the table and leaning forward, my fingertips turning pale. 'I-I needed some time to myself. I regret not bidding you goodbye.' Waves of guilt intertwined with the pain and shame of my predicament.

Bessie pawed Anthony's leg, wagging her tail, her brown

doe eyes looking for a rub. It was funny how dogs knew you were in distress. He smiled weakly at her as she licked his hand. For a moment, he had the same strong jawline as our father. Tears formed in my eyes as my shoulders sagged at the weight of memories of my mother.

Anthony picked his teeth with his nails, and I noticed a scab on the back of his hand.

Staying silent for a few minutes, looking at the dog and feeling like a mouse caught in a trap, unable to escape, I busied myself washing the plates, dipping them into the sink and placing them on the side.

'I won't be staying. I must get back to London.'

Anthony stood silently, coming over to the sink for a cup of water.

I continued, 'Don't talk me into staying. James will help you – he's been like a father to us.'

Anthony cut me short. 'Our father!' His face reddened, and he leaned forward and spat the words. 'James was better than our father. Daddy, our so-called father, was going to leave us the night of the fire. I saw them, Kitty.' He pointed to the kitchen door. 'His brown suitcases sat there on the mat.'

I shook my head. Anthony's words made little sense. A lump formed in my stomach as I saw the image of my father's coat on fire and James beating the flames. I tried to get the words out. 'No, Anthony, you made a mistake. You're lying! Why did you never say until now? Did Mother tell you to say these things?'

He stood staring out the window, shaking his head. 'Don't be ridiculous, of course she didn't. She never spoke of him after he died.'

His words didn't make sense. How could our father have done such a thing?

'Why are you only telling me now? Do you think that will make me stay?'

'Kitty, I didn't remember. We were so young. I was only just seven years old. I must have blocked it out, but when I was in Spain and got injured in Guernica, I lay for weeks in the hospital tent. I slept a lot, but I also had time to think.'

He turned to face me. In the shadow of the Tilley lamp, he seemed to have shrunk again.

The memories of that night filled my mind like a flood. I was drowning in a sea of red and blue flames leaping up into the night sky, engulfing the old barn.

I rose shakily from the table, my legs wobbling from shock or betrayal. My beloved father, my shield, had shattered my trust. My head throbbed, my hands massaging my temples, seeking a moment to process this revelation.

'Perhaps you're mistaken,' I said.

'No, Kitty. Two suitcases by the front door.' Anthony's eyes fell on the scars that marked his hand.

That sight struck a deeper chord of pain than any physical torment I'd suffered.

'Anthony, you must be mistaken,' the words stained to break free. Betrayal surged through me, quickly overtaken by a wake of dread that morphed into anger.

We sat in silence watching the fading fire. I wrestled with my rage, trying to digest the bitter pill Anthony had forced me to swallow. My fury was compounded by the treachery of both parents.

Anthony's hand suddenly captured mine, his rough skin cold, his nails gnawed to the quick. 'Kitty, you can't leave me,' he whispered, his eyes pleading. 'You can't leave me. We only have each other.'

I remained silent, offering no promises.

I pushed open the gate to James's farm, my father's betrayal swirling in my mind. The secret Anthony had revealed about Daddy felt like a leaden weight in my chest.

James stood in the side field with his back to me, talking quietly to a calf – a black and white patchwork of fur, munching on the grass and oblivious to the human dramas unfolding around her. He turned as he noticed my approach and gave me a wry smile.

'She's lost her mother,' he said sadly. 'It's been three days since she disappeared and she is so lonely without her.' His hand rested on the cow's back, a gentle, rhythmic patting. 'She's my responsibility now – I can't abandon her. I'm the only family she has now.' His gaze was steady on mine. 'Kitty we have to look after those who can't look after themselves.'

The double meaning of his words weighed heavily on me, emphasising the responsibility.

'James I'll stay for a while until Anthony gets better.'

He patted the calf, it wagged its tail at the comforting touch.

James's gaze was steady, searching. 'Is something else troubling you?'

I bit my lip, the confession hovering at the edge of my tongue. But I held it back, the truth too raw, too painful.

'It's nothing,' I deflected, turning my gaze to the calf, seeking refuge in her calm demeanour.

James nodded, though his concern clearly remained. 'I've

been thinking. Mrs Kearns in town needs help in the shop; her shop girl went off and got married and is with child.'

A shiver ran through me as I thought of Kearns's shop, of Mr Reilly's leering gaze.

James reached out, his hand gripping mine firmly. 'You're running out of food, Kitty. This job... it's necessary.'

A sigh escaped me. The choice was clear, even if unwelcome. 'All right, I'll do it.'

'Good,' James replied, a hint of relief in his voice. 'And perhaps Anthony can help with Two Piece here. It might be good for him.'

A faint smile crossed my lips. 'Thanks, James.'

I picked up a broom and began sweeping, each stroke a distraction from the growing sense of despair and the betrayal that now seemed more complex.

Later, Anthony's face appeared at the kitchen door, etched with concern. 'Kitty, are you all right?'

I looked at him, seeing the years of worry that had aged him prematurely. How long had he been alone in carrying the burden of our father's plan?

'I think I'll work at Mrs Kearns's shop. We need the money,' I said.

His eyes softened. 'Thank you,' he said quietly, the relief in his voice mingling with a deeper, unspoken gratitude.

That evening, James returned. 'You start tomorrow at the shop,' he announced.

I nodded, my heart heavy yet determined. This job was our lifeline, a necessary step in facing the challenges that lay ahead.

7

Swinging my leg over the bar, I coasted the High Nelly down John Street on one pedal, towards John's Bridge. James had told Mrs Kearns in Irishtown that I would work in her shop for a few weeks. St John's church rang the quarter of the hour, and I hurried on.

As I propped my bicycle up against the shop, Mrs Kearns flipped the closed sign to open. Mr Reilly emerged from the side door, holding a box of turnips against his stomach.

'Morning, Kathleen, you're looking well.'

My stomach churned at the sight of him. His moustache fringed his mouth, ornamenting a few black teeth, and I shuddered at the memory of his leering gaze when we had passed each other on the way home from school. I forced an uneasy nod, smiling politely.

Hold your tongue. Children are seen and not heard. Some things my mother had taught me could be put to good practice. I'd get through a few weeks of this and be on my way back to London. I exhaled, held my head high and walked past, smelling the tartness of his breath.

'Kathleen,' Mrs Kearns said with a smile as I stepped into the shop. 'I was delighted when James called to tell me you would be happy to work.'

She stood back from me, hands on her hips, examining me from head to toe. 'My goodness, look how you've grown, and so stylish, with your fashionable hairstyle – just like Vivien Leigh!'

Mrs Kearns was anything but boring. When I'd called at her shop on my way home from school, she'd always had her hair set and wore red lipstick with matching rouged cheeks, just like the ladies in the magazines. I'd envied her auburn waves of hair, soft and delicate, falling in natural ringlets around her shoulders. Now she wore light lipstick and stroked her hair lightly with her hands as she spoke. The light, sweet scent of fragrant flowers surrounded her, with a hint of cherry blossom and jasmine in the air.

The shop was small and dimly lit, with a few bare light bulbs hanging from the ceiling.

It was filled to the brim with goods. The walls were lined with shelves stacked high with jars of jam, jelly and sauce, boxes of tea and coffee, and tins of biscuits and sweets. In the centre of the room, there was a long wooden counter laden with sacks of flour, sugar, oats and other cereals.

'And, Kitty, I was sorry to hear about your mother. James said you couldn't get back because of the war. That must have been hard. But you must be glad to be away from those bombs.'

I nodded and feigned my practised sorrow. 'Yes, Anthony and I will just have to get on with things.'

I took a brown shop coat from her. I thought she had finished, but she said, 'It must have been so hard to miss it. A daughter only has one mother.'

Nodding again, I looked down at the sawdust on the floor.

She took my silence as grief and her face clouded with worry. 'You poor girl, I'm so sorry. I didn't mean to upset you. I've only boys and they've all gone across the water. I hoped they would come home when the war started, but they all have families in Birmingham.'

She smiled and the flecks of her brown eyes glistened. 'Ten grandchildren now, but all away, across the water.' Her face turned to sorrow. 'And now this awful war on, they'll never get across to see me. Those Germans are blowing up ferries and whatnot. They dropped a few bombs already. Mistake, they said, thought it was Wales.'

She shook herself and forced a smile. 'No rest for the wicked, eh? Enough blabbering for one day.' She hummed as she buttoned her shop coat, covering her cream blouse and showing only the slip of a hem of her blue skirt, so it looked like one long brown dress.

'Today, you can watch how to serve the customers – but first, sweep the floor.' She pointed to the brush leaning against a sack of potatoes. 'And be polite if anyone talks to you, and always treat people with respect.'

She smiled. 'Kitty, no need to be nervous, it'll be grand.'

The bell tinkled and the door opened, letting in the clatter of hooves as a farmer passed on the way to the mart. A woman dressed in a red coat and matching headscarf stepped into the shop, a faint breeze blowing in behind her. She held a basket close to her chest, its handle covered with a handkerchief.

'Mrs Daly, what can I do for you today?' said Mrs Kearns. 'This is Kathleen Flinn. You remember Kathleen, Mrs Flinn's daughter?'

Mrs Daly nodded. 'Indeed I do.'

Sam Daly's mother. She eyed me with disdain, her nose wrinkling. 'And Anthony, Kathleen? Is he well?'

'He's well, Mrs Daly,' I stated, my words strained through clenched teeth as I focused on sweeping the floor. 'He's working hard on the farm.'

Her lips tightened into a thin line and she nodded slowly. 'My Samuel has a good job and is soon to be wed. His fiancée is a wonderful girl from Blessington – her father is a respected major general in the army. A very reputable lineage, highly esteemed in their community. Samuel has joined the Garda Síochána.'

Her hazel eyes, reminiscent of Sam's, sparkled with unabashed pride.

Resentment simmered within me as I tried to overlook her pointed remarks, knowing full well they were aimed at me. She had always been critical of the friendship between Anthony and Sam. To her, we were beneath them, mere commoners unworthy of associating with her son, a Daly. At the age of twelve, Sam had been enrolled in Clongowes Wood, an esteemed boarding school in County Kildare run by the Jesuit priests. It was later that I learned from James how the school marked the line between those who were privileged and those who weren't. We belonged to the latter. Sam's father was a solicitor, like his father before him, and carried on the tradition of educating his son for success, like a farmer breeding pedigree cattle. Sam's future had been decided at twelve years old.

'Well then, I've got a list here with my messages. Bread, tea, the usual things,' Mrs Daly said, looking around the shop.

Mrs Kearns took it and handed it to me. 'Kitty, get Mrs Daly her messages. There's no rationing of bread, but the tea leaves are in demand, I'm afraid, Mrs Daly. People are stocking up on them.'

Glad to not have to talk to her, I busied myself getting Mrs Daly's messages. After she left, customers came and went, with sounds of pleasant chatter and the till opening and closing. Maybe the job wouldn't be so bad after all.

The church bells tolled midday. Mrs Kearns blessed herself and stood clasping her hands, her lips moving as she silently said the Angelus. Mr Reilly stood at the front door, his hands resting on the sweeping brush, also with his eyes closed.

Mr Reilly opened one eye and surreptitiously looked my way, and I quickly bowed my head, his ogling making me shiver as if someone had walked over my grave.

As the last bell tolled, Mrs Kearns said, 'Kitty, will you go in the back office to get some letters I need posting? I want them in the first post. Mrs Comerford is known for her early lunches. She's a law unto herself, closing the post office whenever she feels like it.'

The office at the back of the shop was dark, the frosted window letting little light in. The air was musty and old, as if bottled a hundred years before. The bell tinkled and through the window I saw a thin silhouette moving towards Mrs Kearns, a figure that appeared to be wearing a large hat.

'Afternoon, Sister,' said Mrs Kearns.

It was one of the nuns from Loreto, my old school. I slunk back, not wanting to face her. I hadn't expected to see a nun. I needed time to think. What if Mrs Kearns suddenly called me? I'm sure they knew everything that was going on.

On the desk, the letters were propped against an Underwood typewriter, and beside them was a brown medicinal bottle. I picked it up and read the label. Bayer Aspirin: Headache, Neuralgia, Toothache.

'Kitty, it's 12.30, will you hurry?' Mrs Kearns's voice rose an octave, the way voices did when talking to clergy.

Neuralgia was some sort of nerve pain. This was what Anthony needed. A few of these and he would be right as rain. My heart beat faster. Would I dare?

I glanced again at the window and held my breath, debating whether to take this risk. Mrs Kearns now stood on the small shop step, reaching up to the shelves for some sweets kept behind the counter, out of reach of the prying hands of wayward schoolchildren.

It was a risk I would have to take. Steadying my shaking hands, I unscrewed the top and poured five pills into my palm. The shop bell tinkled as a customer came in. I dropped the aspirin into my cardigan pocket and put the bottle down.

'Kathleen Flinn.' It was Mr Reilly's oily voice. His round body filled the doorway. His beady eyes narrowed, his breath heavy. 'What's keeping you?'

I grabbed the pile of letters. 'Nothing, I've got the letters.' I waved them in his face as I pushed him aside to pass. He leaned on the sweeping brush, his eyes like pins lost in the rolls of fat. He wiped his hands on his shop coat. I slid past him into the shop.

Seeing Sister Brenda from Loreto, my heart pounded like a drum in a marching band, and a cold sweat enveloped me as if an icy hand had clamped around my soul.

'Sister, do you remember Kathleen Flinn?' Mrs Kearns enquired.

A wave of anxiety crashed over me. My mind raced with all sorts of questions – had she somehow found out that I had been in a home for unwed mothers, and ran away? Did nuns have a system to exchange such information? As I shifted my feet, her eyes narrowed and a silent force of disapproval seemed to settle in the room.

'Ah, yes, Kathleen. How are you?' Sister Brenda asked, her eyes scanning me. They lacked the urgency of someone about to alert the authorities, but that did little to calm my racing heart.

'I'm well, thank you, Sister,' I replied, my voice barely concealing the turmoil within as I painted a forced smile on my face.

'Kathleen, what have you got up to since leaving school?' Her question felt like a trap, each word echoing ominously in the silent shop.

The room seemed to contract around me. I took a moment, gathering my thoughts to fabricate a believable story. 'Nothing much, Sister. I've been in London, volunteering, helping in the hospitals.' My voice was steady, but inside I was a tangle of nerves.

Mrs Kearns efficiently packed Sister Brenda's order. She handed over the bag, which disappeared into the depths of the nun's habit without any exchange of money.

'Good day, Mrs Kearns,' Sister Brenda said, her attention never quite returning to me as she turned to leave.

'Sister, will you tell the girls in the school kitchen that I heard there will be more tea rationing at the end of the month, so get the weekly order in soon,' Mrs Kearns called after her.

'I hope not,' Sister Brenda replied, making the sign of the cross. 'As we pray for the sinners on this earth, we also get the girls to say an extra rosary at evening prayers that there won't be any more rationing. I don't know what we would do without our cups of tea.'

As the door closed behind her, I let out a breath I didn't realise I'd been holding. The fear of discovery, the weight of my secret, remained a heavy cloak around my shoulders, even in the mundane setting of Mrs Kearns's shop.

Hot breath brushed the back of my neck and I turned around.

'No rationing for God's workers,' Mr Reilly muttered, then leaned into me, a sneer spread across his thin lips. 'Ye've turned to a right beauty.' I tried to move past him, but he put his hand on my breast, his grip firm, and squeezed it.

Holding my breath, I stood still. Heat flared inside my chest and I inhaled sharply. And then, without thinking, I delivered a powerful slap, the sound reverberating through the shop.

He bellowed, 'You little bitch!'

The imprint of my fingers stood out on his cheek like a fiery brand, and my fingers stung like I had plunged them into a nest of ants.

'Kathleen, what are you doing?' Mrs Kearns shouted.

'Sister Brenda, I am so sorry. I can't apologise enough.'

The nun stood frozen in the doorway. I hadn't heard her come back. She blanched as her hand flew to her mouth.

'Come here, ye brat!' Mr Reilly leaped forward and tripped on the sweeping brush, steadying himself with one hand on the counter, knocking a bag of tea onto the floor. Brown leaves spread across the wooden boards.

Nobody else spoke or moved.

Then Mrs Kearns screeched, 'Kathleen Flinn!' The rouge on her cheeks seeped across her face and down her neck.

I looked from her to Sister Brenda, whose mouth now hung open.

'You'll go to hell,' Mr Reilly spat the words at me. 'Won't she, Sister?' he said, rubbing his face.

'Fetch your coat,' commanded Mrs Kearns, her voice cutting through the atmosphere as sharply as a blade. 'And don't dare return or have any hopes of getting paid for today.'

Her body swayed towards me, as if on the brink of collapse, yet her voice maintained a strong and unwavering tone. 'Miss Flinn, I'm seriously considering summoning the Garda Síochána,' she said through gritted teeth.

My cheeks burning, I grabbed my coat. 'I'm going, don't worry. I'm going.' I pulled the door after me, the bell chiming angrily.

As I shakily untied my High Nelly from the lamppost, I took one last glimpse at the shop. Through the window, Mrs Kearns, Sister Brenda and Mr Reilly were standing in a line like statues with their arms folded across their chests. A wave of triumph surged through me at finally having some revenge for all those poor schoolgirls that he had taken advantage of over the years.

I cycled past Mrs Comerford's post office. It wasn't yet one o'clock but it was already closed, sign hanging on the door.

Oifig an Phoist
Dúnta 1–2 p.m.

I cycled down the high street and up John Street. The shopkeepers were putting *Closed for Lunch* signs on their doors, and like falling dominos they pulled the doors shut as I passed. My fingers curled around the handlebars as the January wind bit.

8

The letters were still clutched in my hand, and I buried them deep in my coat pocket as I hung my coat in the front hall. Anthony came down the stairs one step at a time, and one hand firmly on the banister.

'You're home early, or is it dinner time?' He glanced at the grandfather clock beside him in the hall.

'I'm not going back,' I said. My heart sank as I took in his appearance. His blisters had reopened, causing pus to ooze from the corner of his lips. His face was yellow and sunken, contorted in agony.

'Come, Anthony, you need to rest,' I said, guiding him into the kitchen. I reached for a cup and dipped it into the pail of water. From my cardigan pocket I retrieved two aspirin and held them out. 'Here, Anthony, take these,' I urged, and handed him the pills. 'It's medicine.'

His eyes met mine, searching for answers. 'Kitty, where did you get these? Did you manage to go to the doctor for me?' His voice trembled.

I averted my gaze, my focus shifting to the teapot.

I stirred it before pouring the weak tea into a cup. 'No. I got them from Mrs Kearns,' I said, still avoiding direct eye contact. 'They might offer you some relief. Take them with your tea.'

With a gentle squeeze of his arm, I added, 'Rest for a while. Go back up to bed. I'll prepare the dinner.'

When he was gone, despair crept over me like a dense, slow-moving fog. It was time to go back to London. Could I persuade Anthony to come with me? My gaze drifted to the kitchen table. Beneath the sugar bowl, a small pile of letters lay. They were most certainly filled with words of sympathy for my mother's passing. The thought of reading words of condolences left a bitter taste on my tongue. Slowly I drew one out and began reading it but it wasn't what I expected.

YOU ARE TO PAY ME THE SUM OF £35 BY JULY. FAIL TO DO SO, AND I WILL INFORM THE AUTHORITIES OF YOUR DEVIL HOMOSEXUAL RELATIONS WITH MEN. PAY UP BEFORE THE END OF JULY. ALSO I WILL TELL THE NUNS OF YOUR SISTERS RETURN THEY WANT THEIR £100 PO BOX 35.

I reread the words and each one seemed to suck the air from the room. *Anthony was a homosexual?* The dread, icy and intrusive, wormed its way through me. Six months. I quickly crumbled the note. Father Fitzpatrick had promised me not to tell the nuns. No one else knew about my child, so who had written it?

But then the blackmail note unfurled in my hands, its vile threats unmistakable. Failure to pay meant ruin for

Anthony. And if the nuns discovered my return, there'd be no mercy, only condemnation.

I remembered the personal ad in the magazine.

Anthony seeking clandestine meetings with men? So in the article I read, Tony had been Anthony. It couldn't be. My knees buckled as I grabbed the table to steady myself.

Anthony, my gentle brother who hardly played with other boys, preferring his books and imagination? The boy who clung to me as our only shield against Mother's wrath.

Surely this was some dreadful mistake.

Gasping for breath I was drowning in fear, in fury at this unjust world that would see my brother hanged – me arrested if the nuns got to me. Tears streamed down my cheeks. I grieved for the innocent boy Anthony had been, barefoot and carefree. And I wept for the man denied light, forced to live in shadow and shame. But I would fight for him with my last breath before I let them hurt him, let them crush the beauty of his spirit.

Who was aware of my return? Only James, Father Fitzpatrick, Sam Daly and those from the shop. None of them were in need of money. Why would they, or anyone else, resort to such measures?

The humiliation Anthony would face cast a dark shadow over my already heavy heart. As I considered the limited choices before me, it became clear that I needed to choose a path to avoid public scandal. We were without the means to pay. The task in front of me was as unmistakable as it was daunting: I had to protect him. A whirlwind of questions filled my thoughts as I grappled with the inconceivable predicament that I had stumbled into.

'Anyone home?' James shouted. 'It's only meself.'

He sat down at the kitchen table and placed his cap beside the teapot with a sigh as if ready to give a sermon.

'Kitty, what have you done? I heard what happened with Mr Reilly. You slapped him in front of a nun. Sister Brenda, of all people. You could have killed her with the shock you gave her.'

He chewed a piece of twig, rolling it from side to side. 'I don't blame you though. Mrs Kearns can't sack him, he's her sister's husband. I thought he had stopped all that sort of behaviour. And all that carry-on of his while his own brother's a bishop!'

I shook my head, then moved the breadboard, sliding the letter across the table to James. He read it in silence.

Clasping my hands, I spoke slowly and in a whisper, 'I think... I mean, I know what you meant when you said Anthony will be arrested.' I raised my eyes, looking straight at him. 'What will we do?'

James shook his head. 'I don't know who knows.' He reread the letter. 'What does that mean? And about the nuns?'

Tears fell onto my hands as I told him about the nuns and the money I owed them after my baby died.

'That's why I went to London to get away from everything, from here. There is nothing but bad memories, and nothing good happens.' I looked up at James waiting for his judgement.

James's face was impassive, I couldn't read it.

'I actually thought I could be a mother – in some fantasy world where I could have kept my child.'

James then took my hands in his, rubbing them as he spoke. 'And you would have made a wonderful mother.'

Bessie barked, as if a warning to my thoughts.

The kitchen door opened and Anthony came into the room, looking from me to James. His sudden entrance broke the taut thread of our conversation.

'What's wrong, Kitty? You look like you have seen a ghost.' He took a chair and sat beside me. 'That medicine was good, Kitty.' He stopped, his eyes resting on the letter on the table, then he looked to James.

'Anthony, we need to talk about... the letter, and what it says. Who knows about you, about me,' I said, my voice barely a whisper. I took a deep breath, trying to gather my thoughts. The words felt heavy on my tongue, but they needed to be said. 'Anthony, I saw the magazine... about you and other men.'

His face ashen, he looked down, avoiding my gaze. The silence seemed to stretch on forever.

'Anthony,' I began again, my voice barely rising above a whisper. The air was heavy in the dimly lit farm kitchen. The flickering candlelight cast elongated shadows across the rustic stone walls, while the crackling fire in the hearth added a sombre warmth to the scene. 'You need to understand. This... this is wrong. The Church says...'

'I know what the Church says,' he interrupted, his voice sharp and raw, cutting through the tense atmosphere like a knife. He looked up at me, his blue eyes shimmering with unshed tears, reflecting the fire's glow. 'But, Kitty, I can't change who I am.'

Then, with a hesitant pause, he added, 'You can't talk about the Church saying it's wrong. You had a baby. I guessed as much when you disappeared so quickly after that Seamus McGinty lad scurried off to America. Am I judging you for that? No, I'm not. We all have our crosses to bear, don't we?'

His words lingered in the air.

I replied, my voice strained with the pain. 'My baby died, so I just escaped... we are supposed to pay the nuns even if we have no baby, but me and my friend Eve left in the middle of the night.' A lump formed in my throat as I remembered that night. 'But, that is in the past, we have to concentrate on the present.'

Taking a deep breath, I continued, 'But, Anthony, you must understand the dangers. People who live like this... they're severely punished if anyone ever finds out.'

'I know, Kitty,' he repeated quietly, his voice a mere echo in the spacious kitchen. His eyes, now clear from the pain, widened as he reread the words that threatened to unravel our very existence.

James, who had been silently watching and listening to our conversation, stood up, his chair scraping harshly on the stone tiles. He walked towards Anthony, each step heavy with foreboding. Afraid of what was about to unfold, I held my breath.

Anthony moved back, his mouth agape, as James stood in front of him, his figure imposing in the dim light. James placed his large hands on Anthony's shoulders, enveloping them like paper soldiers.

'Anthony,' James said, his voice surprisingly gentle, like a soothing balm. 'You are like my son; I won't abandon you. I'll give you all the support you need. We'll just keep to ourselves.' He turned to face me, his eyes searching. 'Kitty, we'll try and sort this out.' But his voice was hollow, echoing the dread that filled me, a chilling premonition of uncertain futures.

Outside, Bessie's relentless barking sounded like a warning bell to the urgency of our plight. We had to find a solution, a sliver of hope in the encroaching darkness, or risk losing everything. Anthony stared at the letter, his fragile fingers trembling as they held the damning words, and a profound sadness seeped through my bones for him, the life he chose, and what would become of us.

9

Alone in the kitchen, I ruminated on my choices. Would I have to swallow my pride, bow my head in shame and go back to Mrs Kearns and say sorry to the fat Mr Reilly with his leering red-rimmed eyes? As I folded the newspaper, methodically tidying the kitchen, a job advertisement caught my attention:

January 10th
KILDARE BOARD OF HEALTH AND PUBLIC ASSISTANCE
NAAS COUNTY HOSPITAL
NURSE'S AIDES REQUIRED URGENTLY
The Board invites applicants for the position of nurse's aide in the Naas County Hospital at a salary of £55 per year. Immediate appointment. Apply no later than 4 o'clock on Friday 24 February, with experience – Respectable unmarried woman. References essential.

I reread it. *Experience*. Would anyone check? With little choice, I had to try.

Required urgently. Immediate appointment.

I tapped my fingertips on the table and looked around the kitchen. The silence was broken as the tap dripped, each drop getting louder.

Drip.

Drip.

Drip.

I looked around the kitchen: the breadboard with one slice of bread, the empty shelves. The fire was cold; even the snowdrops on the windowsill drooped. A ray of weak light fell on the tiled floor. Mesmerising dust danced in the funnel like little coloured crystals.

I exhaled slowly, counting to ten to slow my beating heart. I bit my lip while rereading the ad. I had two of the credentials. I knew my way around a hospital – not intimately, but from a few weeks volunteering and first aid training.

I scanned the paper for another job. Nothing.

I needed to find the first-aid certificate. For the next hour I searched the house for it, looking under my mother's bible on her bedside table, moving her rosary beads covered in thick dust. I pulled her bedside table drawer open, saw the knitting patterns she always carefully cut out of *My Weekly* magazine. Nothing.

I threw the contents on the bed. Her diaries spread across the eiderdown. These black leather books held her thoughts. They were guarded secretively. Every night, she would sit in her armchair in front of the fire and scribble for a few minutes, then close the diary and bring it up to her room. Even when she left one downstairs, Anthony and I never dared open it to see what she'd written.

At the end of the year, when she finished a diary, a new one would appear for the next year. I'd thought she had thrown them away. Some of the once black covers were now grey with age, and my fingertips traced the lines on the cracked leather. There were twenty diaries, notebooks with the year scrawled in pencil. Pencilled hard.

I held my breath and stared at the words inside.

7 März 1920
Fühle mich in Ordnung. Wetter schlecht. Wieder Eintopf
machen. Mrs Comerford rief an...

I grimaced as I read her words. Of course she wrote in German. I shuddered; I could hear the manic scratching of her fountain pen on the paper like she was sitting beside me. I translated into English in my head as I read, making her presence less tangible.

7 March 1920
Feel fine. Weather bad. Making stew again. Mrs Comerford
called with...

The day I was born. What did Mrs Comerford call with? Flowers, maybe? A cake?

Nothing about me. I flicked through the diaries; she didn't have one for every year.

7 March 1921

Blank. My birthday.

Endless pages of her moods and how she slept. Nothing of me or Anthony. Mention of our father was sporadic, vitriolic: him talking rubbish, lazy, selfish.

25 December 1924
Con talking rubbish again.

12 April 1927
Frost but sunny, bright day.

That was the day my father died.

15 April 1927
Bit warmer today. Must bake something nice.

The day my father's coffin was lowered into the permafrost.

24 April 1927
Sleeping better.

Was this the mind of a warped woman? Her twisted, sick mind. And no mention of my father on the day of his funeral. Just the usual list of her moods and the weather and cut-out knitting patterns. I flicked through more diaries. There was no mention of me or Anthony. As if we had never existed.

I stopped at the diary entry from one week before her death. Her handwriting hurried and messy, unlike her normally meticulous script.

23 Dec 1940
I met him.

Him. Who was *him*? A week before her death! Did she mean Anthony? A relative perhaps.

My hands trembled, reading her words was like she was in the room with me, and I threw them to the bed to continue the search for the first-aid certificate. I couldn't find it.

I rifled through the papers again but still couldn't locate it. A thought struck me – maybe it had been intercepted by the wartime censors. I knew from the red 'Passed by Censor' stamp on James's letter that outgoing mail was closely monitored. It stood to reason that incoming mail would be as well, although a first-aid certificate was hardly interesting enough to censor.

The rushed diary entry nagged at me as I tidied the papers. Who was this mysterious "him" my mother had met just days before her death? And what had prompted her to scribble it down so hurriedly? My mind raced with questions, but I forced myself to refocus on the task at hand. The certificate had to be here somewhere.

I moved on to search the rest of the room, thoughts of my mother's diary entry lingering in the back of my mind. The "him" continued to gnaw at me, an unsolved mystery tied to her final days. Some puzzles around her might be better left unsolved, I decided.

Downstairs, I opened the kitchen table drawer and rifled through the papers until I found the thick yellow vellum paper – the same writing paper Mother had written to Father Fitzpatrick with, requesting a meeting for her and me.

A piece of crinkled brown paper landed on the cold stone

tiles. I picked it up and smoothed it out, laying it flat on the table beside my fountain pen. It was an envelope addressed to my mother, written by me last year. I inhaled. The only letter I had ever sent her was my first-aid certificate.

Tears tried to fall, and I banged my fist on the table, knocking the inkpot over, the black ink oozing across the table towards the writing pad. I cursed, grabbed the paper and ran to get a dishcloth from under the sink. An iodine bottle and a rusty tin of Jeyes cleaning fluid sat ominously on a piece of white paper with a red pattern. It was my certificate, used to soak up stains. I put it up beside the gaslight, running my fingers over my name and the red crest of St John Ambulance.

I found two sheets of rough paper, and inhaled as my fountain pen scratched on it:

Dear Mr Rodgers,
My name is Kathleen Flinn. I am a single woman of twenty years of age. I have experience working in Charing Cross Hospital, gaining a first-aid certificate.

References. I stopped to think. My coat, the one I had worn to Kearns's. Sure enough, there was a blank page in among the stationery. I began writing again.

Kearns's General Grocery and Confectioner
1 Dean St
Kilkenny

Dear Mr Rodgers,
Kathleen Flinn is a respectable, valuable and honest

employee. She worked in my shop, and occasionally in the office.

I reread it and added:

She is a great worker and gets on well with the other staff.

Yours faithfully,
Mrs Kearns

When I'd finished a wet nose nuzzled my leg. I petted Bessie, rubbing her floppy ears as if wishing for a magic spell, thinking, *I hope he believes that I have experience.* I thought of Mr Reilly and his sweaty, red, fat face, and prayed Mr Rodgers wouldn't write to Mrs Kearns.

I put the reference letter in with the application and sealed the envelope. The paper was a few days old, so I needed to get to the post office without delay. I was soon cycling into town, an icy breeze in the air, freewheeling down the hill, inhaling the freedom. The wind rushed through my hair, only slowing at St John's church, where I silently said a Hail Mary.

The wheel refused to turn smoothly, and when I inspected it, I saw the slow puncture.

'What's wrong, miss? You look like you're in a spot of bother,' a lad shouted across the street. He stood on his toes looking over a cart that seemed abandoned by its owner, grass growing around the wheels.

It was Brian Clarke.

'You've grown since I saw you last,' I said. I hadn't seen him since the day I'd left school, and he'd been just starting.

He had a brown hessian sack slung across his shoulder, a goat's head peering out of it, its tongue hanging slightly as if smiling.

'I've a puncture, Brian,' I said.

'I'll get me da to fix it for ya. When do you want it?' He shifted the goat in the sack, and we looked at each other with the same amount of curiosity.

'I've just to post this, but I can walk the High Nelly home.'

'Here's me da,' Brian said, nodding to the man walking towards me. He had the same grin as Brian, and he thrust out his hand.

'Kathleen, good to see you. I heard you were home.' He clasped my hand in his. 'It's really good to see you.'

'And you too, Paddy.'

He was younger than James but his face was brown and leathery, from working on the bogs in Laois. It had aged him far beyond his years.

'I'm home for a little while. Longer than I thought.'

He leaned to one side. 'I heard you were in London. Dangerous place, bombs all night. We've listened to the BBC radio,' he said, with pride that he could afford a radio licence. Most people kept their sets hidden in the shed in case the licence man called.

He shifted and folded his arms.

Brian stood to the side, watching us. He said, 'My daddy is joining the army. He's going to fight the Germans, and he's going to get a gun.'

Paddy ran his fingers through his hair. Unusually for a man his age, he had the same thick hair as his son. 'Brian, I'm not in the army. I'm in the local defence force. You just never know what's going to happen with these Germans.'

He rubbed his chin, and said, staring at my flat wheel, 'Kitty, give that to me and Brian will drop it up to the farm for you this afternoon. It'll keep him out of trouble.' He scowled at his son. 'Always getting up to no good. Caught him nicking apples the other day.'

It would be easier than walking the bicycle all the way home. 'If it's no bother, that would be great.'

Paddy took my High Nelly. As he walked away, he lifted his hand with a wave, Brian walking beside him with the still-smiling goat's head bobbing up and down.

I took a shortcut through Kieran Street, passing Malloy's bakery, the sweet smell of morning bread lingering in the air as I turned left up the narrow steps through the arches of the Butter Slip. It had once been flanked by stalls of butter vendors on market day, centuries ago. Now it was a walkway from Kieran Street to the high street.

The clock above the courthouse struck two. I would be just in time when the post office reopened after lunch. But hanging on the door was the closed sign. *Dúnta.* I cupped my face, squinting into the blackness of the shop, and rapped on the window.

There was no answer. I rapped again. I didn't have money for the train. Maybe I could hitchhike to Naas and hand deliver the letter to the hospital? But there were so few cars on the road.

'Hello, Kathleen.'

I turned. It was Mrs Daly. Her red lipstick bled into the lines around her mouth.

'Mrs Daly, I was hoping the post office was open.' I turned the letter over in my hand, not wanting to show her prying eyes the address.

'You look like you're in a bother. I heard you left the shop already. Have you been ill?'

She was so nosy, knowing what people had for their dinner. Gossip was her only currency.

I straightened up, squinting in the sun.

'No, I'm fine. I just wanted to get a stamp and post this letter. I need it to go today.'

She fixed her headscarf and glanced again at the letter in my hand. I put it into my coat pocket.

'Mrs Comerford has closed the post office today to go and see her sick mother. She probably took her to see the doctor.' Her head rose a little higher. 'She's good like that. You know, good to her mother.'

I held my tongue. I knew exactly what she meant.

'My Samuel is going to Dublin this evening. He can take it if you like,' she said nonchalantly.

I smiled my best smile.

A crow hopped near her feet, pecking at the grain that fell from the farmers' trailers. Her smile disappeared, and her face settled back to its usual disdain. 'Awful birds.'

A man walked towards us. Different than the ordinary farmer in the streets of Kilkenny. His clothes were tailored, clean, not workmen's clothes. His navy suit was the kind bankers in London wore.

'Ah, here he is,' said Mrs Daly.

Sam stepped towards me, holding out his hand. I took his hand, his grip strong, and I waited for him to mention he had been out at my house with Father Fitzpatrick.

'Kitty, it's so good to see you again.' He looked as polished as his accent sounded. Any trace of Kilkenny was gone from it.

Was I wrong? Had it been him standing against the car? I wasn't too sure now if he had been in our yard.

He was handsome, his brown eyes still his most striking feature. He looked sharp in his suit and smooth, crisp white shirt, everything neat, absolute perfection. Except for the tip of his left ear, which was slightly misshapen, as if it had been clipped with a knife.

'Miss Flinn...' she looked at me like a piece of mud on her shoes. 'Kitty needs a letter posted, Samuel. Maybe you could take it for her. Where did you say it was to go?'

'I didn't.'

Sam smiled at me, his teeth shining white against the tan on his face, raising his eyebrows at his mother. 'Now, we don't need to know Kitty's business, do we?'

'Sam, enough of these pleasantries, you'll be late for your train,' said Mrs Daly, clearing her throat to hurry up the conversation. 'He has a fitting for his wedding suit in Dublin. He's getting married to a lovely lady, from Blessington. Her father's a major general.'

'I know, you told me already,' I said, impatient with her constant snobbery. Sam was never going to marry a girl from Kilkenny; he had been bred for better stock.

Mrs Daly had some cheek. She was born only two fields away from my house, in a one-room cottage now in ruins. All that was left was stone walls with a thatched roof that sagged in the middle.

'Congratulations, Sam,' I said. 'When is that?'

Mrs Daly answered for him. 'It's not until next year. We have so much to do, don't we, Samuel?'

She flicked a bit of dust from his lapel, afraid any bit of

me might contaminate him. 'And Anthony? I don't see him around the town at all any more.'

'He's busy,' I said and looked down the street to see if there was any sign of Mrs Comerford. I'd had enough of Mrs Daly and Sam, and was glad when the Denny's van tooted its horn for Mrs Daly to get off the road.

As I passed St John's church, distant thunder and black clouds rolled towards the hills. The beech trees that had been still on my way into Kilkenny now pulsed and pushed in the wind. Clouds rolled fast. I wished I had my High Nelly for speed.

The quickest way home as the crow flew was through the fields. The wind moved faster on my face and my heartbeat thundered, my shoes pushing into the swampy spikes of grass. Time wasn't on my side. A flash of light lit the sky. I counted, and it was eight seconds before thunder vibrated in the distance. Going through the small wood would shorten my journey.

Something caught my attention in the trees. It looked like a bedsheet had come loose from someone's washing line, billowing in the wind, but as I neared, I saw it more clearly. It was the largest piece of cloth I had ever seen, a silky white between the branches of two trees, long straps hanging from it. I had seen nothing like it before. I stared at it for a moment, getting lost in it as it billowed like a giant balloon. There was something soft about it, gentle.

It dawned on me. It was a parachute, empty straps dangling, waving in the wind. Was this what I had seen falling from the sky that night?

German? English?

The briars cut my legs. The wind threw branches and

leaves at me and seemed to pick up speed with every passing minute, the rain punishing everything it landed on, flattening and breaking it. In protest, the trees creaked and moaned. I didn't know which frightened me more, a German or a tree crashing on top of me.

I stumbled on an exposed tree root, grabbing a branch for balance, but slipped on smooth stones, falling with the rivulets of water down an embankment. A loose branch tore my skirt, and I finally stopped in a labyrinth of branches and clump of nettles. Dazed, with painful scratches on my calves, I heaved myself up, but didn't waste time in case the airman appeared. I ran through the field, my stockings offering little protection against the stalks. My heartbeat thumped in my ears.

As promised, Brian had left my High Nelly in the yard. As I pulled it out, I saw the tyre was still flat. Cursing that you can't trust anyone, I brought it to the barn where I found Anthony.

He sat on a bale of hay, pulling on a wellington boot. He grunted, beads of perspiration forming on his forehead.

'Anthony, what are you doing? You're not fit to go anywhere,' I said and thought how different Sam and Anthony's lives were. 'I met Sam Daly in town today.'

Anthony didn't say anything. I turned to see if he was all right.

'He's not our sort, Kitty – too posh for us. It's a wonder he talked to you at all.' He spat and it landed on the floor, he rubbed it with the toe of his sock.

I didn't tell him Sam had offered to post the letter. I didn't tell him about the job.

10

A week after posting the letter, I stood on the platform of Kilkenny Station, still not believing my luck at being called for an interview at Naas County Hospital. Clasping my bag tight to stop myself shaking, nerves and questions undulating through my body at speed, I thought I might get sick, or even faint.

The station master at the end of the platform glanced at his watch, then looked anxiously down the line. Kilkenny Station was unusual in that the train tracks ended here and the train had to reverse out to go on to Dublin or Portlaoise. Young men in overalls, smoking cigarettes, looked anxiously down the tracks.

'Excuse me, when is the train coming?' I asked as he passed. 'I've got an appointment in Naas at eleven o'clock.'

The station master looked over his glasses, assessing me, his eyes travelling from my red hat to my polished shoes. He nodded, as if I'd passed an exam.

'Don't worry, miss, it's on its way; it's often late and nobody telephoned to say it wasn't coming.'

Finally, the train inched into the station, its slow arrival matching my mounting anticipation. I watched as the driver disembarked to switch ends, preparing to guide the train back on to its route. Settling into an almost vacant compartment, I felt a sense of relief when the train began to move.

Opposite me, a woman with mottled red hair was engrossed in her knitting. Her needles moved with an enviable speed, that I wished the train would match, the needles clicking rhythmically at the end of each row. Strands of white, blue, and orange wool trailed from her lap, intertwining in a colourful dance. She glanced up, offering a brief nod of acknowledgement, before I turned my gaze to the blur of hedgerows and fields outside, mentally rehearsing for the encounter ahead.

Abruptly, the train jerked to a halt. Peering out, the sign for Sallins and Clongowes Wood confirmed my destination.

'This is my stop,' I announced, hastily collecting my coat and handbag. Disembarking, I got the connecting train, finding a spot next to a mother and her daughter.

Shortly afterwards, I got off the spur train at Naas and looked at James's map, turning the paper around. He'd drawn the road clearly, marking the arrows heavily, as he knew map reading was not a strong point of mine. After a few hundred yards on Corban's Lane, I turned left.

'Make sure you have plenty of time, Kit, and if ye get lost, just ask. Friendly enough around Naas, and I think the hospital is close to the old workhouse,' he had said. 'If those stones could talk, they could tell you a thing or two that would make your stomach turn.'

I reached the hospital in under twenty minutes, racing against the swiftly changing weather. The sky transitioned from a clear blue to a foreboding grey. The leafless cedar trees swayed in the wind, and its bite cut sharply against my face. I cast my red-and-white scarf around my face.

Unlike the grey stones of Kilkenny Hospital, which looked hundreds of years old, Naas County Hospital was shiny and new. The windows on the three floors glistened and spoke of prosperity. I dusted my coat sleeves and swept my hand over the hem of my skirt where it had crinkled. I had to do this for Anthony. I stepped into the hospital. My shoes clicked on the tiles. I adjusted my hat, took a deep breath, held the neatly folded letter and entered, unsure of what lay ahead.

The sharp smell of disinfectant seeped from the white-tiled floor, beneath the stark white walls.

A nun's expansive black headdress was an intimidating sight, making my heart leap into my throat and my stomach perform an uneasy flip.

A wave of anxiety coursed through me as I quietly contemplated the conversation I was about to have – would she recognise me? Could she be one of the sisters from St Margaret's? Perhaps this was a mistake; perhaps I should just leave and put this all behind me. But the haunting figure of £35 from the blackmail letter materialised in my mind's eye, pushing me to advance, praying that the nuns were blind to the broken woman standing before them.

I stepped forward and greeted her with a respectful curtsy, despite being nervous and uncomfortable in her presence.

Her suspicion was evident as she looked down her long nose at me, clasping her hands under the folds of her habit.

'Good morning, miss, what can we help you with?' she asked in a guarded tone.

My palms began to sweat and my tongue stuck to the roof of mouth, I struggled to find a suitable response.

'Do you know where I could find Mr Rodgers?' I managed, offering a practised smile.

The veil shadowed her face and her mouth didn't move, but her beady black eyes travelled from my head to my shiny shoes.

'It's the last door on the left.' She pursed her lips and pointed, her finger entwined with a string of worn rosary beads. On the wall at the end of the brightly lit corridor there was a picture of Jesus on the cross. Drops of red blood dripped down his face, a reminder for us to suffer.

I knocked. The room smelled of furniture polish mingled with something sweet that I couldn't quite name. A man sat by the long windows at a wide mahogany desk laden with neat piles of letters and a flowered teacup.

'Sit down,' he said, without looking up from his paperwork. 'I'm Mr Rodgers.'

I sat down and took off my gloves, folding my hands on my lap. The light bounced off his round head, and the metal glinted on his round spectacles. All of him was round and tightly pulled in by his waistcoat; the buttons strained, ready to pop. He scanned over my letters. My heart was racing, blood rushing in my ears, my armpits clammy. My eyes followed a fly walking along the edge of his leather mat, and Mr Rodgers reached for the ruler and swiped it away.

'Ghastly things. No place for them in a hospital.'

He leaned back, taking off his spectacles and rubbing the red line on the bridge of his nose.

'Now, my dear.' He put his spectacles on, leaning towards me and squinting, his eyes falling into the folds of fat. 'You are a slip of a thing, aren't you?'

He looked at a few papers and picked one up. 'We need nurse's aides urgently. All the local girls upped and left for England, to work in the munition factories. Can you believe that?'

His glasses slipped to the end of his nose. He looked over the top of the frames.

'We're trying to improve. We want well-organised girls; neat, who aren't impulsive. And who are, above all, honest. Have you got children?'

He picked up my letter, my neat cursive writing. 'No, you wouldn't. You're not married.'

I straightened and pressed my shoulder blades into the back of the chair. 'No children,' I replied, digging my nails into the palms of my hand.

'The last girl…' He lowered his voice conspiratorially, as if we were old friends. 'She had to leave rather suddenly and get married. Is there any sign of you getting married?' He lowered his voice further, more of a whisper now. 'I don't really think it should matter that a woman gets married, but when children come along, that's another matter.'

He flicked through some papers. 'Your reference is excellent. When did you go to England?' He lifted a sheet of paper. He took off his round spectacles. 'Why did you return?'

My head was dizzy from the questions. I lifted my bag

off the ground to take out a clean white hanky. 'My mother passed away suddenly.' I blessed myself.

'You poor, poor thing. That is absolutely awful,' he said. 'Nurse's aides must have self-discipline and be dependable. And foremost, they have to deal with any emergency. They must help the nurses. A nurse is the link for the patient to the outside world. It really is one of the greatest professions.'

His face turned serious, and he cleared his throat. 'Why do you want to be a nurse's aide?'

I wanted to say: I need the money to help my sick brother, who is in fear he will be arrested because of who he is – he likes men – and the nuns will have me arrested.

But instead I said, 'I want to help people, make a difference to their lives. I have lots of empathy and want to make the lives of the doctors easy, and also the nurses. Maybe, one day, I will be afforded the opportunity to be a nurse.'

I swallowed and continued.

'I love working with people, especially the elderly.' My eyes stared to the crucifix for redemption for the next lie: 'I loved looking after my sick mother.' And I continued with the truth: 'I'm eager to learn more and develop my skills.'

He nodded, whether in dissatisfaction or approval, I didn't know which. He lowered his eyes, his lips moving silently as he read the next question before speaking. 'Give me an example of a time you went above and beyond for a patient.'

This was not one I'd expected. I thought, what had I really done? I hadn't done much in my volunteering in Charing Cross Hospital. Remembering the boy on the steamer I said, 'I helped a young child who had a bad head injury, and stayed with him until his mother came.'

I needed to say something else. I remembered blind Simon Brennan, the loner.

'There was a blind man who had no friends, and I used to read to him in the evenings,' I said, hoping to keep my face deadpan despite these exaggerations.

His face melted into a smile and his brow glistened, as if this conversation was hard work.

'Do you know Father Fitzpatrick? An incredibly good man, incredibly good indeed.'

'Yes, he is my parish priest.'

'I've such fond memories of him. He was so kind to the younger children. When he came here, we had a lot of the poor things. Couldn't look after themselves. I will give him a call and make enquires about you.'

My heart stopped, and the air was pulled from the room. I hoped he didn't notice the blood rushing from my cheeks. I was thankful I'd carefully rouged them for the interview. I couldn't risk Father Fitzpatrick telling Mr Rodgers about the predicament I had found myself in.

'Now, I'm sure I have his number somewhere – I'd love a catch-up as well.' He pulled open his desk drawer, taking a black leather diary out.

I lowered my eyes, putting on my sorrowful voice again. 'It's a shame he got so sick and had to go to the sanatorium in Waterford.'

I was digging myself deeper than I had expected, and was glad I hadn't taken off my gloves. I imagined them bleached white as I tightened my grip on the handles of my bag.

Peering over his spectacles, he looked at the wall clock. 'I'll be in touch in a day or two. We're short-staffed.'

I took a deep breath before I stood to steady my legs. 'Thank you, Mr Rodgers.'

He followed me out into the corridor and glanced at his watch and the empty chairs. He looked at me, nodded, and went back into the room. I thought he would immediately come out shouting 'This reference is a fake!'

Just as I reached the front door I heard the fast clicking of shoes on the tiles behind me. Mr Rodgers was calling, 'Miss Flinn, Miss Flinn!'

I debated whether to run or just own up, but I turned around to confess and waited my fate. He ran towards me, waving his arms, but I couldn't hear his words. Had he phoned Father Fitzpatrick? Had he told Mr Rodgers I'd run away from St Margaret's?

I readied myself to run. He caught my arm. 'Miss Flinn, you dropped this.'

From his hand dangled my white-and-red scarf, looking like a white flag of peace, or maybe a red rag to a bull. I took it quickly and hurried through the hospital and on to the train station.

I I

Every day, with a growing sense of anxiety, I swept the yard, hoping to see and hear Mr Hardy the postman's familiar whistle. It was his way of telling the farm dogs he was friend not foe. As the days turned into a week, my hope had begun to dwindle. Then on Monday morning I was throwing the last of the sheets on to the washing line just as Mr Hardy whistled, cycling to our front door.

'Morning, Kitty, you're looking well.' His moustache moved as he spoke. 'James said you were home from London. Terrible, all the bombing over there.' He lowered his voice. 'I've a wee wireless in the shed at the bottom of the garden. I sometimes get the BBC.'

'No need to quiet your voice, it seems everyone in Ireland has a hidden wireless. It's only me and the dog, and I don't think she's going to tell the Post and Telegraph that Mr Hardy has a radio but no licence.'

'I've only the one for you today, Kitty.' He opened his postbag and gave me a brown envelope, my name written in black fountain pen.

After he left, I sat at the kitchen table and stared at the envelope. I had never been good at rejection. My stomach was somersaulting.

'What's that, Kitty?' asked Anthony.

'It's nothing.'

I stared at the postmark: *Co. Cill Dara*. County Kildare.

'Will I make tea?' he said, yawning and filling the kettle.

I nodded and asked, 'Did you not sleep?'

He shook his head and settled in the armchair, watching the flames dance, licking the base as they turned from white to red.

My hands shook as I slit the envelope with the knife and let the page fall onto the table, not wanting to touch it.

29 January 1941

Dear Miss Flinn,
I am delighted to offer you the position as nurse's aide, starting on Monday 10 February with a wage of £55 per year.

   You will be required to work weekends and night shifts every three weeks.
Yours,
Mr C. Rodgers

The letter trembled in my hands as I scanned the words. £55.

Anthony sat in the armchair, his face drained and expressionless. I knelt beside him and carefully placed my hand on his knee, trying to offer some comfort from the agonising worry etched on his forehead.

'Anthony,' I said gently, 'I've got a job. Everything will be fine, I'll be getting fifty-five pounds a year, that's twenty shillings a week,' I began, trying to sound more confident than I felt.

'I would need to save twelve shillings a week. It's tight, I know. I haven't figured out the lodgings yet, but it's a start, isn't it? And who knows, maybe they'll just leave us be, or... or perhaps we could make it to London.'

Anthony's face was a picture of despair. 'I am so dreadfully sorry to put this burden on you,' he said, his voice heavy with guilt.

I reached out, placing my hand gently on his arm, offering a fragile smile. 'Don't worry, we will be all right,' I whispered, more to convince myself than him. The words felt hollow, echoing my own doubts and fears.

But my assurance didn't erase my own worry. It would be a stretch to cover the blackmailer's demands, and I still needed to pay for lodging. It seemed like an impossible task.

12

February

Stepping off the train in Naas, I was thankful James had arranged a room for me. The February chill nipped my cheeks as I navigated my way my way down Main Street, past the looming courthouse, and left onto Basin Street. A housewife nodded as I passed, her curious eyes boring into me.

I turned left at the bottom of the street. Leading to a red door was a neat flagstone garden path flanked by crocuses. A few had braved the February weather with purple and white flowers. I fixed my hat, exhaled and knocked.

Within seconds, a key scraped on the other side of the door. The woody smell of perfume greeted me, worn by a cottony-grey-haired woman. Smiling, she said, 'You must be Kitty. I got James's letter.'

The little round woman was bundled in a taupe wool cardigan, and a beautiful champagne headscarf made her face appear even rounder and gave her skin a warm glow.

'Come in, dear, out of that cold. You are most welcome.' She opened the door, gesturing to me to come in. The hallway was dark and narrow, and the little light coming through the fanlight fell on the hallstand. I followed the earthy smell of her perfume, and that of fresh floor polish, into a bright room.

'Sorry, I'm Mrs Brady. But please call me Alice. Everyone does.'

She pulled off her headscarf and checked in the mirror that she hadn't upset her curlers. It was a large room with deep comfortable chairs and a wall lined with books and cluttered with porcelain figurines of pink ballerinas and brown and white dogs.

'Sorry, it's a bit stuffy in here. I forgot to open the windows.'

She motioned for me to sit on a velvet, hard-back chair beside a table. As I settled, my gaze landed on a silver picture frame on the mantlepiece. A family portrait – two adults and a child. 'That's Peter and me,' Alice said, her eyes briefly clouding with unshed tears.

The child, Peter, sat in a corner, absorbed in a thick book. His short trousers revealed knees reddened from the carpet, hinting at his youth. Alice's gaze lingered on him, a mixture of love and concern etching her features.

She folded her hands on her lap. 'Tell me about yourself. James said you have a job?'

I smiled. 'Yes, nurse's aide, at the hospital.' I opened my bag and tried to hand her the letter, but she held up her hand.

'Put that away. Any friend of James is a friend of mine.'

Mrs Brady's hands twisted as she looked back at Peter. 'He doesn't talk much. He prefers his own company. He's a little different from boys his own age and can get confused easily.'

She paused. Her eyes glazed over with tears.

'He doesn't know any other boys, so it's just the two of us. He loves the garden. Spring will be here shortly, and birds sing so early; he gets up and goes out to the garden.'

She lowered her voice. 'He's nearly fifteen. I was a late mother.'

Her voice was soft and gentle, like her eyes.

'And I hope you will be all right with him. I'm sure you will, especially as you are a nurse.'

'Nurse's aide,' I corrected her.

'That's such a good job as well.' She nodded as she spoke, and her eyes glistened. 'Nurses can't do their job without assistance, and isn't it lovely to be able to help others? You must be proud of yourself. The doctors in Naas did their best for Maurice, but in the end there was nothing they could do. James said your mother died just before Christmas. I imagine that must have been so sad.'

I nodded, hoping I appeared mournful.

'You only have one mother, isn't that right, and it's so recent, you must still be grieving.'

Again I nodded, this time lowering my eyes. The grief was not for my mother. I coughed, and with my sweetest and saddest face said, 'It's tough to lose a mother.'

'Tea. I'll make us some tea. Peter, I'll be back in a moment, I'm going to make this nice lady a cup of tea.'

She went over to him and put her arm around his shoulders, leaning in and giving him a peck on his head. I'd never seen a mother so tender with their child. I felt like an intruder.

Alice's voice broke my thoughts. 'Kitty, make yourself comfortable. I'll be back in a tick.'

Peter didn't acknowledge his mother or seem aware she was gone but stared out the bay window. While she was gone, I took in the room, the neatness, the comfortable home.

Soon the door opened and Alice came back with a silver tray and white fine-bone China. There was a small silver sugar bowl and a matching jug. As she put the tray on the table, sunlight fell on its chipped edges. Spidery cracks ran through the green leather, though only someone with good eyesight would notice. She took off her horn-rimmed spectacles and rubbed them with the white serviette.

'Old age isn't nice, is it? My eyes seem to be getting weaker.'

Her face was like porcelain; there was no sign of old age on it, her cheeks naturally glowed against her ivory skin as if painted with rouge.

She handed me a gilt-edged cup, the kind I saw through the windows of hotels in London.

'The company will be nice. Peter, he's quiet.'

She paused, looking down at her wringing hands, then sat up straight and took a deep breath.

'He doesn't like change. He likes routine. It's just been the two of us for such a long time. But he doesn't talk, and...'

She looked at her son again. An orange and white cat jumped onto his knees and curled up on his lap with a low, vibrating hum.

'James spoke really highly of you. It'll be a big change for Peter, I...' and she got up and went over to Peter. 'Sorry, dear, that's my neighbour's cat,' she said then resettled herself in her chair. 'Sorry, I got distracted. What was I saying?'

I looked down at my hands and silently prayed she

would say yes. This house was in a perfect location, not too far from the hospital. I could still go back to Anthony on my days off.

'I'm used to being quiet,' I said. So true, that was. Anthony and I never knew what our mother would be like. Every morning we would ask each other, 'Is she in good humour, or bad?'

Alice looked at the silver-framed photo and sighed. 'When Maurice, my husband, died, we survived on his pension, but now things are so expensive. I hate taking money off people. Would three shillings a week be too much?'

Her eyes dropped a little and she wrung her hands again. 'I hate taking too much money from a young girl like you.'

I would be able to save eight shillings a week. After tea, I agreed to move in the following week. It wouldn't be enough, but it was a start.

13

'Anthony.' I squeezed his shoulder lightly. 'Wake up, I'm leaving soon.'

The room was still dark. He stirred, eyes fluttering, and rubbed bits of sleep from the corners of his eyes.

'Kitty. What time is it?'

'Early. James is waiting to bring me to Kilkenny Station.'

I lifted his head and pulled his pillow up, encouraging him to sit up.

'Remember, I'm leaving today for my new job.'

He nodded. 'When are you coming back?'

'When I can. I don't know what my rota is, and maybe I can get extra shifts, but I'll send money to James for you.

I ran my thumb down his cheek, his stubble hard against my skin. He looked so small in the bed. He leaned his face into my palm. I hoped he would understand when this was all said and done that I couldn't stay here – too many memories.

'Anthony, look at me. We have been through so much already. We'll get through this.'

'Kitty,' James shouted from below, 'the train! You'll miss it if we don't leave soon.'

'Anthony, promise me one thing.'

He nodded, and I felt he knew what I was going to say.

'Keep to yourself, don't go wandering, especially in town, and don't meet—'

He lifted his hand. 'Kitty, it's all right, I know what you mean; I'm going to stop all that.' He laughed a little. 'Maybe I'll find a wife and settle down.'

I closed my eyes, a wave of relief washed over me, as if a heavy burden had been lifted. 'Thank God, the last thing I want is for you to be arrested and sent to prison. I'll save money when I get my wages and we'll get that bloody blackmailer paid, and I might even be able to get you a prescription at the hospital. Maybe one of the doctors will write me one.'

It sounded like false hope, but it might be something positive for him to think about.

I looked into his eyes, finding a flicker of strength in my resolve. 'I'll send the money to James. We'll find a way to work it out. But, Anthony, you have to promise me something.'

'Anything, Kitty.'

'Please look after yourself. Stay out of trouble. Keep to yourself if you have to. I can't bear the thought of losing you too.'

Anthony nodded, his expression solemn. 'I promise, Kitty. I'll be careful. For you and for James.'

I squeezed his hand. The path ahead was uncertain, but in that moment, I had a sliver of strength.

The window reverberated with the sound of a pebble

striking it. James's voice pierced the air. 'Kitty, where in heaven's name are you?'

I joined James in the trap, my small suitcase resting on the seat behind him, my fears on my face.

As the pony and trap made its way along the road to Kilkenny, James, skilfully guiding the reins, glanced at me briefly. I held the crumpled piece of paper he had given me. After calculating the weekly savings, another worry crept into my thoughts. 'James,' I started, a hint of trepidation in my voice, 'do you think we could find out who the blackmailer is?'

James looked at me, his eyes reflecting a mix of concern and caution. 'Kitty, I've considered it. But it might be safer to just pay up and be done with it. Delving into it might bring more trouble than we're prepared for.'

I murmured, the reality of our predicament sinking in. The challenge of saving was one thing; dealing with the blackmailer was quite another.

James's voice pulled me from my thoughts. 'We'll manage, Kitty. It's a tough path, but it's the only one we've got.'

I folded the paper, tucking it into my pocket. The journey to Kilkenny, accompanied by the steady rhythm of the pony's hooves, felt more daunting than before. But James was right. We had to confront our challenges, one step at a time. For Anthony, for our dreams.

He interrupted with a reassuring smile. 'Kitty, fear has a way of making shadows loom larger than they are. You've got a sharp mind. Trust yourself. And remember, you're not alone in this. Send some money to me, and I'll ensure Anthony gets the help he needs.'

His words, a blend of caution and hope, echoed in my

mind as we stepped down from the trap into the station. Taking a deep breath, the cool morning air filled with the scent of coal and damp earth, I stepped forward into my future, murmuring to myself, 'And I'll keep saving, keep everything close.'

James's hand reached out, grasping mine firmly. 'It's going to be all right. Alice will look after you.'

I boarded the train in the first of its two carriages. Settled in the seat, I took out the paper with the saving calculations, wondering if I could do it.

Now that turf had replaced coal to power the train, the journey was slow. Green field after green field littered with grazing cattle chewing the cud, the whitethorn hedgerows dotted with white flowers of spring. Changing at Sallins for the spur train, I was in Naas before tea time.

At Naas I gathered my bag and coat, my heart beating fast. The platform was narrow, and I waited as two men hurled a large trunk onto the back of a waiting horse and cart, like hurling a sheet over a washing line.

Walking quickly down Corban's Lane, I turned onto Main Street. I stopped at Lawlor's Hotel on Poplar Square and looked at my new town. It was smaller and quieter than Kilkenny. The streets were empty; the only sign of life was the sound of a fiddle player coming from a bar across from the hotel. Two black cars were parked in front of the hotel, and rows of bicycles leaned against the wall of Daley's Lounge and Bar.

'Daley', spelled differently to Sam Daly. So many things look the same but are different.

The door to the bar opened and the fiddle got louder, and two men wobbled out, arms around each other's shoulders, singing. One took a High Nelly, throwing his leg over it, but then thought better and instead walked it down the road.

Within minutes I stood outside Alice's house. A thin sliver of light escaped from beneath the door. Closing my eyes briefly, I gathered my thoughts, wondering if I had the strength to see this through. As I hesitated, the door swung open.

'Kitty, come in. You're here! I was so worried when you didn't arrive. I thought I'd got the wrong day. Come in and we'll get you sorted for tomorrow.'

After a restful sleep, the following morning I walked rapidly to work in my sensible navy skirt and tights, and my hat pinned tight, my icy breath trailing behind me. Soon I slowed, as the hospital came into view. The white windows glistened in the low February sun, and the brilliant white building looked sterile.

My heart beating fast, I counted slowly, breathing in and out, my breath clouding and scattering in the frosty air. Near the entrance, an ambulance driver leaned against the green vehicle and nodded to me. He inhaled his cigarette down to the butt and threw it onto the gravel, rubbing it into the ground with the toe of his boot.

'New, are ye?'

I nodded, my mouth dry.

'Cat got your tongue, has it?' he said, and laughed. 'Don't worry, I don't work for the hospital. I'm with Naas County Council.'

Under his black overcoat he wore a blue cardigan and white shirt. He opened the door of the ambulance and took out a little piece of paper to hand to me, with a few lines in pencil:

I stand here before you, begging that you present to the Lord our God these requests that I confidently present in your hands today.

May these graces that I now request help me to always seek the Kingdom of God and His Righteousness, knowing that God – who dresses with beauty the flowers of the field and abundantly feeds the birds of the sky – will give me all other things. Amen.

St Cajetan, pray for us!

'Oh, thank you,' I said, taken aback by his kindness.

He rubbed his chin as if embarrassed by my gratitude, and brushed away my thanks with a wave of his hand. 'It's a little prayer I give to all the new girls. Saint Cajetan, patron saint of good luck. It's something people should all have.'

He nodded to an old grey stone building to the right of the hospital. 'Well, at least it's better to be in the hospital than over yonder. Nobody in there any more. The workhouse may be gone, but memories of people still linger in those stone walls. They say crying can be heard at night; they say it's the souls of children looking for their parents. Those poor people had no luck. They went in looking for shelter and food.'

He blessed himself. He took off his cap and ran his hand over his head as if he had a full head of hair, not just a few greying wisps.

'Poor creatures were buried somewhere over there.

No markings, just dumped behind that stone wall in the field.'

'That's awful.'

He pointed to a small grove of trees – no flowers, let alone headstones, to mark their graves. There was a stream running near the boundary.

'That stream, Millbrook, often floods, taking away the souls of the lost children.'

I shuddered at such a strange thing to say.

'Anyway, dear, I don't want you to be late on your first day, and that little prayer will bring you all the luck you need.' He hopped in the back of the ambulance, which held a stretcher and a few boxes of medical supplies.

Slowing to let two nurses walk from the other side of the walkway, I avoided eye contact, hoping I was invisible with my brown skirt and my wavy hair tied up. They wore their navy and white uniforms like a badge of importance, displaying that they were professionals. They had bright red lips and pink cheeks.

A car door opened nearby. The nurses paused, their attention drawn to a man stepping out onto the gravel path. He removed his fedora hat, revealing black hair that glistened like his white teeth, showing off his tanned skin. The sun bounced off his freshly shaved face. He had the confidence of knowing his looks could melt any heart. The nurses stepped aside, allowing him walk ahead of them. Their heads came together as they whispered something, their shoulders moving in a giggle.

When we reached the front door, he stood aside and held it open. They chorused in unison: 'Thank you, Dr Smith.'

Nerves got the better of me, and I started to question

what I was doing in this strange place. In London I hadn't had time to think, always on edge, running when the sirens resonated through the dark London air, grabbing a gas mask, following Eve to the Underground for shelter. There, I knew what I was doing. I was trying to stay alive and following everyone else. Here, I didn't know anyone.

I walked through the front door and looked around the shiny white walls. Steel-capped shoes echoed in the hall as nurses and orderlies in their white uniforms passed me, pushing patients in wheelchairs.

'Miss, can I help you?'

I turned. A thin man holding a brown file towered over me, his head slightly bent, as if his long neck was too weak to hold it. I stepped back to look up at him.

'I'm sorry, I'm new.' I clicked open my bag and handed him my letter. He read it slowly.

'See Miss Hardy. The clerk's offices are up on the second floor now. Third door on the left. Go through the double doors, keep going to the end of the ward and ask for Matron. Just follow those nurses.'

The pungent smell of disinfectant burned my nostrils as I followed the girls down dimly lit corridors. The echoes of pained moans and machine beeps filled the dreary ward, reminders of the countless wounded souls who passed through these halls.

We walked past a row of beds that ran up and down a long beige-walled room. Thin white curtains cordoned them off. Glaring bulbs on thin wires hung from the ceiling. The thick air was full of antiseptic and moaning men. Trainee nurses wore starched white uniforms, carrying shiny tin bowls in one hand and sheets or towels on the other arm.

I didn't want to look at the men but their eyes followed me, watching me, and despite myself I stared at them.

I didn't see the woman until she snapped at me. 'Miss, what are you looking at?' A wide woman dressed in black and white, she snatched the letter from my hand, scanned it, then pointed to a tall, thin woman in black.

'That's Matron. Go to her. Stand behind those nurses and listen.'

Matron was surrounded by a group of trainee nurses, her eyes moving over them one by one. Her thin lips moved silently as if counting; her most prominent feature was her nose, strong and angular, set on sharp thin cheekbones, her skin the shade of tallow. I knew not to cross her.

She thrust her chin out and pursed her mouth before speaking. 'Ladies, you are going to be by their side all day, and if they need help with a patient when they are changing their dressing or bed linen, you are to help them in any way.'

She pointed to two other women dressed like me in navy skirts and blouses. 'Ethyl and Harriet are the two other nurse's aides in these wards on the second floor.'

The two women gave me smiles, but dropped them when Matron's already thin lips became non-existent and her eyes darted between them. She took a clipboard from the end of a bed, read the chart, nodded and turned on her heel.

'Follow me, no dilly dallying,' she said and thrust her head forward, moving past the beds. She meant business. We fell in step behind her, our shoes clacking in rhythm on the tiles as if marching to the beat of a drum.

'I'm Ethyl,' the smaller girl whispered quickly to me, 'and

this is my sister, Harriet.' She whistled her 's' through a large gap in her front teeth.

Matron led the nurses through a long ward, their heads bobbing like ducks in a pond, listening and watching. Harriet, Ethyl and I were at the back, giving me time to look at my new surroundings. Men sat in bed, some reading. Stinging disinfectant hung in the air. Patients' wounds were visible, heads wrapped in bandages, arms or legs hung from a strap. Two nurses changed the dressing of a young man whose leg ended at his knee. He caught my stare, and his face reddened. The nurse looked at him and patted his hand. She followed his eyes to me, stood and pulled the curtain.

A nurse about my age had a thermometer in a man's mouth. 'Now, now, Mr Bradbury, you can't smoke for another hour until Dr Smith checks your lungs.'

Mr Bradbury's hair was the colour of tobacco.

I watched silently, following the nurses. A doctor in a white coat, his hair slicked back, wrote *Fluids-Faco-Max* with chalk on a blackboard, and gave it to a nurse to hang over a bed. The patient's blue striped pyjamas opened, and along his chest was the zigzag of stitches. An orderly with a thin black moustache, dressed in a brown jacket, winked at me, and my cheeks burned. I pulled my eyes back to the nurses.

Matron, with her stern face, long nose and navy hat, looked like a bird of prey, ready to pounce. When she spoke, the nurses eagerly listened, wide-eyed and open-mouthed like young chicks getting food from their mother.

She enunciated every syllable. 'Every time you see a patient, you must record on this sheet what you are doing.

And any medication he gets, you must, and I stress *must*, record what it is.' To emphasise this, she lifted the clipboard with a sheet attached to it and pointed to the top of the ward. 'Then return it to the desk for the next nurse.'

I listened just as zealously as the nurses, getting a thrill from everything she told them. My head was dizzy by one o'clock, when she finally put the clipboard on the nurses' station.

'Girls, take your break. The nurse's aides' – she nodded to us – 'will take a break as well.' She turned to Ethyl. 'Miss Corrigan, show Miss Flinn what duties are expected of her.'

Ethyl gave me a tour of the hospital instead, along wide corridors and up flights of stairs, pointing to a tea trolley. 'We've to give out tea and mop the floors, but that's easy work. Just look busy, you'll be grand.'

I didn't want to be just grand; I needed the job and wanted to make the best of it. I surveyed the bright white walls, the gleaming tiled floors, the air tinged with Dettol, clicking heels echoing through the corridors. The efficiency and professionalism sent an exhilarating thrill through me, and I looked forward to embracing it.

Ethyl took a pin from her hair; it fell loose, and she shook it out before sticking the pins back into it. She looked at her reflection in the window and twirled a single strand around her finger. 'I can't wait to get it cut, and maybe put colour in it. Have you seen those posters in the hairdressing windows? I'd love a hair wave. And some go blonde! Mousy brown hair is so dull, don't you think?'

Not really – it was better than my strawberry-blonde hair.

'Me and Harriet started here a few months ago.'

She opened a door for me to go through, throwing

her arms out wide and pirouetting. Harriet was already inside.

'This is the most important room. The tearoom. Lots of chats in here, and a chance for a break when Matron is giving out!'

'Sit down,' Harriet said. She moved magazines from the table, lifted the teapot and frowned. 'Cold and empty.'

Ethyl looked at her wristwatch. 'We don't have time to make another. No rest for the wicked, as my grandmother would say.'

'Ah, Granny,' Harriet said. Her hazel eyes clouded. She tied her brown hair around her head in a long braid, like a bronze crown. 'I hardly remember what she looked like, but there are certain things I remember as if she was here only yesterday.'

'Isn't it amazing that there's some things we never forget?'

The girls looked at each other and smiled. We tidied up the dirty teacups and saucers.

I followed Ethyl through the wards, pushing the tea trolley, lifting the teapot for her as she took empty cups from the patients, chatting to them with a smile and promising to be back with bread and butter at five.

Finally, after eight hours, my day was over. My head was spinning from giving cups of tea to patients, fetching clean sheets for the nurses, mopping floors and trying to remember the names of staff. I wondered if I would ever get used to it, and be able to keep up the charade.

Outside the front entrance, I leaned against the stone wall, the cool stone kissing my back. I took off my shoes and rubbed my aching feet, swollen after a long day walking through the hospital. It had been busier than I'd expected.

From the windows above, long lines of light broke the graphite night. I inhaled the cool air, filling my lungs, and exhaled slowly, watching my white breath lingering in the still air until it dissipated into the night.

14

Over the next week, at 8 a.m. sharp, I joined Ethyl and Harriet in the staff room, tentatively pulling on my white hospital apron to begin my day. In the hospital there was a colour-coded hierarchy. Doctors at the top wore pristine white coats; nurses wore navy and white uniforms, a blend of authority and care; nurses aides tied a white apron around their cream blouses. The porters, distinctively separated from the medical staff, often went unnoticed in their brown coats.

The most important in the hierarchy, the nuns, wore black.

On the third day, I checked the rota stuck on the staff room wall, using my finger to run over all the names and dates. I had three shifts that week, the weekend off, and two twelve-hour night shifts the following week. Calculating when I could go back to Anthony, I jumped when I felt a hand on my shoulder. I turned around to Ethyl's toothy grin.

'Sorry, didn't mean to give you a fright! We're on together today,' she said, 'but first we'll have a cup of tea.' The sisters both looked relaxed, their hair messy from the blustery morning. They had a comfortable ease about them. Ethyl poured me a cup of tea.

While finding my way through the hospital corridors, my stiff, white apron felt like a second skin, closely clinging to me. Thoughts of Eve in London surfaced, and I sighed. Had she begun her training without me? This thought lingered, since the letter I sent to her had been returned from London with *Not known at this address* written across the envelope.

Looking at a chart hanging from the end of the bed, I handed a cup to the patient. 'Time for breakfast, Mr Peters,' I said, my voice tinged with forced cheerfulness.

Each grimace that crossed his face as I assisted him into a sitting position struck at my conscience, stirring memories of Anthony. With a trembling hand, I gave him his medicine, feeling a turmoil churning within me. What about Anthony? The blackmailer? Anthony should be here getting medicine, not lying at home in pain. I stared at the clock over the medicine cabinet. Each tick echoed my internal dread.

That evening I joined Alice in the sitting room, the fire blazing, the lamps dim, as she listened to the gramophone. She sat by the fire, humming as she darned. Sleepy from our tea of fried potatoes, I settled back into the soft cushions in front of the fire, reading, and soon the words began to blur. I closed my eyes, wondering if I would ever get back to London. Alice lifted the sock to the lamp, rolling her fingertips over the patch, and removed the needle with a final stitch.

'Kitty.' She broke my reverie. 'Tell me about the farm, and what your family life is like.'

I smiled. 'Well, it's just me and Anthony.'

Her eyes travelled to Peter, sitting on the floor in front of the fire as he flicked through his picture book. 'That's nice. Peter missed out on having a brother or sister. And is Anthony working at home on the farm?'

She continued before I could answer. 'It's nice you have each other. James said your father died when you were small. That must have been so hard for your mother. It's not easy rearing children without a man.'

Silence was the best way to deal with that statement. It would be difficult to explain how hard it had been without our father, and not for the reason she thought.

I told her a half-truth. 'Anthony isn't well, so I got a job to help and send him money.'

'My Maurice was never the same when he came home from the Great War. He would be up coughing during the night. Pneumonia – that's what killed him in the end.'

'I'm sorry to hear that. It must have been hard for you,' I said.

She looked at the bookshelves beside the dresser. There were two rows of red leather books, embossed with gold writing.

'Maurice bought a set of encyclopaedias when Peter was born.' She lifted a book from the shelf, leafed through it and sighed. She carefully put it back. 'There's twenty-nine of them altogether.'

Memories of my father and how difficult he'd found reading came to my mind.

'Funny, James sending you to us,' she said. 'He's been so

good to us since Maurice died. He's not a blood relative, but he's like an uncle to Peter.'

'James is like that to Anthony and me,' I said, speaking slowly, not sure how she would react. 'Our mother was very hard on Anthony.'

She didn't say anything. The gramophone crackled and she put her darning on the side table, then got up to slip the needle from the turntable. The yellow glow from the lamp fell on the daffodils like a shawl.

'It's nice here,' I said. I wanted to explain the difference in her home, how warm it was, the words flowing in my head but stumbling and tripping at the tip of my tongue.

She nodded. 'We had waited so long to have Peter, and Maurice loved him.'

'Did it not make you angry?' I asked, and stopped. 'I don't mean to be rude. I'm so sorry, Alice.'

'No, Kitty, it never made me angry. I felt complete when Peter was born. Life is a challenge, and we have to adapt, accept and move on. We all thought we were going to be speaking German, but thankfully Mr de Valera said we were to stay out of the war.'

She hummed as she knitted. 'It's great to keep the hands busy; then the mind is busy as well.'

Looking at her and Peter, I felt if I put my hand out in front of me, it would touch the love she had for him.

'Maurice would sit there every evening when he came home from work and put Peter on his knee, telling him tales, little stories.' She smiled at the memory. 'He was so patient with Peter. I know of men who would run a mile from their child. I often read the encyclopaedias to him. The names of birds – wrens, robins, thrushes – pointing them out in the book. I tried to teach him the alphabet, but I don't know if he understood. But when we saw a red robin in the garden, I'd get the encyclopaedia. He often picks them up and looks at the pictures.'

Later I lay in bed, thinking about how we don't always need words to express our emotions. How at ease Alice was with Peter. The house was calm, no drama, no noise. Her love for Peter was unconditional. I'd thought all mothers put conditions on their children.

My eyelids suddenly heavy, a wave of tiredness surging through my body, my head sank into the lavender-scented pillow.

15

March

On the way to work for my first night shift, I pedalled to work under the cloak of darkness, the triangle of my bicycle light cutting a solitary path on the road. I turned right past the courthouse, past Daley's pub. In another few weeks the first fingers of spring would stretch its fingers, coaxing the days to unfurl their light a little longer.

Standing outside the hospital, catching my breath and watching it mingle with the cold air in front of my face, I leaned the High Nelly on the side wall. Looking around, I saw nothing except the dark outlines of a few trees. The doctors' cars were gone, as were the nurses' bicycles.

Something unsettled me. A tremor ran over my skin, making the hairs on my neck stand up. I felt an unsettling urge to pay closer attention. A thin stream of light escaped from the hospital, revealing the murmurs of moving shadows.

A voice cut through the cold air, its breath momentarily visible. I found myself an unintentional observer of a hidden conversation. Holding my breath tightly, I leaned against the wall, trying to blend in, but a stone pressed sharply against my shoulder, reminding me of my presence.

Three men.

'Right, you wait here, and I'll be back in a few minutes.'

I quickly covered my face, muffling my breath and any noise, fearful of being discovered. The hospital door opened with a creak, letting light fall on the three men standing near the ambulance. At first glance, they could have been mistaken for hospital orderlies in their matching clothes. However, their attire was more suited to business than healthcare – they wore sharp suits and fedoras, a stark contrast to the plain uniforms of hospital staff.

The light suddenly fell away, and the hospital door banged. To the left, two or three nurses chatted, thankfully soon their voices faded. I stood frozen with cold and fear. How embarrassing it would have been if I were found spying on these men – what would they think of me?

I reached into my pocket and pulled out Saint Cajetan's prayer, from the ambulance driver. Holding it tightly, I prayed for courage as more whispered words came from the shadows.

'Upstairs… room 5… operation.'

The words seemed to hang in the air like a fog around me. My heart raced as I strained to hear more.

'After operation bring… to the Curragh Military Hospital.'

This voice sounded familiar, but I couldn't place it. Inhaling deeply, I closed my eyes tight reprimanding myself for being silly; nothing untoward was happening.

Suddenly, all was silent again, except for faint whispers and murmurs of conversation coming from inside the hospital building. As quickly as possible, without making any noise or revealing myself, I exhaled slowly and opened my eyes.

Only to find myself looking directly at Sam Daly.

He looked deep in thought, but then he noticed me looking at him. Our gazes locked for what felt like an eternity, until he nodded in recognition and turned back to the men without uttering a word.

With one heave they lifted a stretcher out of the ambulance and into the light of the door, the thump breaking the silence of the night. The patient's bandages were wrapped around his head, his face covered in a once white dressing now splashed with red patches. The men lifted the stretcher inside the hospital, muttering.

Another man got out of the ambulance, closed the door, and looked around into the darkness. His hat hung low over his face. The light from an upstairs window fell on him. He wore a military-green army uniform, with a peaked hat and long black boots.

I made my way inside, not understanding why Sam was there, and sought out Matron in her office. She sat ramrod straight behind her large oak desk, scrutinising a stack of papers. Clearing my throat, I approached hesitantly.

'Matron, might I request additional shifts? I could use the extra wages.'

She eyed me over her spectacles. 'Extra shifts are for the senior nurses, Flinn. You're still in training.'

My hopes sank, but I pressed on. 'I'm a hard worker and a quick learner. I know I can handle it.'

She pursed her lips, the red lipstick incongruous with her pale face and the wisps of thin grey hair sticking out from her cap. She looked at her watch; her wrists were as thin as the rest of her.

'You're late for your ward round,' she said, then paused. 'Wait. Where are the Corrigans?'

Her eyes bored into me. 'Miss Flinn, don't lie to me. Do you know where either of the Corrigan girls are?'

'No, I'm afraid I don't,' I said.

Was I going to be reprimanded for Ethyl and Harriet's tardiness? Or would she give me extra shifts?

Matron pushed her spectacles up her nose. 'Miss Flinn, since the two Corrigan girls haven't turned up, you will have to assist in theatre.'

I was shocked. I just stared at her.

'Have you lost your tongue?'

'Sorry, Matron. Of course I will assist.'

She folded her hands as if in prayer. 'Miss Flinn, this operation is extremely important. Dr Smith demands full attention in surgery. He has the hands of the Pope. All you have to do is help Sister Maria with the instruments to give to the theatre nurses and Dr Smith. Nothing more. It's a simple task, but important. See Nurse Stewart at theatre and she'll give you a gown, gloves and mask.'

'Now? In the middle of the night?'

'It's not the middle of the night. It's not yet nine. Don't give me cheek, Miss Flinn. Go now, straight to Nurse Stewart in the scrub room. It's an emergency operation, so be quick, will you, and get a gown. You will assist Sister Maria.'

Matron shook her head and rolled her eyes. 'I don't know where those other two went to. Some girls are a such a waste of time. I've a good mind to sack them.'

★

My heartbeat pounded in my ears as I followed Nurse Stewart to the theatre. Inside, it was bright and stark. A sterile smell hung in the air and my eyes watered a little. The doors whooshed open behind me and Sister Maria beckoned me to her side of the operating bed. Like the nurses, she wore a white gown. Her black shoes peeking out underneath were the only evidence that she was a nun.

She spoke while laying the silver instruments on a white table. 'Now, Miss Flinn, pay attention and don't speak unless you're spoken to. In fact, Miss Flinn, don't even speak if you are spoken to. Dr Smith demands complete silence. And attentiveness. And absolute precision.'

She pointed to the trolley. 'The scissors are kept in the silver bowl. Dr Smith will ask you for one of these. Just move forward, hand it to him and move back. He doesn't want to be disturbed. Surgery is extremely complex and demands full attention.'

She could hardly be precise and attentive with her glasses permanently steamed, I thought to myself while I washed my hands. I needed to concentrate. This felt like a promotion. Maybe one day I would get to be like the nurses here in the theatre.

Sister Maria spoke again. 'Miss Flinn, don't forget that we work in silence not just to respect the patient, but also to respect the sterile environment that we created for the patient's safety. Just stand here beside me and do what the doctor says.'

The double doors opened and an orderly pushed in a trolley with the patient on it, a white sheet draped over him. The only visible part of him was his face. He wore a surgical cap. The theatre was silent except for the ticking clock on the wall.

The operation began. I waited beside the trolley. The nurses passed instruments and worked in silent coordination. Dr Smith expertly worked away in the intricate duties of surgery. I watched their confidence and how skilled they were, wishing I had had the chance to be a nurse alongside Eve. Maybe here, I would get that chance.

'Miss Flinn,' Sister Maria hissed. 'Quick, give Dr Smith the scissors.'

Shaking myself out of my reverie, I picked up the stainless-steel scissors and handed them to his outstretched gloved hand, but I caught the trolley as I did so. It fell over, and a silver bowl crashed to the ground. The instruments scattered across the tiled floor, the sound of steel cutting through the theatre.

Nobody spoke. I still had the scissors in my hand, mid-air, paralysed. Dr Smith took them and continued with the operation. Sister Maria brushed me to the side and picked up the bowl and instruments from the floor, dropping them one by one into the stainless-steel bowl. It seemed to take her ages, her movements slow and unsteady.

She waved her hand and mouthed to me. 'Over there.' She pointed to the back of the theatre. Cursing silently, I moved to the wall.

Finally, at midnight, Dr Smith stepped away from the operating table. Ethyl wheeled in a laundry trolley. She didn't acknowledge her tardiness but instead said, 'Kitty, get the gowns and sheets to bring to the laundry for washing.'

I looked down at the crumpled gowns. 'Oh, Ethyl, I'm going to get sacked. I knocked the instruments on the ground in the middle of the operation. I really didn't think this job was going to be so stressful. I really need this job.'

Mother's niggling came again: *Useless girl.*

'We all need a job,' she said.

'But, I need it.' I couldn't say *or I might get arrested*, but she cut me off anyway.

She threw her head back and laughed. 'You won't get the sack. They're used to it. Sister Maria is always dropping things. Sure, isn't she half-drunk most of the time.'

Did this explain her slow movements? 'But this is a hospital. They can't have somebody drunk working in the theatre.'

'I suppose she's not drunk in theatre. She doesn't really drink until the evening time, but Dr Smith is always nicking medication, so it's a happy relationship. If you look at the chart, she never writes it down and she misplaces the keys half the time.'

'Does nobody smell the drink?'

Ethyl rubbed her back and stretched. 'This trolley is so heavy, pushing it around all day long. Peppermint sweets. Sister Maria doesn't leave her room without them.'

She looked over at Nurse Stewart taking the instruments out of the autoclave, and lowered her voice. 'I think they're going to get rid of her soon.'

'Who?' I asked. 'Nurse Stewart? She's one of the best nurses.'

Ethyl laughed again. 'No, Sister Maria.'

'Why, they can't. She's a nun.'

'Some nun she is. My sister Peggy said she's a shame to the nuns.'

Ethyl blessed herself, a swift left to right, and threw a gown into the trolley.

'Oh, don't worry, Kitty,' she said in a conspiratorial tone, 'you won't be dismissed. My sister lives in Rathmullen, right next door to Sister Maria's mother.'

With a flourish, she pushed the sheets down in the trolley and folded her arms.

'Sister Maria visits her mother once a month for a night or two. According to Peggy, during those visits they have ear-splitting arguments in the middle of the night. You could hear them through the walls. Like two alley cats screeching at each other. And guess what?' she said, not waiting for a response. 'They're both drunk. How scandalous! Screaming at each other with no shame whatsoever. The next morning, Sister Maria's suitcase is at the front door, and soon after that, Sister Maria herself. Peggy is mortified that a nun could behave in such a manner.'

Once again, Ethyl blessed herself, this time with a deep sense of sorrow. 'But there is something funny about it, isn't there?'

I interjected cautiously. 'Perhaps there's more to the story, Ethyl. Maybe there are reasons for Sister Maria's behaviour that we don't know about.'

I thought about my reasons for being there, the journey I'd taken, lying to the girls and to Alice, the consequences for me and Anthony if I lost this job.

Ethyl shrugged dismissively. 'You think too much, Kitty. Watch Sister Maria for yourself. She sips gin all day long, pretending it's tea by blowing on it like she has a hot drink. We all know what it really is, though.'

Her voice dripped with disdain. 'She's going to her mother's again for a week. The cycle will repeat itself. They'll fight, her mother will kick her out, and then she'll be back again in no time, starting the whole process all over again. It happens every few weeks.'

She paused for dramatic effect. 'And do you know what she has in her room?'

I shook my head.

'A picture of Saint Matthias on the wall. Right above her bed. The patron saint of alcoholics.'

Nurse Stewart closed the autoclave and turned to us. 'Ethyl, will you stop that gossiping and go find your sister, and clean the theatre properly.'

She hummed to herself while gathering fresh starched white gowns. She gave them to Ethyl, frowning as she tried to clip her fob watch to the front of her uniform.

'Kitty, I'm going to get this fixed. Will you come with me to the recovery room and wait with the patient until I get back? I won't be long, I've a spare watch in my bag.'

16

Nurse Stewart held the door open for me, and we left the ward, going into a part of the hospital I had never been to.

'It's the second door, Kitty. It's... unusual for a patient to have a room on his own unless he's somebody important, like a priest.'

The patient groaned, his eyelids fluttering, his tongue moving across his cracked lips, and shifted slightly in the bed.

The patient shifted and muttered something, voice thick with anaesthetic.

I looked at him with my best apologetic face. 'I'm the nurse's aide. Nurse Stewart will be here in a few minutes.'

She and Dr Smith hovered just beyond the doorway, their heads bent together in deep discussion. Stripped of their surgery gowns, they seemed distant. The light hanging above the bed flickered as if casting my mother's silent judgement on me. *That's right, you're only an aide, not a nurse.*

The man moaned in discomfort once more, a thick slurred muttering that snapped me back to reality. I steadied myself with a deep breath before pushing through the double doors into the private recovery room.

Kneeling beside the man, I peeled back the blood-soaked bandages to assess the damage. Angry red gashes were carved across his stomach, hastily stitched together. Beads of sweat pooled on his forehead as his body fought against infection. I laid a hand gently on his arm, wishing I could absorb his pain.

'You're in good hands now,' I murmured. Though he couldn't hear me, it felt important to offer some small comfort. This man depended on the care I could provide. I set to work changing his dressings, keeping a watchful eye on his breathing and heart rate. He seemed stable for the moment. His eyes fluttered open, glazed with delirium. They focused on me briefly before falling shut again.

Then to my surprise, he spoke again, too quietly for me to make out, and not in English.

'Wo bin ich?' his voice scratchy and thick with morphine,

'Ruhe dich aus,' *Rest*. I said softly, my German emerging awkwardly yet instinctively from a place I'd long forgotten.

His eyes reopened, this time sharper, locking on to mine.

'You speak German?' he rasped.

'Only a bit,' I replied, repelled by uttering words in the language that had brought so much grief into my life.

Seemingly content, he relaxed into the pillow. But I felt exposed, a secret part of me laid bare, and hoped this revelation would go no further. The past should stay hidden, even if it had a way of resurrecting itself when least welcome.

I redirected my attention to his IV drip, purposely avoiding his scrutinising eyes. A potent blend of antiseptic and blood filled the air. Outside, the hospital hummed with the rhythmic beeping of machines and the shuffle of nurses going about their duties.

'Danke, Krankenschwester,' he said softly. *Thank you, nurse.*

I regained my composure. 'You're welcome.'

His eyes softened. 'I did not mean to unsettle you. Hearing my own language just offers a sliver of comfort in an unfamiliar land.'

I couldn't allow my personal feelings to compromise my professional duty. 'Rest now. You need to regain your strength,' I said.

The moment was interrupted as the man I had seen outside the surgical theatre entered. His piercing blue eyes, a sharp contrast to his pockmarked complexion, instantly fixed on me, feeling like a physical force.

'A word, nurse,' he said tersely, motioning for me to join him in the corridor with a sense of urgency that left no room for refusal. I followed him out, my heart pounding with a mixture of curiosity and apprehension. We stopped in an alcove, secluded away from listening ears.

'I overheard your German in there,' he said, his voice tainted with accusation. 'Quite the curious skill for an Irish woman.'

His accusation lingered in the air, a silent challenge that demanded an answer.

'And under what authority have you the right to question my language skills?' I asked, my voice steady despite the rapid drumming of my heart.

He scrutinised me for a moment, as if weighing my words against his own suspicions. 'Authority?' he echoed, a wry smile briefly softening the harsh lines of his face. 'Let's just say my interest is... professional.'

The word 'professional' hung between us, heavy with unspoken meaning. It was clear that his role here was more than just that of a mere observer.

'My mother had a German background. I learned a few words as a child.'

'Really?' His tone was dripping with scepticism. 'And where might this German mother of yours be now?'

I clenched my jaw. 'She's dead.'

'Convenient,' he sneered, his eyes narrowing, his eyelashes so white it looked like he didn't have any.

Drawing a deep, calming breath, I stifled the surge of anger rising within me.

'If you're insinuating something, say it outright.'

He looked me over as if he were peeling back layers, his face tense with scrutiny. His words sent a chilling ripple through me. 'Very well. Your ties to the enemy make you a person of interest. I'll be keeping a vigilant eye on your activities.'

'If you must know, I despise the Germans,' I retorted, anger flaring in my voice. 'Don't mistake language for loyalty.'

He paused, taken aback by my vehemence.

'I have nothing to hide,' I added, struggling to regain my composure. 'Now if you'll excuse me, my patient requires my attention.'

He stepped nearer, his red hair catching the light.

'Were you dispatched to rendezvous with him?'

He leaned in even closer, breath wafting stale tobacco. His accent was sharp and distinct, south Kerry. His steel-capped shoes clicked against the floor as he began pacing around me, sizing me up. I felt my palms begin to clam up, and I wiped them against my skirt.

'I have no idea what you're talking about,' I replied evenly, my voice unwavering despite my nerves.

The man snorted derisively. 'Let me put it this way then, nurse. If I discover you have any further contact with those with whom you share a mother tongue, then your services here will be terminated, and you will be arrested.'

He pinned me with his icy blue gaze. 'Do we understand one another?'

I nodded mutely, my throat too constricted to form words. He looked at me for a few seconds longer then abruptly turned on his heel and walked out of the alcove without another word.

My head spun as I made my way back to the ward. What could this man possibly want from me? Was this merely an idle threat, or something more sinister? What possible connection could I have with the enemy of another country?

In a sudden rush of realisation, it dawned on me. The stranger was the same man I had seen standing behind the ticket inspector when I got off at Rosslare. My mind was flooded with questions as I returned to my position next to the patient's bed.

As I did, the German patient bellowed in agony, ripping away his bandages.

Dr Smith rushed to his aid. 'Miss Flinn, get Sister Maria's assistance quickly,' he commanded, his voice laced with urgency. 'We desperately need more morphine.'

I sprinted down the hospital hallway, my feet barely brushing against the tiled floor tiles. My eyes darted from ward to ward searching for Sister Maria. At last, I glimpsed her silhouette, bending over the medicine trolley. In one hand, she held a vial of clear liquid, and in the other, a bottle of pills.

I inhaled, preparing to call out to her when an icy draught sliced through the corridor like a harbinger of chaos. The bulbs above flickered, a prelude to darkness, as shadows leaped to claim dominion over the space.

Then, as abruptly as it had retreated, the electricity coursed through the hospital once again.

Overhead the lights flickered erratically, as if they were performing a wild dance, before regaining their normal brightness and illuminating the hallway with their sharp, sterile light. Shuddering, it was like my mother's ghost was reminding me to be careful.

Gathering my wits, I raised my voice. 'Sister Maria, Dr Smith urgently needs morphine.'

Nodding her head, Sister Maria tightly held on to her medical supplies. Together, we went back into the room of the patient.

A sense of unease washed over me.

17

At four on Friday, I met Ethyl in the tearoom, the round tables already set with teacups and plates for the nurses' tea at five o'clock, a vase with two tulips on each table. Poor Ethyl, her face worn and etched with fatigue, sat there massaging her ankles.

'At last. I need a rest. God, I'm so glad the week is over. I've worked five twelve-hour days in a row. Matron has it in for me ever since I turned up so late for the night shift,' she said. 'I'm hesitant to take off my shoes. I'd say my feet are so swollen I'd never get them back on, and I've a dance to go to in Lawlor's Hotel tonight.'

She inspected her feet. 'Jesus, they're a sight. I'll never be able to dance in this state.' She wiggled her toes. 'I'll never get a man tonight. Are you coming tonight, Kitty? Please say yes,' she implored.

With a heavy heart I shook my head. The thought of frivolously squandering my savings on a dance was unfathomable. It was a luxury I would have to do without, and I had taken on a few extra shifts.

'How can you not fancy a dance? Think of the music, the gaiety, and, I daresay, the handsome men!' She paused, a knowing smile dancing on her lips. 'And there'll be Germans, believe it or not.'

'Germans?' I echoed, my voice a mix of surprise and scepticism. 'Here, in Ireland?'

Ethyl nodded. 'Crash-landed, the lot of them. The army's got them interned over at the Curragh Military Camp. Just imagine the stories they'd have to tell. Isn't that enough for curiosity?'

Ethyl smiled. 'And think of it this way, not every German is the enemy. Many are just young men caught in the tides of war.'

I sighed, feeling the weight of her words. 'All Germans are the same, Ethyl.'

She tilted her head, eyeing me. 'You sound like you don't like them. Why?'

'It's nothing,' I murmured, and gestured to the wards. 'We've still a bit of work to do.' I looked at her wristwatch. 'Thank God, nearly finished.'

She turned her hands over, her knuckles red-raw. 'I'll never get a man tonight,' she said. 'Matron made me scrub sheets and gowns all week. There was so much blood on one of the patients' clothes.'

As we left the tearoom, Ethyl frowned, biting her lip. 'Now I think of it, it was some sort of military uniform, but not green like the ones our army wear. The jacket was blueish and torn. I would have thrown all the clothes in the bin, but Matron made me wash and dry them. When I brought them back to her office, she told me to give them to a man.'

I stopped and looked at her. 'Ethyl, just curious, what did the man look like?'

Her brow creased and she tapped her finger against her mouth like she did when she was trying to remember something.

'Red hair, and his skin was really bad. My brother had the same after chickenpox, his face was so bad, covered from head to toe. My da clipped me around the ear when I said he'd turn into a chicken. But this man's was the worst I've ever seen.' She laughed at her own chicken joke.

But I didn't laugh, I was sure that was the same man who had confronted me after I spoke German to the patient, and at the docks in Rosslare.

Ethyl stopped in front of the window to look at her reflection, she puckered her lips and dabbed on lipstick, then smacked her crimson red lips. Down the hall the clatter of the tea lady's trolley echoed through the halls.

'Ethyl Corrigan, you're a sight for sore eyes,' I said and smiled. It would be lovely to dance away the night, but I shook my head. 'I feel a headache coming on.'

Sister Maria rushed past us, her face squashed as she squinted down at the corridor tiles.

'Are you all right, Sister? You look as if you've lost something.' Ethyl said.

'No, I'm fine,' she said. 'Don't bother with me, just get on with your work.'

'We're finished for the day, Sister,' Ethyl said, mimicked holding a cup and taking a drink.

When Matron was gone, Ethyl whispered, 'She probably misplaced her cup of gin somewhere, or lost the keys to the medicine cabinet. She's supposed to keep them in her room, but Matron found them in theatre last week. The week before that, in the broom cupboard.'

As I walked up Main Street, a few drops of rain began to fall. Three boys in short trousers huddled in a doorway, one last chat before going home for tea. Passing Daley's bar, I nodded to the brewery delivery man. A man cycling past skidded and fell off his High Nelly, embarrassed for me to have seen the incident. Two dogs yapped at him from a puddle flowing into a drain. At the top of Basin Street, a gust exposed turf under a cart's tarpaulin.

Saturated, I stood in Alice's hallway with puddles coming from my coat.

'Kitty, I'm in here,' she called from the sitting room. She put her knitting needles down on the armchair rest when I poked my head in. I didn't come inside, not wanting to wet her carpet.

'I'm going up to change, Alice.' Cold was beginning to seep into my skin.

She turned the volume dial on the wireless.

'Don't go just yet, just listen to this nonsense. He's on most days.'

My clothes were damp, and I just wanted to go upstairs to change.

Through the crackles on the wireless, an Englishman spoke: 'Germany calling, Germany calling.'

'Mrs O'Connell said it's broadcast from Germany. This fellow calls himself Lord Haw-Haw, and he said that he was attacked by Jewish communists after a conference or something in England. Now, he's a real fascist. He hates

Jews and the English as well, and I know he doesn't sound it, but he's from the west. Galway.'

'I've never heard of him.'

'Listen to his rubbish, saying the Germans should attack Dublin. I think he said we're supplying the British with beef, or butter.'

Giving up on my wet clothes, I sat down beside her, listening to the man with the strange accent speak, trying to make sense of his words. Lord Haw-Haw spoke with an exaggerated English accent.

Alice sat back and picked up her knitting. 'I don't support the war, but talk about a traitor. Sorry, that man makes me so mad. I don't know why I listen to him.'

As I listened to the radio, disgust washed over me. The voice of Lord Haw-Haw slithered like a snake into my ears, each word carrying the stench of German propaganda. It was impossible not to think of my German mother, who had inflicted so much torment and suffering during my childhood. Every syllable that flowed from the radio speaker was like a lash against my skin, reopening old wounds that I thought had long healed.

'God, Kitty, sorry! You're soaking. Go and change, and I'll make us some nice cocoa.'

She shooed me out. The wireless faded to silence while she bustled about in the kitchen, and my heart thumped wildly as I stumbled towards the door, leaving a trail of water droplets behind me. As I went up the stairs, the echo of 'Germany calling, Germany calling' reverberated in my mind.

Upstairs, I slipped into a skirt and soft wool cardigan. Thoughts of that uniform, the red-haired man and the strange broadcast swirled in my mind. Anger simmered in me, and resentment towards Germany. Ireland was neutral, we were supposed to be distant observers of the chaos, yet somehow the war had seeped into our lives, staining them like the blood on that uniform.

Sitting at the desk in the dim glow of my room, I got my pen and paper to write to James and Anthony. Opening my tin box, I counted the money I had managed to save – it was only two pounds and four shillings. This would not be as quick as I thought.

Leaning back, I felt the full weight of our predicament pressing down on me. The uncertainty of the blackmailer's demands were like a whisper in the room, insidious and persistent.

Taking a deep breath, I confronted the arithmetic. I still had twelve pounds and sixteen shillings to save. If I continued saving eleven shillings a week, it would take around five months to save the full amount. The prospect was daunting.

To calm myself I took in the room, clean and smelling of lavender from the fresh sprigs Alice put on my pillow every day. Soap sat in an enamel dish, beside a fresh towel under bright yellow curtains. The tranquillity of my surroundings soothed me.

The silence was broken by three impatient raps on the door. I heard Alice opening it and the murmur of voices, followed by Alice's gentle footsteps on the stairs.

'Kitty, there's a man downstairs for you,' she said, speaking quietly. 'He's very smartly dressed. And he doesn't sound local,' she lowered her voice, 'maybe down south, somewhere, like Kerry, I think.'

She raised her eyebrows in a knowing way. 'Are you expecting company?'

'I'll be down in a minute.' I brushed my damp hair, tucked in my blouse and went downstairs.

A man stood in the hallway. The man from the hospital.

'Miss Flinn. I'm Commandant Doolin,' the man said as he removed his black leather gloves. The man from the hospital. 'Can I have a word in private?' It seemed more of a statement than a question.

Alice had changed into her gardening coat. 'Commandant Doolin, you can use the sitting room. I'll leave you to it. It's stopped raining, and I've lots of planting to do.'

His tan trench coat was darker around the shoulders with rain, and he wore a similar navy suit to the one he had worn when I met him in the hospital. He followed me into the sitting room.

Did Alice think I had a suitor? I frowned, searching my memory to see if I had given him any word of encouragement. He had been aggressive with me at the hospital, and the patient had been gone the following day.

He looked around, then sat in Alice's armchair and cracked his knuckles. His hands were like boxing gloves, and his nails were bitten down to the quick. He took a silver cigarette case from inside his trench coat and lit a cigarette. A Lucky Strike, the same as Eve smoked. He took out a brown notebook and cleared his throat.

'Miss Flinn,' he said, positioning himself comfortably in Alice's chair. 'Can I call you Kathleen?'

Stiffening, I said, 'Kitty is fine. If you don't mind me asking, who are you, Commandant? And what exactly is a commandant?'

'Apologies,' he said, his smile failing to reach his frost-rimmed eyes. From the recesses of his coat he extracted an identification card, its surface a worn, mottled brown.

Irish Military Intelligence
Commandant Frank Doolin
G2

'It's a sort of police force of the army,' he said matter-of-factly.

Intelligence. A bead of sweat made a slow, treacherous journey down my spine. Surely they couldn't know about Anthony, his flirtations with communism or his sexual preferences. My heart clenched at the thought of what they would do to him. Hitler's notorious orders to arrest homosexuals had set tongues wagging in London, but would the Irish government care? And if so, how could they know? Most perturbing of all, what did this man want from me?

'Please, Miss Flinn, do sit.' His tone was insistent. 'This won't take long. I've only a few questions to ask you.'

His brown notebook lay open in his hand.

'You speak German,' he stated, a thin plume of smoke escaping his lips and veiling his face.

'So?' I retorted, my pulse fluttering like a trapped bird. 'I already told you at the hospital. My mother was German, and I learned a bit from her. I really don't understand what this has to do with you.'

His legs crossed, then uncrossed. 'G2 is military intelligence. You're aware there's a war on?'

'Yes, but what does that have to do with Ireland? We're not at war.'

He reclined in Alice's chair, his cigarette smoke spiralling up like a spectre. The rhythmic tap of his pencil against his notebook echoed in the room.

'Tell me, what were you doing in London?'

'I never told you I was in London,' I retorted, feeling a sudden chill. His knowledge of my time in London was unsettling.

He stubbed out the Lucky Strike.

'Another question, then. Have you met or spoken to any other Germans living in Ireland?' he asked.

'No. I am not German.' Shock washed over me, sending a wave of revulsion through me, mixed with a surge of anger.

Unbothered by my reaction, he looked up from his notebook slowly, his eyes meeting mine.

'Have you ever heard of or met anyone from an organisation called Friends of Germany?'

'No. I can't help you at all, I don't know any of these people. What do you mean Friends of Germany? I'm not some sort of Lord Haw-Haw.'

'You listen to him?' he raised his eyebrows and uncrossed his legs, sitting up straight.

Even though he didn't raise his voice, this sent a chill through me.

He went on. 'Has anyone from any German organisation been in contact with you?'

'No.'

The evening breeze blew against my cheeks as the French doors opened from outside. Alice stood there, trowel in hand.

Soil dropped onto the carpet. She took off her gardening gloves and shook clumps of dirt off them. She frowned.

'Kitty, are you all right? You look flushed.'

I ran my fingers through my hair, now dry and frizzy, and tugged it over my left temple.

Comdt Doolin's knees crackled as he rose.

'Don't worry, Mrs Brady, I'm on the way out.'

We followed him, Alice throwing silent questions with her eyes to me. I shrugged. Comdt Doolin retrieved his hat from the console table in the hallway and rested his palm on the doorknob, pausing for a moment before swivelling to confront us. His brow was slick with perspiration. The edges of his lips twitched upward, yet it was anything but a grin.

'Kitty. I've confirmed your identity already. I simply had to inquire about a few things. We're constantly on the lookout for German linguists. You may prove useful to us.'

I felt a knot tighten in my shoulders at the thought. My response was shaky.

'German linguists? I told you that I lack the necessary fluency.'

His eyes scrutinised me, narrowing.

'It seemed to me as if your manner of speech demonstrated fluency, and your articulation was more reminiscent of a native speaker than of a textbook learner.'

'Nevertheless, I have no plans to reside in Ireland permanently,' I said with a confidence I didn't feel. 'I want to return to London as soon as possible, once my brother...' I trailed off into silence. I didn't want to bring up Anthony.

'So, Miss Flinn, do you have a travel permit?' he asked, raising his eyebrows.

I froze with the enormity of his question as it sunk in.

'And keep in mind, there's a Stop List.'

'What's a Stop List?' I asked.

'The Stop List decision is for others to make. It doesn't concern you right now, it concerns me. My job is to make sure that all citizens are safe and accounted for. Especially those who cause trouble wherever they go.'

He turned to look at himself in the mirror, adjusted his hat, and left. The slam of the door seemed to rattle the house. I took a deep, slow breath.

Alice broke the silence. 'What was all that about?' she demanded. 'The nerve of him, barging in here and upsetting you like that. For all his semblance of cordiality, he didn't seem pleasant at all. What was he talking about?'

My hands trembled.

'Honestly, I don't know. A patient at the hospital spoke a few words in German. I was in the room with him post-operation.'

I recounted the tale to her. Feeling numb, I followed Alice into the kitchen, where she busied herself making tea, a cure-all for life's problems.

'Tea is a much better pick-me-up than cocoa. Let's have a strong brew. Sit down, you look like you've seen a ghost.'

She warmed the teapot and spooned the leaves into it. After placing it on the table, she left the room, only to return a moment later with a newspaper. Pushing a vase of lilacs aside, she spread it across the table and pointed to an article.

Evening Herald
30th March 1941
German plane down. Four pilots injured.

The plane had crashed during a forced landing at Lady's Island in Wexford.

'Kitty, the patient must be one of the pilots! You do read every so often about crashes here. I think they used to let them go. Now I wouldn't know the ins and outs, but they built an internment camp in the Curragh. Any German or British airmen that crash-land are kept there. It's only an hour on the bicycle from here.'

They must be the ones at the dance, but how strange they are out and about.

Alice took off her spectacles, rubbing her eyes. 'Why are they interested in you? There's a local German teacher here in Naas already, I think. What do they want with you?'

I shrugged. So, they are the men Ethyl was talking about.

'When Maurice was alive, some Saturdays he used to take Peter to the Curragh to look at the horses, and I'd go shopping. It's such a beautiful place. You'd never think the ornate red-brick buildings were a military camp.'

I stopped pouring my tea as the image of the parachute entangled in the trees, dangling from the branches in the woods, came vividly to mind. I put the teapot down. That was last January. I wonder where he had gone and if he was British or worse – German.

'Shopping in a military base?' I asked.

Alice laughed. 'It's like a small town. There's a large department store, Todd Burn's, with everything a household would want. Curtain material, clothes for men and women, and at Christmas the store windows would be ablaze with lights. We'd bring Peter there to look at the toys.'

She frowned, remembering days gone by.

'There's even an Eason's bookshop. There are a couple of butchers, and a fruit shop. It's really something else, Kitty. There is even a golf course, and a swimming pool, but that's only for the people who live on the camp. And Kitty, the post office is quite breathtaking – a beautiful red-brick building on a crossroads.'

I couldn't imagine a post office being beautiful.

She frowned and tapped her fingers on the table.

'When the British built it, they say it was supposed to be in India.' She chuckled. 'Imagine making that mistake, and shipping the materials here instead.'

She bit her lip, something she did when she was thinking.

'A lot of the families have been moved out to make way for the new recruits. I suppose Mr de Valera is preparing, just in case Germany decides to invade us.'

I thought about the German patient and the questions, and my head started to throb, a steady pulsating beat.

'You should take a cycle through it sometime. Honestly, it's worth a visit. You can't miss it, there's a huge tower sticking out of the middle. There's a lovely view of the Wicklow Mountains.'

I shuddered. I didn't think so – a place full of Germans was the last place I wanted to go.

Why would he come to my home? How did he know where to find me? the questions began flooding my mind.

Alice shot me a concerned glance as I began to pace, my fingers twisting in the hem of my blouse. How had Comdt Doolin traced me from the hospital to my doorstep?

Had he followed me? And was Sam Daly somehow involved with them? He was a guard, Special Branch. Was he just a guard, or something more?

The realisation sent a shiver down my spine. I halted abruptly, my gaze darting to the window. The curtains were drawn, but I felt the urge to peek through them, half-expecting to see him still lurking outside.

'Kitty, just ignore that man,' Alice said as she gathered the teacups. 'Just keep your head down and don't say anything, for your own good.'

After tea, I took the newspaper up to bed and laid it flat on the bed, studying it. There, at the bottom right-hand corner, was a small article:

> All persons going to the UK need a travel permit
> and to apply in writing to their local garda station.

At the desk, I set about writing my letter. With the pen held thoughtfully between my teeth, I read over the lines again and then purposefully corrected the number: two travel permits, not just one.

18

Three weeks later there was no sign of the permits, and to take my mind off my quest Alice took me up on my suggestion to go to Dublin to the Easter Monday Parade. After breakfast the three of us swathed ourselves in coats and scarves against the blustery April winds and shivered as we joined the crowd in Poplar Square, waiting for the bus to Burgh Quay. Alice fixed the Easter lily adorning her tweed jacket and straightened Peter's woolly hat.

In Dublin, we slipped in with the swarm of people walking to O'Connell Street. Mothers pushed prams with babies in yellow Easter bonnets. Overhead, bunting fluttered in the cool breeze, as if cheering us on. Alice and I held Peter's hands, shielding him from the bulging crowd, and we moved like sticky treacle along the footpaths.

Participants in the parade were already at attention. Men with trumpets and gleaming faces stood tall, their instruments poised, ready to start at the beat of the drum. Planes roared overhead as they swept across the bright summer sky, trailing colourful smoke behind them. People cheered and whistled, pointing up at the streaks of green, white and orange that billowed like chiffon scarves in the breeze. Peter's eyes were wide with wonder, his mouth agape as he took it all in.

'Kitty,' Alice shouted, 'we'll stay here, in front of the GPO.'

Just then, a rhythmic clatter of steel-toed boots broke through the din of the crowd: the Irish army had arrived. Everyone erupted into applause once again, and Alice grabbed my arm excitedly.

'See her?' She nodded towards an older woman who I recognised as Kathleen Clarke, a famous activist, and blessed herself. 'Her husband was Tom Clarke, God bless him. We probably wouldn't be free from the British were it not for those good men in 1916, all executed for their part in the Easter Rising.'

She sighed, her face crinkled with worry. 'I hope the Germans don't come here,' she said, and blessed herself again.

A whistle shrilled through the air, and the soldiers and firemen began to march with a steady swing of their arms. Nurses followed, led by a matron with her chest puffed out like an emperor penguin. I smiled at the nurses; they seemed to glow with pride. All around me, children waved tricolour flags as military armour wheeled along the street. Peter, hands firmly pressed against his ears, stared at the vehicles as they moved past.

The podium was filled with dignitaries: President Douglas Hyde, Taoiseach Éamon de Valera, Kathleen Clarke, the mayor. I imagined pride in their eyes as the cavalcade of firemen, soldiers and nurses turned their heads to the podium as they passed.

I wondered what it felt like being a woman with such important men. Now, in 1941, Kathleen was as important as she had been all those years ago during our fight for freedom. She stood out with her bright red hair and her poise, the centre of attention.

Alice took my hand and gently tugged me forward. 'Let's go, Kitty. The parade is almost over, let's enjoy what time we have left before it gets dark.'

We walked, taking in the sun's last rays. We passed a bakery, the windows open. The sweet smell of bread filled the air.

'I always wanted to be a baker,' Alice said. 'Maurice even mentioned that maybe when children didn't come along at first, it might be a good idea. He was afraid I'd suffer from my nerves as my mother had. We were going to adopt. But then Peter came along, and the emptiness was gone. I didn't need anything else.'

The streets were peaceful. A few pieces of greasy newspaper drifted along the footpath in the spring wind, and the scent of salty chips filled the air.

Alice cast a glance at her son. 'What do you think, Peter? How about some chips before we return home?'

'Kitty!' A voice came through the shrinking crowd, but I ignored it; there must be lots of Kittys here.

'Kitty Flinn!' Nearer now, and more insistent. A woman in a bright red dress waved from the opposite side of the road.

'Eve!' I shrieked as she crossed to me. Her soft mahogany-brown curls hung loose around her face, shining like a treacle crown. Her cheeks were rosy from smiling; tears fell and she wiped at them with the back of her hand. She hugged me.

'Kitty, I'm so happy to see you.'

'Eve, when did you get back? I thought you were in London.'

She hugged me and smiled knowingly, took off her glove and gave a mock curtsey. Her brown eyes twinkled, and she gave me her ungloved hand. I laughed.

'Kitty, it's a long story. I came back home about a week after you left. My da wrote and said my ma was unwell. I thought she was pregnant again. I wrote to tell you I was going home.'

'I wrote to you, too, and when you didn't write back, I thought you were mad at me because I'd left you. I was so worried, especially as we had made so many plans,' I said and smiled.

We hugged; we were sisters again, sisters who had sailed a winter storm, the world around us at war. I pushed her away and our eyes locked, speaking the words we need not.

'You girls know each other?' Alice asked. We probably looked a sight, crying and laughing at the same time. 'Are you from Kilkenny as well?'

'This is Eve,' I said. 'She's a friend, we met in London.'

Eve hugged me again and laughed.

'I just got chips.' She crinkled her face. 'The smell will be stuck to my dress for days.'

She looked at Peter, who bent his head and shuffled his feet in the dust.

'This is Alice's son, Peter,' I said. 'I'm staying with them. I'm working in Naas County Hospital.'

'Nursing, Kitty! Isn't that what you always wanted?'

Eve's brown eyes shone with a happiness I had never seen.

'Not quite. I'm a nurse's aide.'

'Kitty, it is so good to see you. You look wonderful! Come back to Dublin another time soon.'

I stood back, taking in her fashionable burgundy pompadour, just like the girls in the magazines. 'Eve, you look amazing. You look so happy.'

She threw her head back and laughed her throaty laugh again. 'Please, you have to come to Dublin, Kitty. Number 14 South Circular Road. We could even go to a dance.' She swayed her hips a little and gave me a dig in the ribs. 'Remember?'

Alice put her hand on my arm. 'Kitty, we must be going. The last bus is leaving soon.'

Eve winked at me. 'And wear your green dress. You never know what luck you'll have.'

We hugged, the tight hug of friends who share a past left behind. As she walked away, she tossed the strap of her bag over her shoulder. The last vestiges of sun receded, and the sky darkened.

A small hand slipped into mine, Peter's. He was smiling. As we reached the bus stop, I felt a sudden wave of optimism come over me. Perhaps things weren't so bad after all. Maybe I could spare a few shillings to visit Eve in Dublin and go to a dance.

19

I had hoped to sleep late the following morning after the parade, as I had three days off for Easter before switching to night shifts, but I woke at the usual time, seven o'clock, lying in bed listening to Mr Casey's milk cart rattling on his morning round. Packing my case to go and see Anthony for a few days, I hoped I would be greeted with an improvement in his health. I'd get the one o'clock train to Kilkenny.

After breakfast, I joined Alice in the sitting room. 'Was there any post today for me?' I said, praying my travel permits had arrived.

She motioned me to her side by the wireless. The news was just ending, and she turned it off. Her grey eyes glistened.

'Kitty, something awful has happened. The Germans bombed Belfast again last night. Hundreds are dead, and more wounded. Bombs dropped on streets of houses. I couldn't follow what he was saying, but it was chaos.'

She turned to me, and tears flowed. 'Those poor families. The Germans have no hearts.'

She looked over to Peter sitting on the floor with one of his encyclopaedias, the picture of innocence. Was life simpler for him? Would I want his world? I couldn't imagine being locked inside my head all day long. I'd miss the joy of reading a book, or even watching the sun falling through the trellis and casting the shadows of the climbing clematis along the rug in the sitting room like dancing ballerinas. Did Peter see those? He spent his days looking at the pictures in the encyclopaedias; maybe he had stories going on in his head all day long.

There was a sudden rap on the front door. Alice looked at me and frowned. 'I'm not expecting anyone.'

Her knees creaked in protest as she got up, flattened her skirt, and had a quick look in the mirror. Her forehead creased in worry as she went out. 'I hope it's not that nasty man Doolin.'

Or maybe it was Sam Daly. Did Doolin tell him about my German heritage?

Muffled words were followed by the sound of a closing door. Alice walked back into the room and handed me a brown envelope without a word, her knuckles pale white. I opened it hesitantly, my hands trembling slightly.

Telegram an Post
James Died – Heart Attack – Father Fitzpatrick

Time seemed to stand still as I stared at those words, a lead weight pressing down upon my chest. All noise faded away except for the sound of my heart beating in my ears. I put my hand on my chest, a sudden pain ripped through my heart, splitting it in two. Tears welled in my eyes but didn't fall. Alice sat beside me, wrapping me in her comforting embrace. As she rocked me gently, I finally allowed myself to cry. Tears streamed down my face and soaked into her dress.

She eased me back, then stood. I watched her through blurry eyes, as she walked to the cabinet. Opening it and getting a canister, she poured a rich amber liquid into a glass. I nodded my thanks as she handed me the glass. It was reassuring to be with someone who also cherished James, a man I had grown to love like a father. The drink warmed my throat as it went down, easing away some of the pain in my heart.

Alice held my hand in hers and allowed me to cry. For a moment, we just sat there in silence, two people united by tragedy yet unbending against grief. In that stillness I found solace – a brief reminder that life is fragile yet full of beauty, if we can take the time to appreciate it.

'Poor James,' she said, 'he was kind to me when Maurice died. And he sent you to me, Kitty.'

I looked at the family photo on the mantlepiece. There was another picture of Peter in a pram. A vase of dried flowers was delicately placed between the two, like it was joining them in something beautiful. Family.

The whiskey began to take effect, and my eyelids were heavy. I tried to resist sleep, but it claimed me soon enough.

When I woke up, Alice stood by my bed with her hat clenched tightly in her hand. Her cheeks glowed with a reddened tint.

'Father Fitzpatrick knows you're coming home,' she said quietly.

Later, as I boarded the one o'clock train, she said, 'Kitty, the pain will ease in time. But let your tears fall. I'm so sorry I am not able to go. I have to get back to Peter.'

Blinded by grief, I didn't acknowledge any of the other passengers; I just stared out the window. My eyes hurt from crying all day. A farm labourer about my age smoking a cigarette wouldn't stop staring at me. I didn't care – all he saw was a woman with red-raw eyes, not the pain in my heart. It was like somebody had opened my chest, pulled out my heart out with their bare hands, and ripped it in half.

Anthony met me at the station, his face pale with anguish rather than sickness. We silently hugged, knowing words were inadequate. As we trundled onward in our horse-drawn trap, Father Fitzpatrick's black Morris Fourteen pulled up and flagged us to a stop. He stepped out and rubbed the pony's coat, before speaking softly.

'I'm sorry for your loss. Kathleen, you're a good girl. Remember that your father and James would both be proud.'

He looked at Anthony. 'I know you didn't steal. It was Brian Clarke, Paddy Clarke's young lad.'

He shuddered as a gust of wind blew up John Street from the river. He looked at his wristwatch and opened the car door, heaving himself in with a grunt. We watched him drive away.

We should have been relieved, but instead of joy our hearts were overwhelmed by heartache. As the horse moved, something soft rubbed against my ankle. It was

James's hat, wedged underneath the seat. I picked it up, feeling its velvet rim between my fingers. He had only taken it off for Mass or to go to bed – now he would never wear it again.

20

We arrived at the church early, sitting in the pew we had sat in with our mother for eighteen years. The church was packed with mourners coming from all corners of the parish. Everyone wore their Sunday best. Even Anthony looked respectable: clean-shaven, with washed hair, wearing pressed trousers and a jacket.

The coffin sat in front of the altar. It was a lonesome sight. James's death was like a spring tide during a storm. It stretched forever, and I could see no end in sight.

After the ceremony, we all watched the coffin being lowered into the grave. Father Fitzpatrick dropped a handful of earth onto it, and Anthony squeezed my hand as we listened to his words. Our heads bent, and our tears fell.

Ashes to ashes. Dust to dust. We rose from the earth and to the earth we return.

Neighbours and friends took my hand and sympathised with me and Anthony, many with tears in their eyes. 'I'm so sorry for your loss,' they said. 'He was a wonderful friend to you and Anthony, and especially your father.'

Near the end of the line of mourners I saw him, walking towards us. Sam.

Anthony and Sam locked eyes, both pictures of strained civility. Sam held his hand out, but Anthony turned away without a word, extending his hand to another mourner.

Sam turned to me. 'Kitty, we meet again. The loss of James is a terrible thing. I know how dear he was to both of you.'

Conflicting emotions tugged at me. I wasn't sure what to do. I wanted nothing more than Anthony and Sam to make peace. Wasn't there a kind of sacred truce that should pervade these moments, a tribute to the departed? Finally, I grasped his hand. It felt unsettlingly warm, almost intimate. He leaned in to kiss my cheek, the scent of Old Spice mingling with the funereal air.

I stepped back, my pulse quickening as a flush of heat rose to my cheeks. I looked into his eyes and felt a strange, magnetic pull. Then my gaze shifted to Anthony, whose face looked like a storm cloud about to burst. Was Anthony's disdain for Sam justified? Or was it rooted in some past grievance that should have faded along with our childhood?

As I watched Sam mingle with the dispersing crowd, nodding and smiling as though he belonged, a gnawing question seized me: would he reappear later at James's house, to toast a life cut tragically short? And if he did, what web of motives and secrets was he weaving, even in this solemn hour?

The entrance to James's stone cottage was as warm as he had been, the twisted, red-berried ivy over his doorway leading into a low-ceilinged room with beams running its length. The two-room cottage filled easily. The women of the parish poured tea as people nodded their heads, lamenting what a great man James had been, his death a loss to the community.

Tales of James's life went long into the early hours of the morning. His triumphs, his generosity, his strength, and not just physical. Eventually people put on their black caps and dispersed to their homes. Listening to these tales, I took ragged breaths and grief spooled, tightening its grip on me like a coil of rope.

Anthony and I were the last to leave, and as I pulled his door shut, a wave of sadness rolled over me. I looked at his cottage, thinking it might never get whitewashed again. James had never married, and he had no family. What would become of his small farm?

I linked Anthony's arm as we walked the dry-stone path to our home. When we pushed open the front door, there was an emptiness in the kitchen. I turned on the wireless to break the silence, but it only emphasised it.

Unpinning my hat, I shook my hair loose, catching a glimpse in the mirror. My face looked stark white and weary. I didn't think I could deal with my brother on my own.

Anthony sat outside on the back step. I joined him, wiping the dust from the step before I sat, gathering my thoughts.

'Anthony, I can only deal with one grief at a time.'

'What do you mean?'

'It's just...' I felt the weight of sorrow sitting on my shoulders. 'First Daddy, then our mother, and memories of my faceless child. Now James is gone.'

*

The next day I got up early before I left for Naas. I cleaned the house and looked through the shelves in the pantry. Rows of pots piled up high, dishes, nothing matched. I lifted a plate; it was all chipped and cracked.

I opened the flour jar: empty. There were some crumbs on the small cutting table, from the bread James had brought to Anthony most days. I lifted the lid on a bell jar and my stomach flipped at the sour smell. A long, slimy, purple slab. Liver. I stepped out the back door and threw it into the ditch.

Anthony brought the pony and trap to the front of the house, and I began the lonely journey back to Naas again. We travelled in silence, my thoughts swaying with the cart as it went down the Ballach. I watched Friesians chewing the cud in the field, moving in an easterly direction across the field then turning south, like they had compasses guiding them. Even cows needed routine. Mr Sheridan lifted his hand, saluting us as we passed, then returned to filling their water barrel.

As the trap shuddered up the ridges to the station, I put my hand on Anthony's arm. 'I'll send you more money for food.' It would mean we wouldn't be able to put enough away for the blackmailer.

'Has the blackmailer contacted you again,' I asked, feeling the concern lacing my words.

He shook his head. 'I doubt they will simply disappear and leave us in peace,' he said.

My mind went back to the aspirin I had given him. 'I'm just wondering... the aspirin I gave you, did it really help?' I thought of Sister Maria and her medicine trolley.

Anthony took my hand, holding it lightly. 'Yes, thank you, Kitty, I mean it.'

I held his hand. His palms were hard and lumpy with callouses.

'You would do it for me,' I said. 'Anthony, don't worry. But promise me you won't bring any unwanted attention to yourself.'

The halter rattled as the horse moved impatiently.

'I'll be back as soon as possible on my next few days off. I'll stay a day or two with you. But it was hard to get the day off; they asked if James was a blood relative. They didn't understand, and we can't live on fresh air.'

Anthony embraced me, then I pushed him away and stared into his eyes. His irises were like little mirrors that captured the fading twilight in their depths.

My heart quickened as we stood on the platform. The train engine rumbled. Just as I was preparing to board the train, Sam appeared from the waiting room, wearing a smirk that suggested he had been watching us all along. Anthony's eyes narrowed instantly, and he took a step towards him.

'Stay away from her.' His voice was low but filled with unmistakable warning.

Feeling Anthony's tension, I laid my hand on his shoulder, shaking my head gently. This wasn't the time or the place for confrontations or old rivalries. We had other matters to focus on.

Sam slowly stepped away us, and then walked confidently towards the first-class compartment. I breathed a sigh of relief as I boarded the train, and I watched Anthony as the station slowly faded away into the distance, pondering the complex web of emotions and secrets that linked these two men.

21

Over the next few days, the pain of James's death intensified to a deafening, pulsating roar in my head, like a dam ready to burst its walls after a storm. The only way to push away the insanity of grief was to throw myself into work and volunteer for every task, from mopping the floors, washing the bedpans and scrubbing the bedsheets, to cleaning the windows until they gleamed like polished ice; so clear it was hard to tell if there was glass there at all.

By the time Friday came, I was exhausted, fit to fall in a heap, and I slept late on Saturday morning. After breakfast, resting in the living room, I sank into the armchair and ran my fingers down the golden velvet armrest, watching as the fibres momentarily flattened, only to spring back to their former shape. I wished life could be that simple.

The door opened, and Alice came in carrying a silver tray. The three teacups rattled as she set them down.

'Here we go, a nice brew for us all,' she winked and smiled mischievously. 'Don't tell anyone, but I got some extra tea on the way to the shop. Hugh McBride's son got him some on the black market, and the flour rationing is only going to get worse; we could have the black bread for a bit longer.'

Alice chatted away while stirring the tea, but I merely saw her red lips moving and didn't hear her words.

She held the leaf strainer over a cup. 'This will make you feel better.' Once poured, she tapped the strainer, emptying it onto the saucer, careful not to let any tea leaves stray, treating them like precious gold dust.

'This is my favourite tea set. Maurice got it when we married. It's called Paragon.' She ran her index finger around the auburn rim of her teacup.

Her movements seemed more delicate than usual. Old age waited for no one. She lifted a matching plate which had black bread with a thin sliver of jam on it, offering me a slice, but I couldn't eat; hunger had evaded me since James's death.

Alice sat silent for a moment in her chair, watching Peter as a painted lady butterfly walked across his fingers.

'Peter, look, more butterflies are in the garden.' She opened the French doors, and a light breeze dusted the room with lavender scent.

Peter put on his scarf to go out, even though the warmer days of spring demanded no such garment – but he was a creature of habit. As I watched him approach the dancing butterflies, I admired Alice's strength and commitment to him. She never broke down or got frustrated with him when he didn't respond or acknowledge her. Her patience was admirable. I hadn't known Alice long, but she seemed to find a silver lining everywhere. This house had everything I had ever wanted in a family – most of all, happiness and peace.

'Kitty, drink your tea.' She sighed. 'I would love to be

able to take away your pain, but it is something you have to go through. Time – it will take time. I know that sounds so daunting.'

'I'm just tired, Alice, tired of it all,' I said, looking out at Peter, now sitting on the grass, surrounded by white butterflies, the sun on his back. He looked like an angel.

'My mother used to say the storms are not calm until they break. Challenges and changes are there to be confronted. We often have to weather the storm, and watch the sunset before we see the dawn.'

She cocked her head to one side. 'Kitty, you're a kind and gentle person, and I know Anthony is a worry now.'

'Oh, Alice, if you knew what I had done… I'm an awful person.'

I couldn't look at her. Could I tell her the truth?

'We have all done things we regret,' she said, her eyes now on Peter watching the butterflies rise up to the sky.

I looked on the rug for the painted lady, but it was gone. Its life was simple. Why was mine so complicated? I was barely twenty-two, and seemed to have been on an adrenaline train since I was a child.

I inhaled, bracing myself.

'You really have a lovely life. Can I share something with you?'

She put her cup down on the saucer delicately balanced on her lap.

'Of course you can. What is it?'

'I look at the way you treat Peter and his difficulties, and I feel jealous. Not in a bad way, just envious of the love you give him. It's unconditional. He was lucky to have a loving father, even though he was taken away from him.'

I lowered my eyes to my clasped hands on my lap.

'I never had that. My mother was so cruel to me and Anthony. Our father died when we were young.'

I let that linger in the air before my next words, unsure how she would take them.

After a moment, I continued. 'Anthony was just so confused about things. He seemed angry at life. And I didn't help him. I escaped to England. I often wished my mother dead. I thought when I left home, all those feelings and unhappiness would disappear. To be honest, it was an enormous shock when they didn't. My mind was bombarded with them, and I was so self-absorbed, I didn't give Anthony a thought or consider how he might have been feeling. I thought that I would come home and return to London after a week or two.'

I tried to choke back a memory, but tears flowed down my cheeks. Alice sat beside me on the couch and held my hand.

'What's wrong?' she said, rubbing my hand with her delicate, papery fingers. 'What do you mean, you escaped to England? When did you go?'

I sat with my eyes closed, not wanting to face her judgement.

'I was in love with a local boy. I believed he felt the same, and when I found out my stomach was growing...' I ran my hands over where my bump once was. 'I told him, and that was the last I saw of him.'

Alice hadn't pulled her hand away in disgust. Her grip was still firm and warm.

'Kitty, if this is too much for you, tell me another time,' she said, her voice as soft as a feather.

I shook my head.

'It's fine. Father Fitzpatrick collected me and brought me to St Margaret's in Laois, a home for unwed mothers. His sister was a nun there. I had no idea what to expect. There were girls as young as thirteen and women as old as forty. Sister Assumpta was kind, but most of the nuns were strict. We were constantly working with little food and our growing baby bumps. Despite that, I made some wonderful friends.

'My mother wrote to me often, her words full of vitriolic hate for me, saying how useless I was. She was glad I was gone, stabbing me with her pen. She often said she wanted to throw me into the River Nore and would watch me drown.'

I steadied myself, wondering if the words would even reach my throat. I looked down at my glistening hands and wiped them. Alice handed me a handkerchief.

'I dreamed of running away with the child and giving it all the love I never got. But as I read one of her letters, the pain started. I knew it was too early. But I kept bleeding, the pain was unbearable. The girls called for the nuns and they dragged me to the delivery room, telling me to stop screaming. They strapped me to a commode for the birth.'

I couldn't stop a deep sob from escaping. It felt like my heart was crumbling, and I could no longer control my emotions. All the pain, grief and anger flooded through me like a wild river. Alice pulled me closer, wrapping her arms around me and holding me tight, protecting me.

Alice looked at me with so much compassion that it brought more tears to my eyes. She held my hands between hers and said softly, 'It wasn't your fault, Kitty. You didn't know what consequences would come from your choices.'

I shook my head vehemently. Alice nodded in understanding and hugged me tightly once more, before pulling back a little so she could look into my eyes.

'You are strong, Kitty.'

'You're the strong one. Look at you, Alice. You coped on your own, without Peter's father.'

She stared at me for a moment. 'Kitty, we all do things that are not right, and we may regret them at the time, but they often work out. We all have secrets,' she said, glancing at the family photograph on the mantelpiece.

'I feel guilty that I'm sometimes angry at Anthony for not doing anything to help himself,' I said. 'We need money, but he just sits around the house.'

I couldn't tell her about his preference for men, or the blackmail letter.

She sighed and twisted her fingers.

'We all do things we regret. I want to tell you something. Don't judge me for this. I've carried it with me for so long, and I need to share it with someone.'

She inhaled a long slow breath and turned to face me, her face hidden in the bright rays of the sun.

'I met my Maurice when I was fifteen, and we married a year later. We couldn't wait to start a family, but after years of marriage, no child had arrived. I felt like a failure. And then the Great War started, and like many men from Dublin, he signed up.'

Again she looked at the photo, eyes glistening.

'I felt I had failed him. He said it wasn't my fault, but

it was. When he came back from the war, he wasn't well. He was failing quickly. The glint in his eye was gone.'

She stopped and sat back down in the chair, listening to whether Peter was still upstairs.

'Still no children came. By the time I was twenty-five, I'd accepted I was barren.'

Children's laughter drifted in from outside. A dog barked wildly as they kicked a ball up and down the street. Alice took off her shoes and stood on the bay window seat, closing the window. She sat back down.

'The doctors said it was mustard gas. He couldn't breathe properly. We had to make do with so much less. He spent a lot of time in the hospital. In time he came home, with good care and medicine.'

She paused, carefully choosing her words.

'His younger brother Richard came to lend a hand. He was entertaining and a welcome addition to my dull and stressful life, full of charm. Maurice spent all day in bed and rarely got up, and sometimes it was only to listen to the radio. He used to love to read, but he stopped doing that.'

She lowered her eyes to her clasped hands and twisted her wedding band.

'One evening Richard took me out to dinner in Dublin. We went to see a play at the Abbey. It was lovely to have the company, especially as he paid attention to me. He listened to me. Well, one thing led to another, and I became pregnant.'

She stopped talking. I thought for a moment she had finished.

'One night after dinner, I told Richard. When I woke up

the next morning, his suitcase was gone and I never saw him again.'

Tears ran down her face. I went to comfort her, but she motioned for me to sit.

'When I started to show and couldn't hide it from Maurice, I had to tell him. He took my hands and said everything would be all right. When Peter was born, Maurice's health improved. New medicines were introduced. When he looked at Peter, his eyes brightened once again. He even took him for little walks in the park. Men didn't do that sort of thing.'

She smiled at the memory.

'When Peter didn't start walking or talking... I'd never noticed he hadn't babbled. I assumed it was normal. It was the jubilee nurse who spotted it and got him seen by a specialist. The specialist said Peter would never be like an ordinary child. They wanted to take him away. The department came and insisted he be put into a home, but Maurice refused. There was an awful scene. But Peter stayed.'

She retrieved her handkerchief from her pocket.

'And then one summer morning, while Maurice sat in the sun, his blanket fell from his legs. When I picked it up to cover him, I knew he was gone. Peter was seven years old. Richard didn't even attend the funeral. Kitty, we all have secrets, and sometimes those secrets carry the burden of guilt. What could I do? I had to keep going and look after Peter the best I could.'

She lifted her eyes to meet mine.

'When Peter was born, I feared the love wouldn't come

due to the guilt. But it flowed like a tap that was stuck open, never turning off.'

I sat numbly for a few seconds.

'Thank you for sharing that with me, Alice. I really mean it.'

Later, I lay in bed staring at the ceiling. Alice's words echoed through my mind. Her strength in protecting Peter when faced with raising him alone, and her courage in telling Maurice, had been a gamble. She hadn't known how he would react.

The soothing arms of sleep eventually enveloped me, but not for long. All night my dreams left me in a hypnagogic state of wakefulness and sleep. Maurice and Anthony drifted in and out of my dreams, ghosts in a hospital with rows and rows of bottles on shelves. They scattered the contents onto the floor, white pills spilling onto a thick red pile rug.

They vanished when I opened my eyes, hearing Alice's footsteps on the stairs. Trying to make sense of my dream as I dressed and brushed my hair, a thought niggled at the back of my mind, a solution forming to my problems.

But it was a daring one.

22

I began the night shift cloaked in uncertainty over whether I would have the courage to follow through with the plan. The hall was silent; moonlight flickering on the tiles through the shifting clouds. A flushing toilet echoed along the hollow corridor reminding me I was not alone in the hospital. The key to the medicine cabinet, Anthony's lifeline, was within reach, I reminded myself. I just needed to get him medicine.

With my shoes in my hand, I trod the tiles lightly, my stockinged feet barely touching the floor. The moonlit path led me to Sister Maria's room. Pausing, I wrapped my fingers around the brass knob, pressing my ear against the door, straining for any sound. Ethyl had mentioned Sister Maria's absence, but her sudden return, spurred by another quarrel with her mother, wouldn't surprise me.

My heart thrummed against my chest. I reminded myself that the key to the medicine cabinet was Anthony's only chance and turned the knob with a slow, deliberate motion. The room, bathed in moonlight, revealed its sparse, monastic contents: a narrow bed, a small bedside table, a candlestick holder, and above the bed, a crucifix, its shadow a stark contrast against the pale wall. A black robe, hanging over a chair, looked too scant to offer any warmth.

It seemed a lonely room. At least there weren't many places to look.

In the hallway, Thomas the night porter whistled as he strolled past the door. The sound faded and silence filled the air once more. But as I stepped towards the bed, my foot hit a small glass. Liquid spilled onto my socks as the glass rolled off the rug onto the floorboards, the hollow sound of rolling glass resonating in the room.

I stood still, expecting Thomas to return and burst into the room to investigate. My socks were soaked, and I smelled gin. But the hallway remained silent.

I slid the drawer of the bedside table open, my fingertips gliding over the contents: wooden rosary beads, a bible, a notebook. Did she keep a diary? But no keys. She must have taken them with her.

The only other person with a key was Matron. Her hawk eyes watched nurses and patients suspiciously, as though we were prisoners planning an escape rather than people here to get better and staff here to help them.

I closed the drawer and looked around. A small pool of spilled gin glistened on the floor. I bent down to wipe it and under her bed was a wooden box. I lay on the floor to pull it out, then opened it with hope it might have the keys.

Inside was a wooden-framed photograph of a child standing between two sombre-looking adults. Sister Maria with her parents, I assumed. Also, there were five £1 notes – quite a sum for a nun. And there were keys.

My fingers curled around the cold metal of a large black key. I pocketed it and returned the box under the bed, careful to leave the lid as it had been.

The clock in the hall struck four, its chimes a reminder of the dwindling night. I needed to reach the pharmacy before the bustle of the shift change at six.

I left with the cold key in my hand, glancing at the crucifix of Jesus on the wall, and whispered a silent thank you. A grey dawn was beginning to creep across the dark sky. I'd have to hurry to reach the pharmacy. Pulling the door behind me with a soft click, I checked the hall and was satisfied with the silence. With each step I took away from Sister Maria's room, my breathing grew more laboured. My palms sweated against the key in my pocket. Thomas's whistle cut through the silence.

A torchlight blinded me as Thomas appeared at the end of the corridor. 'Who's there?' he said, his flashlight over me.

'I was just getting a mop,' I said quickly. 'There was a spillage in one of the rooms.'

He nodded to me as he passed and continued on his way, whistling loudly into the night air; providing a distraction that allowed me to slip around the corner unseen. A different man's heavy footfalls echoed through the corridor becoming quieter as he neared Thomas. I didn't want anyone else to see me, especially if Sister Maria, in her sobriety, noticed her keys were missing. I needed to hurry. Thomas's whistle stopped abruptly and was replaced by a man's voice.

A chill ran down my spine as I recognised it to be Comdt Doolin's voice. 'Can I have a word, Miss Flinn?' His cold fingers encircled my arm, pulling me towards him.

My heart pounded. 'You gave me quite a start! Sorry,

Commandant, but I must return to the wards. The shifts
will be changing soon, and I need to assist the nurses with
the preparations.'

My voice, I hoped, masked my fear. His grip tightened,
pulling me under the harsh glare of the overhead bulb. His
stale cigarette breath was uncomfortably close.

'You're hurting me,' I said. 'I have to go, the nurses are
waiting to change shift.' I pulled away, leaving him in the
corridor. Walking quickly down the stairs, the sounds of
the awakening hospital echoed in my ears. My plans for the
pharmacy visit, like the night, had evaporated.

As I descended the stairs, the rhythmic squeaking of the
trolley wheels echoed through the corridors, signalling
the start of a new day in the hospital. My mind raced with
the implications of my encounter with Comdt Doolin. What
was he doing lurking around the corridors? His unexpected
presence and unsettling demeanour added a new layer of
danger to my mission. I clutched the stolen key tightly in my
cardigan pocket, its cold metal a constant reminder of the
risks I was taking for Anthony's sake.

Reaching the bottom of the staircase, I paused, taking a
moment to compose myself. The early morning light filtered
through the windows, casting long, sombre shadows across
the hallway. Nurses bustled about, their voices a blend of
weariness and duty. I joined them, slipping into the role
of a dutiful nurse, all the while feeling the weight of the key
against my chest.

In the midst of the morning chaos, I caught glimpses
of patients stirring in their beds, their faces etched with
the strains of illness. Their vulnerability strengthened my
resolve. Anthony, like them, deserved every chance at life.

My thoughts were interrupted by Matron's sharp voice cutting through the din. 'Kitty, attend to Mr Peters immediately,' she commanded, her hawk-like eyes surveying the ward with an air of suspicion. Her gaze lingered on me for a moment longer than necessary, as if she sensed my inner turmoil. I nodded, masking my anxiety with a practised smile, and made my way to Mr Peters' bedside.

As the morning progressed, the normalcy of my duties contrasted starkly with the secret mission that consumed my thoughts. Each ticking of the clock was a reminder of the fleeting time. I needed to access the medicine cabinet, but with the hospital now fully awake and under the watchful eyes of Matron.

23

During the bustle of the shift change, my mind raced. It was one thing to take a few tablets of aspirin from Mrs Kearns, but stealing from the hospital? Doolin's unexpected presence had unnerved me. But the days were galloping at sped I couldn't keep up with.

When things had quietened down, I headed straight for the tearoom. Ethyl and Harriet were sitting at the table.

Ethyl, mouth full of toast, looked up at me. 'Matron is in one of her moods again.'

'Are there more injured Germans?' I asked, lifting a cup and inspecting the inside for dust before Harriet poured tea.

'I wish,' Harriet sighed. 'I thought he was quite the dish when I got a look at his face.'

'But he was German,' I said, my face flushing.

'Oh, Kitty, when it comes to men, nationality doesn't matter. A handsome man is a handsome man,' Harriet retorted. She and Ethyl burst into laughter and clinked their teacups together.

'Do you know why she's in a bad mood?' asked Ethyl.

'I assume Sister Maria has been at the gin again?' I said, glancing at the clock. It was nearly eight o'clock, and with a sudden change of heart, I wanted to return the key as soon as possible.

Ethyl giggled. 'You're not that naive, are you? Matron has been meeting Dr Smith at Lawlor's Hotel.'

My eyes widened. 'But isn't Dr Smith married?'

They both burst out laughing again.

'This morning, a new batch of nurses arrived,' Harriet said, 'and one caught his eye. By the end of his shift, he had his arm linked with hers and off they went.'

The surprise at this revelation momentarily pushed my concerns about the key aside when someone shouted 'Fire drill!' in the hallway.

I spat my tea back into the cup. 'Fire!'

'Fire drill,' Harriet clarified.

The door opened. Matron stood in the doorway, her face as dark as a storm cloud, her knuckles white on the door handle.

'There's a fire drill this morning, girls,' she said, taking in the dirty teacups, biscuit crumbs and spilled milk. 'Miss Flinn, fix your cardigan and tidy this place up. Hurry. And you two,' she pointed at Ethyl and Harriet, 'go to the second floor and help the nurses there. Make sure everyone is ready.'

She turned to me.

'I want you in the children's ward. Remind the nurses about the drill. The bells will ring loudly. We don't want to frighten the children.'

With a final disapproving glance around the room, she shut the door behind her.

We collected the cups and wiped the tablecloth clean. Wearily, I ascended the stairs towards the children's ward. As I pushed the door, I didn't see any children, just infants. Six cots, three on each side. I was in the nursery.

A squat nurse with a soft black fringe, wearing a pink bib, gestured silence with her fingers while cradling a sleeping baby in her other arm. I gestured towards the bell on the wall above the nurses' desk, then pointed at my watch. She gently laid the baby in the cot and slowly approached me, checking the other cots as she passed.

A teddy bear was propped against a vase of blue and white hydrangeas on the desk.

She picked up a crying infant from one of the cots, causing another to wail. 'Here, would you hold him?' She turned to fetch the other crying baby.

The boy looked at me curiously, his head tilted to one side, sucking on his dummy, the blue ribbons of his cap tied neatly in a butterfly knot.

'Thank you,' she said, reclaiming the boy. 'They're all in their prams, me and the other nurse will take them out. You'd better complete your rounds.'

She bounded down the corridor, pushing a pram.

I stopped and read the word on the door opposite me: PHARMACY.

The hall was silent, interrupted only by a fly buzzing against the single light bulb illuminating the long corridor. I watched it for a few seconds, contemplating why it would continuously repeat that action. Flying into the light and then flying away, only to return again. Does it have no memory? What is the point? Does it have a choice, or does instinct propel it?

My fingers encased the door handle of the pharmacy. I closed my eyes; what if I was caught? I clutched the doorknob, turned it, remembered every action has consequences, and pushed open the door.

'Yes, can I help you?' asked a man in a white coat, a cross between the mole from the Beatrix Potter book and the Mad Hatter.

'Matron informed me there's a fire drill,' I said with feigned confidence. The nurse had shown me respect, likely due to my being older, but the pharmacist was easily twenty years my senior. I hoped that in the dim light he saw little of me, only hearing an authority in my voice.

'Yes, yes, but I have to finish this solution first. I'll be down in a minute.'

'Matron said we have to go now.' I held his gaze and didn't move, the silence between us deafening. 'She said I've to check everyone has left. I'll pull the door shut after you.'

He sniffed and adjusted his round spectacles on the bridge of his nose, then sighed and put down the beaker, grumbling, 'All right, I'll go.'

He grabbed another white coat, putting it on over the one he already had on, hiding the iodine stains and grubby black fingerprints on the cuffs. As he bustled past me, I pulled the door towards me but held the doorknob so it didn't latch shut. My eyes landed on a cabinet marked DANGER.

When the sound of his steel toe-capped shoes had faded, I sprang into action. I knew I didn't have much time until he realised the drill hadn't started yet. I moved past rows of drawers, each marked with a label. My trembling fingers skated along the smooth wooden bench, lightly touching cool stainless-steel instruments. A thin stream of light from the corridor seeped in between two wooden benches. A clock ticked on the wall behind me, and water gurgled through the pipes.

I didn't have much time. I moved swiftly to the labelled cabinet and squinted to read the labels on the bottles. No wonder he had mole eyes.

ASPIRIN. MORPHINE.

I extracted the key from my cardigan. It scraped against the lock in my shaky hands. *This is wrong*, a voice in my head whispered, but another voice argued, *But it's for my brother*. Squinting at the keyhole, I felt like I was shooting fish in the dark. The lines between right and wrong blurred in my mind like ink running on wet paper.

Time was not on my side. The key slipped in, and I twisted it. Nothing. I exerted more pressure: lefty loosey, righty tighty. Nothing. *This is a sign*.

Again, I applied more force. I held my breath, then exhaled to slow my accelerating heartbeat. 'Hail Mary, full of grace...' The prayer felt hollow as I uttered it, a feeble attempt to wash away the guilt that was already staining my conscience.

Then I heard the click of the lock opening. My heart leaped, but so did my fear. The echoes of warnings I'd heard in London about addiction haunted me. '*What if I'm opening Pandora's box?*' I grabbed the bottle with the aspirin, but my eyes landed on the morphine bottle. This was the pain relief, but in London I'd heard how people had become addicted to it. I emptied half the aspirin into my cardigan pocket and put the bottle back.

My eyes returned to the morphine. Would I risk it?

My fingers curled around the cool glass bottle. Closing my eyes, I imagined Anthony's pain free face. I squeezed the bottle so tightly that I was afraid I would break it. There was a faint, muffled sound of clipped shoes in the room above. It was now or never.

Taking the bottle, I carefully dropped it into my cardigan.

I rushed outside to find Ethyl and Harriet standing at the emergency entrance. We waited patiently as Matron did a head count to make sure everyone was out of the hospital. Thick layers of smoky turf hung in the air, spiralling upward and then down to the streets below, clinging to the washing as it blew in the wind.

The next day, after work, I nodded a greeting to a grey-bearded man on Craddockstown Road. He was leaning on his walking stick, puffing a pipe, watching his two grandchildren playing with half-sized brooms and saucepans atop their heads.

'Tut, tut, you're dead,' squealed one boy, his companion collapsing to the ground, small hands crossed over his chest. They both erupted in laughter.

War, I thought, *was no laughing matter*.

The older of the two boys caught my frown. 'Miss, the Germans are coming, and me and my brother Hughie will be ready. Our uncle Jimmy has already enlisted.' He moved his arms in a wide circle. 'He's off to see the world.'

I noticed fresh blood on his scabbed brown knees. Their perspective on war might change if they met Anthony.

Casting a glance over my shoulder, I narrowed my eyes and scanned Ballymore Road. A shiver ran down my spine, the hairs on my neck prickling despite the mild evening air. Behind me, Fairgreen Street was devoid of people, save for a few cars. Was that the sound of footsteps?

At home I found Alice in the garden, savouring a cup of tea. Fresh bed linen, secured with wooden pegs, fluttered on the clothes horse in the soft breeze. My mind drifted to the parachute and its missing airman. Had he been taken to a hospital, or perhaps captured? Had he managed to escape?

Spring was in full bloom. Alice was basking in the evening sun, and Peter was sprawled amid the golden buttercups on the lawn, engrossed in *Gulliver's Travels*. I wondered if he saw himself as one of the Lilliputians in a world of giants.

A week of wet weather had left the garden vibrant. The rain, a blessing from the skies, was a liquid magic that revealed nature in her humble brilliance. The sweet, honey-like scent of clematis blooms weaving through the trellis filled the air.

'Kitty, come sit and have some lemonade – well, water with mint and lemon balm. Isn't it a splendid evening?

She smiled looking up at sky. 'Red sky at night, shepherd's delight! I've only just got home from the butchers. I spent two hours in the queue for three meagre rashers and four sausages. But getting out and meeting people is good for me.'

I nodded, noting the red streaks across the rooftops, and stretched, yawning. 'The fresh air makes me so tired.'

'Kitty, why don't you visit Eve? It would do you a world of good. James wouldn't want you moping.'

She turned to her son. 'Don't uproot those. They're lemon balm for the water.'

He popped a green leaf into his mouth, and she reached out. 'Peter, I wouldn't.' He winced and spat it out.

Alice laughed. 'You can steep it in boiling water and drink it. I often have it before bed.' She crushed yellow flowers in her palms, releasing their scent into her steaming cup. 'Lady's bedstraw, good for fleas – not that we have any, but it aids sleep. There's so much in nature that helps ailments.'

I was distracted, thinking of the morphine vial wrapped in tissue at the bottom of my bag. Rising to stretch, the day's weariness eased from my muscles.

'Alice, did any post come for me today?'

She swatted at a midge. 'Annoying creatures. I've been bitten so often these evenings that I'm questioning the merits of sitting outside. They always come out in May.' Her brow furrowed. 'A letter? No, there hasn't been any post for a few days now.'

I groaned inwardly. No letter, and it was May already. The scene around me of Alice and Peter on the beautiful evening, should have been idyllic, but the mention of May pulled my thoughts to the dilemma I was in. James death was more than just emotional, it was a tangible gap that drained my savings. I was forced to divide up half of my salary and send it to Anthony. I'd never get the money for the blackmailer and my only hope was the travel permits.

A shiver ran through me and I looked around the garden as if I expected to see someone – but there were only empty shadows of spring. I looked at Alice. She was smiling at Peter as he stared up at the blue sky, watching the slovenly wispy clouds pass by.

24

I had finally secured some extra shifts. I pushed the tea trolley to St James's ward, the men's surgical ward, hoping to get on with my day without any delay. Patients often pulled you in for a conversation to share their problems, but my usual receptive and sympathetic ear was not available today.

Men in blue-and-white-striped pyjamas were sat up, propped against their pillows, eagerly awaiting their tea. Their newspapers were neatly folded on their bedside tables, with their charts hanging at the foot of their beds. I discreetly read the name of the first patient.

'Here you go, Mr Peters, a nice cup of tea.'

He gazed at me with pale grey watery eyes, leaned towards the table and shifted a vase of daffodils to reach the glass containing his teeth. He inserted them into his mouth. 'Morning, nurse,' he croaked, a smile on his grey face, which was etched with lines of age.

James's face bubbled up in my mind. Suppressing the pain, I managed to force a smile. I set a rich tea biscuit on his saucer, handed him the cup of tea and swallowed back a tear when his frail fingers brushed the back of my hand.

'Thank you, dear, you're all so kind here.'

As I worked, we chatted about his family in Tipperary, his days working the land before old age stole his livelihood and health. I soaked up every word, letting his lilting voice wash over me, using my care to ease his burden.

I adjusted his cardigan around his shoulders. 'There's a rich tea biscuit for you.'

He dipped it into the tea. 'I shouldn't grumble, but I think these are more akin to poor biscuits. Nothing rich about them since they stopped adding sugar.' His shoulders jiggled as he laughed.

'Mr Peters, you're a right devil.'

'Ah, it's good to laugh. When my Susie passed away, I never thought I'd laugh again, but we just have to, don't we, dear? Grief comes in waves. Initially, the wave towers over ten feet tall, and over time it diminishes, flowing into the shore with the ebb and flow. Some days it surges higher again, but soon it's merely a ripple of a wave.'

His eyes grew heavy, and he yawned. I left him to rest as he removed his dentures once more, dropping them into the glass of water on his bedside table. Soon he slept soundly, and I dimmed the light.

No matter how much you cared for people, some wounds refused to heal.

Thinking of his words, I made my way to the train station with a new-found sense of clarity. The gloomy mist that had been shrouding my thoughts with grief was opening like a curtain.

I was Anthony's sole surviving family member. I had the morphine and aspirin to nurse him back to health. With luck, he could get some work and help pay the blackmailer. And I was prepared for any outcome, including the last resort: have Anthony cross the sea and join me in England.

May in Ireland had a mix of sun and showers, but it was overshadowed by the looming threat. I boarded the train with resolve, a plan and a glimmer of hope.

The train ride flew by as I got lost in thought, mulling over the prospect of giving Anthony the morphine. Dr Smith had said it was the quickest means of pain relief while giving it to the German at the hospital, when his agony had filled the night air.

As I stepped out of the carriage in Kilkenny, the smell of peaty turf filled the air on this still May morning and I set off on the five-mile walk home, the aspirin and morphine tucked away in my coat pocket. Usually, I would marvel at the beauty of the countryside – the bright whitethorn and the lush green fields of fresh sweet grass for the animals – but this time my pleasure was overshadowed by doubt.

Stories from London resurfaced; stories about men who had stopped screaming in pain after taking morphine but then kept asking for more and more, becoming addicted to it even though their pain was gone. Would I make that same mistake? Would that be the end result, leaving him in an even worse situation?

Exhausted after the climb up Ballach Hill, I reached out to push open the gate to our yard, just as a feather landed on my knuckles. Before I could take a closer look, a slight gust of wind swept it off, causing it to flutter down to my shoe. I often came across feathers of fledglings once the chicks had flown the nest. A robin? Perhaps a speckled or brown hermit thrush? They say that when feathers appear, angels are near. I pocketed it.

As I passed James's cottage, I decided to go in. Pushing the door open, the house welcomed me with its creaking and groaning. I opened the curtains and morning sun flooded onto the kitchen tiles. James's pipe and tin of Sweet Afton tobacco were in the centre of the table, his overcoat draped on the back of his armchair.

But the air was not what it should be. It had been the coldest May on record so I'd expected a frigid, musty house, but it felt fresh. It felt lived-in. Had Anthony finally been getting up and about and cleaning James's cottage? Maybe he had listened to me after all.

The clock above the fireplace continued to mark time. Had I expected it to stop ticking with James's passing? I lifted his overcoat. It still bore his scent, a combination of Sweet Afton and Pears soap.

I sank into his armchair, succumbing to my grief. My heart felt torn asunder. The pain was relentless; each breath brought fresh hurt as I tried to block out images of James's smiling face. His laughter seemed to echo around me. I could hear the thud of his boots as he cast them aside after a long day of turf cutting. He had always known what to do, always looking on the bright side: 'That's a nice drop of rain' or 'Great day for the hay'.

Craving fresh air, I stepped out into the garden. Shutting my eyes, I tuned into the birdsong, wishing I had paid more attention to my father when he taught me to recognise the different chirps. The thrushes, blue tits and magpies all sounded similar to me, yet perched on James's washing line was a row of crows, their distinctive caw impossible to miss. The branches of the apple tree were covered in brown moss, new green buds of spring wrapping around the trees like a green shroud, contrasted by the sweet aroma of honeysuckle.

The forest floor was soft and cool under my feet with its layers of damp autumn leaves, the air fresh with rain, the safe place of my childhood.

A breaking twig brought me out of the reverie. A wood thrush, a female, her belly almost white. I wondered whether the feather I'd found belonged to one of her chicks. I startled her and she spread her wings, taking flight. From the rich brown hue of earth to the blue skies above, to the vast array of animals, the forest is a wonderful three-dimensional world. Anthony emerged through the trees, and I lifted my hand to wave at him, and shout. But then I stopped. It wasn't him; the man approaching was taller and broader than Anthony.

The man was over six foot tall, his complexion sandy, tawny, and smooth. He wore a kind of uniform consisting of a blue-grey, single-breasted, open-collared jacket with four pockets and flaps, a light blue shirt and dark blue necktie, blue-grey trousers, black leather boots and a blue-grey peaked cap. I moved back, crouching behind a Mayberry bush, thankful to the evergreen bush for concealing me, and that my yellow coat blended in with its yellow leaves. I watched him through the leaves as he moved to the stream. He went more slowly, caution in every step, looking around through the foliage until he came to the open place among the trees. The man's shirtsleeves were rolled up as he cupped his hands to drink water from the stream. I stepped back, my foot breaking a twig, sending a flock of crows squawking up in the sky, and when I looked back, the man had retreated into the trees. He was gone as quickly as I saw him. My feet were chilly as damp kissed their soles, and I moved stealthily but quickly through the trees and towards home.

Anthony was slumped in the armchair, asleep, his legs out straight, his toes resting on the fire's hearth. I watched him for a minute. His face was returning to the pink glow of his youth. His eyelids fluttered, but he was otherwise still. His breathing was soft and even, and if not for the rise and fall of his chest, I would think he had departed to the other side.

He woke up, sensing that I was there. 'Kitty,' he said, his voice full of sleep. He stretched and went to the sink, bending low to splash cold water on his face. When he turned back, rubbing his face with a cloth, the light caught his red cheeks and I saw the blisters were gone, faded to outlines of small circles like faint pencilled drawings.

'Anthony, you're looking better! I thought maybe after James died, you might go off...'

But my words got caught in my throat. The wave of grief washed over me, more tears. Anthony got up and wrapped his arms around me.

I wiped my cheeks with the back of my hand and laughed. 'Would you look at me, crying like a baby. And you're the one who's unwell.'

'I'm actually feeling better than I have been in a long time. The numbness in my thigh isn't as bad,' he said, his voice strong. He ran his hand through his hair, which looked shiny and cleaner. 'And I seem to be thinking clearer now as well.'

A weight lifted with those words. I wanted to push my chair back and wrap my arms around him, tell him he had made the right decision, that the world is not kind to men who mix with other men.

'Thank God. I do worry – your health, your future. Our future.'

I made a pot of tea and cut some bread, slathered it thick with butter and thinly spread gooseberry jam. Sugar was not as plentiful, so the jam hadn't thickened.

Anthony put down his mug and moved his empty plate to the side. He looked towards the window. 'Thanks, Kitty. It's lonely here without James's company. The yard is so quiet without him calling in for a chat. I was so used to hearing his whistle. I didn't realise how much he whistled until it stopped.'

Nodding in agreement, I was just about to say it was great that he had cleaned James's house when he asked, 'Do you like your job? And tell me about Mrs Brady. James said she was a lovely woman.'

I told him about the girls at work, and Alice. 'She is so patient with her son. He's so quiet and doesn't talk. He just watches the birds and butterflies in the garden and looks at encyclopaedias that his father bought him. He died when he was young as well.'

I paused, then continued, 'We went to the parade in Dublin. I bumped into a friend I knew from London.'

His gaze shifted towards the fire, which had subdued down to a low heat. He went over and nudged a piece of turf with the tip of his boot, and the flame hissed and spat back to life.

I washed the plates and took the tea towel from the hook hanging over the sink. After my conversation with Alice about Maurice, I was trying to understand my brother.

'Tell me about Spain,' I said softly.

He looked past me and through the kitchen window. His eyes darkened.

'It was horrendous from the moment we got there, in Catalonia. I didn't even know the name of the small town. It was chaos. There seemed to be nobody in charge, and nobody had any uniforms. I didn't know what I was getting into. I was young, angry with everyone. I wanted to help people who had no voice, but not war, not death.'

He clasped his hands, wringing them as he spoke.

'We had no training. We were given a rifle one morning and told to go and fight against Franco's men. Over time it got worse: no food, no clean water to drink, let alone to wash with. And then the sores began, and I was so weak. The days led to weeks, and then months, and I just got weaker and weaker, feeling like I had fallen into quicksand and there was no one to pull me out.

'The thing I remembered was when I woke in a camp bed in a field hospital. I met some lads who were beside me. I was lucky to get home. I went through the Pyrenees with a small group of Dublin men. We got passage on a ship from Le Havre back to Rosslare.'

'Thank God you did,' I said. 'I couldn't bear to think of you dying.'

'I had to get away, Kitty. I wanted to prove I was a man.'

He raised his eyes.

'I don't know why I think about men. I know it's wrong. I believed if I joined these fighting men, I would prove to myself I'm just like all the other lads.'

My heart was splintering like it was pierced with a dozen tiny needles. Gently, I placed my palm on his face, feeling the warmth of his skin against my hand, and he leaned into it.

'I've been thinking about what we'll do if we can't gather enough money. To be honest, I actually don't think I can,' I admitted. 'So I wrote to the Kilkenny Guards and applied for two travel permits.'

There was a flicker of hope in his eyes as I spoke of our potential future.

'We can leave all of this behind. Together, we can escape the shadows of our past, the confines of this place. We can make a fresh start. We'll go to London. It's our chance for a new beginning, away from the troubles that have haunted us here.'

My words hung in the air, a tentative promise of a different life, one where we could step out of the darkness and into a new light.

The following morning, I pulled my bedroom curtains open, watching sun streaming across the yard, the fields, as if it was a different season than the day before. Anthony joined me shortly after I finished cutting the bread and getting the boiled eggs ready. Sitting across from me at the table, he topped his egg.

'Remember, Kitty, we used to make soldiers from our bread and dip them in our eggs, making yellow hats for them? Why do we forget the good memories?'

'Anthony,' I said, 'I've something for you.'

My fingers explored my bag for the medicine, resting on the cool glass bottle of morphine. I pushed it to the side, and found the aspirin wrapped in tissue. I spilled the tablets into the empty sugar bowl.

'Take one a day, in the morning. And hopefully you'll continue to get better. There are only ten here, but I'll try to get you more. And the permits will come, and the savings I have for the blackmailer will pay for the steamer tickets.'

Back at Alice's, hanging my coat on the stand, I noticed a letter addressed to me leaning against the vase of daffodils. A brown envelope with a tiny harp. DEPARTMENT OF EXTERNAL AFFAIRS.

'You found your letter.' Alice came into the hall with her yellow-flowered apron – she called it her summer apron – dusted with flour. 'I'm making a cake for you to take to Mrs Murphy tomorrow,' she said and wiped her hand on the tea towel.

I carefully slit the envelope, not wanting to damage its contents, anticipation building. But the world stopped spinning when I read the first line, knocking me off balance.

Merrion Road
Dublin
May 1941

Dear Miss Flinn,
Your letter was forwarded to us by the Kilkenny Garda Síochána in the Permit Office section, and we wish to

inform you that you have been refused a travel permit
due to being on the Stop List.
Signed,
Seán MacEntee
Minister for Industry & Commerce

'What the hell?' I muttered.
The Stop List Commandant Doolin had mentioned.

25

The address on the letter had said it came from Dublin. Remembering Eve's invitation to visit her, I told Alice that I would be going to Dublin that same day. I'd go to Merrion Road before I called to Eve's house. I needed to clarify there was no need for me to be on any list.

In Dublin, the bus stopped by the quayside, and I watched from the window how seemingly uncomplicated Dubliners lived – men in suits, women pushing prams, young girls cycling. Clutching Alice's small case tight, I followed two old ladies off the bus.

I set off towards O'Connell Bridge, remembering the bus driver's directions. Merrion Road was fifteen minutes from O'Connell Bridge, and North Strand was fifteen minutes to the north-east. As I crossed the bridge, the breeze from the Liffey brushed my cheeks and I wrapped my scarf twice around my neck.

I followed the brass name plates on the fine three-storey red-brick Georgian buildings of Merrion Road, noting the little iron balconies on the first floors which surrounded a park enclosed by steel railings. I didn't have to look far. A line of people snaked down the street, a mixture of young women like me and men, a lot of them no more than boys.

I approached the two young women at the end of the queue, both wearing knitted cloche hats that matched their red coats. 'Is this the queue for the Permit Office?'

The taller one, with the same green eyes as me, sighed and threw her eyes upwards. Her head moved side to side as she spoke. Her hat slipped, and the sun caught on her shiny black hair. 'Yes, we've been here over an hour already. But it does seem to be moving a bit now.'

We spent the next hour shifting from foot to foot, trying to will the line to move. They told me they were sisters from Wexford, Theresa and Concepta – 'But everyone shortens it to Connie.'

Connie offered me a bull's-eye sweet from a paper bag and popped one into her own mouth. 'We're going to Liverpool,' she said. 'Our brothers are already there. And if they don't give me a permit, we're going up north and going from Belfast, or we'll pay the fishermen. They'll do anything for a price.'

Theresa nodded. 'My brother went up north, going from Belfast to Scotland then down to Manchester or somewhere. Me da nearly had a fit, as he'd been furious with the Free Staters giving away the six counties, but now it's to our advantage.'

'You don't have a job here in Ireland?' asked Connie.

'No, I've a job,' I said, then thought twice as her forehead furrowed. Before she could ask why I was leaving then, I went on. 'But it's only temporary. I thought it would be quicker if I came to the office to get a permit.'

'Same. I worked in a hotel in Wexford, but there aren't many visitors now, with the war and everything. I forgot to send in my birth certificate.'

I was just about to ask why they needed to send in a birth certificate, but we had finally made it into the building. The two girls disappeared up the steps and into a large office, and stepped into a long queue of people leading clerks at desks.

I read the poster stuck on the door:

DEPARTMENT OF JUSTICE TO AN GARDA SÍOCHÁNA
Application for Passports and Travel Permits, Visas, Entry into Great Britain

TRAVEL PERMIT
Persons wishing to travel must fulfil the following:
1. Letter from priest or guard
2. Letter of securement of work
3. Persons must be over 22 years of age
4. The sum of five shillings

I hadn't sent any of the items mentioned to the Garda Station. In London all I'd needed was my identity card. But it was the rest of the poster that really caused my heart to hammer in my chest.

STOP LIST
No travel to the UK permitted for:
Married women
Teachers
Nurses

People in employment
People of German origin

I felt a knot form in my stomach.
People of German origin.
Even though my mother had been born in Germany and moved here as a child, I'd never set foot there. I had no other ties to the country. But now, she had just placed an insurmountable roadblock in my path.

At the top of the room, Theresa and Connie stood shoulder to shoulder, facing the crowd with bright smiles. Spotting me, they waved two sheets of paper triumphantly – their travel permits. I managed to muster a smile and wave back, all the while my heart felt like it was plummeting to my shoes. Clutching my suitcase, I rushed down the steps, my mind a whirlwind of thoughts.

The single avenue of escape I had been banking on was now firmly shut. It was back to saving money, back to the grind. I couldn't afford to stay with Eve for long, I'd have to explain that I needed to get back to work and couldn't take any extra days off. Despair tasted like a bitter residue in my mouth, but I swallowed it down.

Thirty minutes later I was walking past smaller red-brick terraced houses, their windows glinting in the afternoon sun. Like Kilkenny, there was a calmness in Dublin – no sandbags, one or two lamps shrouded in black cloaks, and this calmness I found comforting.

I inhaled, shook the disappointment from my shoulders and walked towards Eve's. I would enjoy myself for one night. Eve opened the door in her stockinged feet and flung her arms around me.

'You look lovely, Kitty. I always said blue was your colour.'

Eve radiated energy. Her hair shone and she wore a deep pink dress that pinched her waist – any tighter and it would have stopped her breath. I followed her along the worn floorboards, dull with age, into a small warm room. I sank into the deep cushions on the brown sofa.

Eve laughed. 'That couch is nearly human. I swear it will swallow me up whole one day. I'm so glad you came up.'

She stood back and smiled, the way she had when we only had each other, under the blankets at night at St Margaret's.

'You look well, Kitty. I'd say it's all Alice's good home cooking,' she said and hugged me.

I would leave all my worries until tomorrow and get lost in the night ahead.

The door opened and a young man came in and looked quizzically at me.

'Kitty, this is my brother, the most handsome man in Dublin – or so he thinks.'

He grinned. 'I'm Edward, but call me Eddie.' He took off his black cap, and put an arm behind his back, bowing in mock courtesy.

I laughed. He bore no similarity to Eve with his mousy brown hair, and blue eyes.

'Eddie, you're a complete eejit,' said Eve. 'Kitty, he thinks he's something special now he has a cap with LDF on it. All the lads joined the local defence forces, it's nothing that special.'

In the kitchen, Mrs Murphy stood at the stove pushing

sizzling sausages in a pan. She turned around, hearing our footsteps on the wooden floorboards.

'Ma, this is my good friend Kitty. I told you about her.'

She was a little round woman wearing a fuzzy housecoat, with olive skin like warm butterscotch you got for Christmas. Like Eve, she had hazel eyes and they shifted from the frying pan to the saucepan of milk, making sure it didn't boil over. It was evident Eve took after her mother.

'Sausage, Kitty?' She took a bite of one and wiped her mouth. 'Denny's – they're the best.'

I shook my head. 'No, thank you.'

There were three raps at the door, and a man shouted, 'Are you in there, Mrs Murphy?'

She untied her apron in a huff and marched to the door. 'Christ almighty, it's the bloody glimmer man. Has he nothing better to do? I'll tell the long thin strip of misery to stop bothering people at this time of night and look after his own family.'

After a few heated words between Mrs Murphy and the glimmer man, Eve and I put on our headscarves and coats to leave for the Gresham.

'Kitty, let's go,' Eve said, flattening the fur around her collar. 'Ma lets me borrow this coat for special occasions. It was her mother's.'

The sky had turned from blue to dusky grey, but there was enough light for the children to play hopscotch on the street, jumping between chalked squares, giggling and laughing. I linked Eve's arm as we walked unfamiliar streets and soon we were in O'Connell Street with women and men our age. The men wore dinner jackets and some of the ladies dressed in glittering satin dresses of blue and red, but mostly, like Eve and me, they wore snug fitted dresses that showed their small waists.

'I haven't been out in ages to dance,' said Eve. She gave a little sway of her hips and we both laughed, just like we did in London. 'Eddie says there's great fun at the Gresham, and lots of parties after. We haven't got dressed up in our finest just to look like wallflowers. Let's dance ourselves silly. Everyone's up for a laugh and a good time.'

I hadn't been out like this since we'd danced in Highgate the previous summer.

She turned serious. 'Kitty, everyone just wants to have a good time. Eddie told me about a lad who joined the Irish Guards and was killed within six months of joining, in Africa of all places, so come on yourself. You never know what's around the corner.'

She put on red lipstick and clasped her bag shut, whirling around. 'Life doesn't have a road map. Don't you agree?'

She was right – life is short and we don't know what path we will take, or where it will take us, and mine wasn't going where I wanted it. The alcohol didn't seem to be rationed, but we kept dancing, never returning to our table, our drinks left untouched. The band played Benny Goodman, followed by the husky Nina Simone, and we left just before midnight, our hearts and minds racing.

'That was such fun,' Eve said, giving me my coat. We waited for Eddie outside as the chattering crowd left and got on their High Nellys or walked home.

In a flash, the moment changed with a loud bang in the distance. White searchlights moved over and back over the city sky reminding us of the fragility of our life.

Eve looked up. 'Eddie, what's this all about?'

'It's nothing. The Germans fly over, and there's the odd exchange of fire between a German fighter and a British Spitfire. But nothing too serious. Nothing more than a dogfight.'

The cloudless sky hummed. I hadn't been expecting this. There was little light. We followed the circles below the lamp posts, and though most people were probably in their beds, faint light shimmered around windows where curtains were pulled tight.

The excitement of the dance evaporated as the sky exploded with three flares – orange, white and green. Air raid sirens screamed through the city. We stood frozen. Would there be more planes?

'Let's get home. It's not far.' Eddie quickened his steps. He held my elbow, guiding me across O'Connell Street. I wished I still had my ARP band.

Eve started to fret. 'What if something happens to Mammy and I'm not there?'

Eddie let go of my elbow, put his fingers into his mouth and let out a long shrill whistle. He shouted and waved to the crowd gathered on the street, women crying, young men jacketless. 'David, over here!'

Tracer bullets whizzed across the sky. A young man about Eddie's age, though much taller, was the only man not looking like he'd been to the dance.

'Jesus, Eddie,' David said, 'I was on my way home from work in the brewery. What the hell is happening?'

'It's the bloody Germans. Will you take my sister and her friend home?'

'There's only space for one on the carrier,' David said. 'Come on, Eve, hop on.'

Eve lifted her skirt and got on the back of his bicycle. The metal carrier looked uncomfortable, but that was the last thing on her mind.

'Kitty, there's a shelter on Kirwan Street. We'll go there,' Eddie said.

The ground shook, the night sky turned red and orange, and the ack-ack guns fired. Eve and David disappeared in the confusion. Eddie grabbed my elbow again, pulling me along the road, now filled with men and women with stark faces, some wearing only their bedclothes. Ambulances were going back and forth in a cloud of dust. A figure was lying on the side of the road – his head was gone. Air raid sirens sounded.

Eddie pulled me close and gripped my hand tight. 'It's too late! We won't get to the shelter.'

My throat constricted and in a second that seemed like an eternity, all around us houses collapsed like a pack of cards. The front of a house lay crumpled in piles on the street. Upstairs, a bed hung from floorboards that seemed to float mid-air, still attached to the stone wall, picture frames knocked sideways, hanging on with a string, and curtains waving in the breeze where once there was a window.

Women gathered on the street, still in their nightclothes, their faces stained with black tears, all unable to speak. A baby cried somewhere.

A woman in an apron, grey with ash, ran to the rubble of the middle house and fell to her knees. 'My baby, where is she?'

The desperation pierced the air.

There was nothing but stones and rubble left. The dresser

lay on the floor, beside what I thought might be the kitchen table, piled high with red bricks.

I ran to the woman. 'I'll help.'

She ignored me and struggled over the bricks, picking some up, ripping her knuckles. 'Daisy! Daisy!' she cried.

'Over here!' an SDL shouted, pulling back a rocking chair lying upside down against the back of the room. He bent down and stood up with a perfectly clean, unharmed baby in his arms. Her mother stumbled over the rubble.

'Everyone stand back now – gas leak.' A man stood beside the crater, his face black, wearing nothing more than his vest and trousers. He ran and threw a match into the crater and, immediately, a blue flame shot upwards.

A man grabbed my hand, pulling me to the side of the road. 'Jaysus, love, what are ya at?'

The air cleared of dust, and the prayers started for the dead. 'Five bodies so far,' I heard a man say.

'Kitty, are you all right?' I turned and saw Eddie's blackened face, his eyes bloodshot. 'Go back to the house, Kitty.'

I looked through the rubble for Daisy and her mother, but they were gone.

'Kitty!' Eddie grabbed my wrist and shook me. 'Go back to Eve. Kitty, will you please go? There's nothing you can do.'

He was right. I nodded and ran through the crowds, breathless. Soot stuck to my clothes and the inside of my nostrils.

Eve stood in the doorway, looking up and down the street. When I finally appeared, her face softened with relief, the lines of anguish gone.

'Kitty, I was so worried. It's awful. There are lots of people dead.'

She brought me inside, and Mrs Murphy brought a basin of hot water and soap.

'Get some rest, and Eddie will bring you home tomorrow.'

Lying in bed and waiting for sleep to come, images of bombed buildings, and the screams of distraught parents looking for their children, filled my thoughts.

I left Eve the following evening with a hug.

'God, Kitty, I feel so worried that you might have been killed.'

'But I wasn't. I'm fine.' I looked at my wristwatch. 'I'll miss the bus back.'

On the bus back to Alice's, I thought of Anthony and the scars of Spain. I turned my hands over; there was not a blemish on them. I looked at my reflection in the windows. All I could see were piles of rubble, the debris, the mother looking for little Daisy.

When I reached Alice's house, the door was flung open before I even turned the handle.

'Kitty, thank God you're safe. I was so worried about you.' She ran her hands over my face, turning my hands over. 'Are you hurt?' She sniffed my hair. 'Peter and I listened to the radio, and it was the first thing I read about this morning, when I got the newspaper. I was so worried when I saw the headlines.'

My hair and my skin had been scrubbed, but it still felt like the residue of last night was embedded deep in my skin. Peter took my bag. His face had the same blank look, but he held my hand. We went into the sitting room, and Alice moved the *Sunday Independent* and her Kerry Blue cigarettes from the sofa.

I took the paper from Alice, my body still in shock. I had been so near death. I couldn't get the image of a fireman holding a child in the rubble out of my mind. Thirty dead and twenty houses damaged.

'Peter heard it first on the radio last night. At first, I couldn't understand why he was so upset.'

I didn't notice he had sat down beside me until I felt his warm fingers curling around mine. Alice noticed it too.

'I thought you could do with the break – have a life, not be cooped up all day with an old lady and her son.' She held my hand, stroking it lightly, and looked out the French doors to the garden. 'I don't know what will happen to him when I'm gone.'

'Alice, you're not old. You have many more years.'

She got up and picked up the picture of her and Maurice, running her fingers around the silver frame.

'You never know what will happen in life. I was an only child and Maurice, well, he had only one brother. Some people say blood is thicker than water, but it's what is in the heart that matters.'

26

June

I sat down in the first free seat on the train, my gaze fixed on the undulating green fields beyond the carriage window, and drummed my fingers on the seat handle.

A man sitting opposite me tried to catch my attention, but I wasn't in the mood for idle chatter. My life seemed to be closing in on me, and now the only escape was for me and Anthony go up north, but now Alice and Peter had entered my life, and complicated my need to escape.

The man folded his paper and readjusted the blanket that had spilled onto the seat. 'Kathleen Flinn, is that you?'

'Father Fitzpatrick, I didn't expect you to have to take the train,' I said.

'Petrol rationing, my dear. I prefer to give the saved money to the less fortunate.'

He shifted his large bulk to face me.

'How are you and Anthony holding up? I can't imagine how difficult it must be after James. He looked after you so well after your father died.'

I didn't want to talk about James, and I wished I could just continue to look out at the passing green fields.

'Kitty,' he said, his hand landing on mine. 'I know how hard it was for you and Anthony. Your mother was... sometimes a difficult woman.'

I interrupted him. 'Father, I don't want to hear your thoughts on my mother. And don't tell me she meant well.'

'Kitty.' He squeezed my hand gently. 'She was a cruel woman. She hurt many people. Kitty, her own father hurt her by appearing and disappearing in her life.'

'I know,' I said. 'Daddy told me about that.'

'And sometimes when people feel unloved or abandoned, they find it hard to give to others.' He closed his eyes, searching for the words. 'They feel they will only be rejected again, so if they don't give any love, they can't be hurt.'

I was speechless for a moment. 'I thought no one knew.'

'Sure, what could people say? Many knew but people have their own worries.'

He sighed and looked out the window. A low mist sat on the purple heather, like soft candy floss.

'Can I ask you something, Father? Why did my father marry her?'

Father Fitzpatrick inhaled and looked at the luggage compartment opposite him. 'Your mother saw your father as easy prey. He was a victim. I've heard lots of confessions over the years. The confessional box may be dark, and I can't see faces, but over the years I've learned to tune in to voices. When people make a confession, if the rhythm changes, it's easy to spot a lie, or anger, but the easiest to pick up on is fear. Your father used to come to talk to me there. It was the only place he could speak freely.'

'You knew? Then why didn't you do something about it? Sorry, Father, but you're a man of God, aren't you?' I asked, trying to stop my anger.

'I know you're angry with me, but we keep our own business, and we don't talk about things that go on in other people's houses.'

His hand felt warm on mine.

'Kitty, I tried to help all I could. I told your father to leave, and to take you and Anthony. I told him your mother was going to die a lonely old woman. I think he was going to leave just before the accident. He had come to me to ask for my advice. My sister Claire – you know her as Sister Assumpta – was going to help. They once had been very good friends, but like me she chose God.'

Sister Assumpta had known my father. Was that why she was so good to me?

'When your mother came to me to say you were in the family way, I knew Claire would help. Believe me, I really tried to help the best I could.'

I got up. 'You didn't, did you? And claiming to be a friend to my father, when you knew how she was? Some man of God you are.'

Father Fitzpatrick's face drained of colour.

'I tried my best, Kitty. But some things are outside of anyone's control.'

The train halted in Kilkenny, and I picked up my coat and bag. Father Fitzpatrick stayed seated, and I looked at him again.

'Father, I'm sorry. I didn't mean to...'

He raised his hand, a look of exhaustion etched into his features. 'It's fine, Kitty,' he said softly. 'Go and find your peace.'

I gave him one last nod before making my way down the aisle and out onto the platform. As I watched the train pull away from the station, I realised that there were some things no amount of apologising could ever undo or make right again.

On my way home, I mulled over Father Fitzpatrick's words spinning in my head. I was eager to talk to Anthony. The bright sun shone down on the farmers cutting hay in the fields, stirring up memories of childhood days when Daddy and Anthony were by my side. An ache in my chest pushed against my ribs, the tears filling my eyes as guilt pricked at my heart for being so angry with Daddy.

27

Finally, I arrived at our little house down the lane, walking under the beech trees, their leaves fluttering gently in the breeze. As my hand brushed the handle of our front door, the unmistakable tremulous voice of Édith Piaf filled the air, singing 'On danse sur ma chanson'.

Stepping into the familiar house I was greeted by the enthusiastic wagging of Bessie's tail and kneeled to ruffle her ears as she smothered me with a flurry of dog kisses to welcome me home. My eyes narrowed at seeing a pair of imposing black boots resting by the door – they weren't Anthony's. Their high-quality leather glimmered in contrast to Anthony's muddied boots beside them.

Laughter drifted from the kitchen. There, at the worn table, sat Anthony and a stranger, both smiling, as they played cards and shared a cigarette. A sudden chill ran through me at this intimacy.

Anthony's eyes widened when he saw me and he quickly rose, the chair behind him overturning and crashing to the floor.

'Kitty! I wasn't expecting you.' He stuttered as a crimson flush crept up his neck.

'Who's this?' I said, side-stepping Bessie and ignoring her questioning whimpering at my sudden change in demeanour.

He gestured uneasily at the man opposite him, his voice barely a whisper.

'Markus, this is my sister, Kitty.'

Markus stood up, his face hidden by bright sunshine pouring in from the window behind him. I couldn't place his face; he was completely strange to me. He wore a navy-blue pullover that I had made for James on my first Christmas in London. The knitting stitches seemed to tell a story that I didn't want to read.

A sense of dread filled me as I looked from Anthony to Markus and then around at the cluttered kitchen. Their easy companionship forbidden in a world where such a thing would be condemned.

'Anthony, who is this?' I demanded, my words heavy with suspicion and anger. 'I'm struggling to keep us safe, and is this how you repay me? Bringing another man into our house?'

Markus took a step back. His face was marked by a silvery scar etched across chiseled cheekbones and an athletic build. I took in his grey wool trousers, the light-blue collar sticking out of the jumper. He was broad-shouldered with blonde hair and olive skin.

As Anthony struggled to explain, the man stood there in silence. I could feel a whirlwind of emotions welling up inside me. How could Anthony put himself at risk by bringing a man here and risk getting exposed as a homosexual?

'Kitty, don't jump to conclusions.' Anthony ran his

hand through his hair, a look of distress on his face as he attempted to explain. 'He's an airman whose plane went down. I met him during one of my walks in the forest and I felt I had to help. He was dirty and really thin. I couldn't just leave him. He would have died, Kitty.' His voice was tinged with desperation. 'His parachute got caught in the trees. A branch tore into his legs and his ribs were broken.'

The parachute.

'What kind of airman is he?' Somehow, I managed to keep a level voice.

Anthony stepped closer, reaching for my hand.

'Kitty, please, sit down for a moment. He's a German but—'

I reached for the bread knife on our kitchen table. I pointed it at them both with trembling hands.

'Anthony, get away from him.' My voice cracked.

Images of the destruction in Dublin flooded my mind – the bombings, the crumbling houses reduced to rubble, the haunted faces of people covered in soot and ash. The mother's anguished cries for Daisy.

'A Nazi, Anthony,' I seethed, my voice laced with disbelief. 'What on earth is a Nazi doing in our home, sitting at our table, sipping tea as if he were a civilised human being?'

'He's not a Nazi. He's a meteorologist,' Anthony said. 'He's not a murderer. He just reports on the weather. He told me things about what goes on in Germany, in Bavaria. He crash-landed here on purpose.'

The mention of Bavaria made my back stiffen.

'Jesus, Anthony, that's where Mammy's people come from. No good has ever come out of Bavaria. And you believe him?'

The words tumbled out of me. I spoke forcefully, 'Anthony, you have to put a stop to this. We're already drowning in debt, and now this. We will undoubtedly be arrested.'

Anthony shook his head and looked at Markus. 'He just takes weather readings, and he was forced to do that. He's been good to me, Kitty.'

Markus sat and lowered his face into his hands. I placed my hands on the table and stared at Anthony, leaning over to catch my breath.

'We can't let him stay. We're harbouring a criminal. The Curragh has a prisoner of war camp full of German airmen. Think of Dublin! Thirty people died when they were bombed. They went to bed expecting to go to Mass the next morning but never woke up!'

'That wasn't him. He's been here for a while.'

The parachute. The strange presence I had felt at James's house. It all fell into place like pieces of a jigsaw. The airman moved behind the table, his face stark.

The air drained from the room. My hands trembled and I pressed my lips together, trying to find the words. 'People like him, killing innocents all across Europe. James would be disgusted if he was here. He was such a good man, and our mother took advantage of him. He would turn in his grave if he knew someone like that was in his house.'

I went on, 'Anthony, we need to escape and get to England, but we're on the Stop List because of our mother's background.'

I told him about Frank Doolin and his request that I work for the government. 'He's Military Intelligence. He arrived at Alice's house out of the blue and asked me to work as a translator. He's a horrible little man.'

He frowned. 'Why? You're not the only person in Ireland who speaks German.'

Then something else struck me.

'Christ, Anthony, Sam Daly lives just up the road. You're harbouring a criminal.'

'Of course I know that! But he won't come near here.' Anthony gazed out the window toward Sam's house across the field.

'How the hell do you know that? We could both be arrested!' I slumped into a chair and buried my face in my hands. 'What a mess.'

I looked at Bessie asleep on the mat in front of the fire. What a simple life a dog had.

'Anthony, I don't know what Doolin wanted. You're right, it's strange that he asked me to be an interpreter.' The mere mention of the language reopened wounds I hoped had healed.

I pointed at the airman. 'And that's another reason I don't want him here – he reminds me of our mother.'

Markus stepped forward. 'I'm sorry,' he said. 'Anthony told me about her. She sounds awful. And I am sorry about Dublin,' His accent was nuanced, with more of an English accent than German.

'It's a bit bloody late to be sorry,' I said as again I pictured little Daisy crying in the rubble.

He blessed himself, his face twisted as if in pain, and his eyes simmered with the onset of tears. 'The people that did that, some were evil, some were young men, and some were old, like me. They were just carrying out orders,' he whispered. 'Kitty, I'm not like them. I swear to you.'

'It's a bit late to be blessing yourself now and pretending

you're all saintly. Did you think about how all those mothers felt finding their child missing, or how it felt to be a child losing their mother? You'll just have to go into Kilkenny Garda Station or the army barracks and hand yourself in.'

'Kitty, he has helped me,' Anthony said. 'Why did you think I was getting better?'

It was true; his sores had healed into faint silver scars. His countenance seemed clearer, his face pinker and fuller.

Anthony sat up. 'Markus explained I had a bad bacterial infection, lingering trench mouth, from my days in Spain,' he said, he drew a deep breath and gazed into the distance. 'We talked about what I saw in Spain; Markus explained it can affect the mind.'

Anthony closed his eyes, reclining in his chair. His mouth hung open, remaining silent. His face turned pale. Rising unsteadily, he clutched his throat as he gasped for air. Suddenly, he lurched forward, grabbing the side of the kitchen table, knocking over the cups and teapot. He collapsed amongst the shattered delph.

Markus hurried to him, placing the back of his hand on his forehead and peering into his eyes.

'Kitty, help me to get him into the armchair.'

Together we carried Anthony, Markus supporting most of the weight. I touched my hand to Anthony's head, it was burning up. He started to shake violently, then stopped. Beads of perspiration formed on his forehead, and his breathing was fast. Feeling his wrist, I detected a faint pulse under my fingertips.

'What's happening?' I asked.

Markus nodded to the stove. 'In the saucepan there is

something I was brewing. It should be hot. It's something to help the fever. Get it, quickly. Pour some into a cup.'

Following his instructions, I watched as Markus propped Anthony up and gently lifted the cup to his lips. He tilted Anthony's head back and dripped some of the brew into his mouth. Soon, Anthony's breathing slowed and his face calmed.

Again, I checked his pulse. It had slowed.

'Your brother will be fine. The blisters, see, they are all dried, nearly gone. I found iodine and put that on them.'

I nodded. Markus filled the cup again.

'As your brother said, he has trench mouth and a septic throat. Each illness led into another, and his body never healed, and neither did his mind. It was easy to fix. He is in need of nourishment. Lots of fresh vegetables and liver. And I showed him exercises for his leg. A splint, will help a bit. But with good food, pain relief, life might be a bit easier for him.'

He let Anthony's head gently fall back in the chair. Thankfully, pink had seeped back into his cheeks like water on wet paper.

'He got it in Spain, from poor hygiene and nutrition. It causes all sorts of problems – your mind goes a bit insane, hallucinations, tiredness, and extremely painful blisters and mouth ulcers, and in turn just leads to more problems. My father got it in the Great War in the trenches. And the images of war don't leave as soon as men decide to stop killing each other.'

He got a mug and lifted the kettle, pouring a little water into the mug. From the shelf, he took a tin of Baxter's bicarbonate of soda and spooned a teaspoon into the water.

'Anthony swirls this in his mouth to keep the gums healthy. But this drink in the pot, that is like aspirin.' He lifted a bunch of white creamy flowers smelling of almond. 'Meadow sweet: they grow in the damp forest and in ditches. Very easy to find in the woods.'

These soft acts of kindness were incongruous with the images I witnessed in Dublin and in the papers. I was in over my head. I was drowning; I was fighting to get to the surface to breathe and I was failing. I did the next best thing: I sat down and cried. After a few minutes of heaving, I wiped my nose with the back of my hand and turned back to Markus.

'Have your people no shame? Did you hear how many people died in Belfast this Easter? Nine hundred. Women and children, whole families. They had to drain the public baths to put the bodies in there.'

'Believe me,' he pleaded, his voice rising in desperation. His eyes glistened with sincerity. He gripped his hands together tightly, his knuckles turning white with emotion. His accent became thicker, more pronounced with anguish as he continued. 'I was conscripted into the Luftwaffe. They needed a meteorologist. One day our plane ran into trouble while we were flying over the Irish Sea, and we had no choice but to land either in Wales or here. We chose the latter because I had already been held captive in a British-run prisoner of war camp at Vilvoorde, where conditions were appalling. Beatings and lack of food were daily occurrences.'

The paraffin lamp flickered, and the room grew still and

cold. He looked over at Anthony and got up and pulled the blanket over him, before placing his hand on his shoulder and speaking in a soft voice, as if to a child, 'Anthony, sleep for a while.'

Then he turned to me. 'Kitty, please, I can't go to another internment camp, I'd never survive.'

His eyes met mine for a few seconds, imploring. Then Anthony let out a groan and he turned to him. He was moving a little, his face soft, his breathing regular and strong.

I sighed. 'I do appreciate you helping my brother. But you cannot stay.'

He lowered his eyes. 'I know. I am truly sorry for what you saw in Dublin.'

Anthony stirred, sat up and stretched. 'What happened?'

He rubbed his head, the blanket falling onto the floor. I got up, taking my shawl from the kitchen hook, and sat beside Anthony the way we used to cosy up in front of the fire as children.

'I told him he can't stay,' I said. 'It's too dangerous.'

Markus sat in our father's armchair, dropped his head into his hands, rubbed his fingers through his hair and looked up at me. 'Kitty, I am not a threat. I hate them. I hate all the Nazis.'

He picked up another mug beside Anthony. 'Smell this.'

I grimaced, the smell biting the inside of my nose. 'What's that?'

'Wild garlic. It grows in the woods. It's good for your immune system. Helps a sick person ward off infections.'

He held up a small green plant with little white leaves. It looked more like a weed than something edible.

'When I finished my final exams at school, my father asked if I wanted to be a doctor like him. But I hate blood. I knew he wouldn't like it if I said I wanted to be a gardener. He would have said that's not a man's profession. So, I said I would study meteorology in England. I had to escape, to get away. I never chose to be one of them. They chose me.'

I shook my head. 'There is nothing you could say that would change my mind.'

'Will you please listen to me?' he pleaded. 'Just give me two minutes. I already talked about this with your brother.'

He cleared his throat.

'In early 1938, I went to see my cousin, a priest in Bavaria. The Nazis, the Gestapo, they ran the place, arresting anyone who was a threat. And a threat to them was someone like my cousin. He acted as a peace negotiator and wrote to journals and newspapers complaining about the Nazis.

'Have you heard of Dachau, Kitty? It's a camp in Bavaria. They built it during the 1930s as a place to put people who they think are not pure. And I don't just mean Jewish. But also political activists against the German regime, even Catholic priests, and especially if someone is a homosexual. It is an awful place.'

The moment he mentioned *homosexual* a pang of fear pieced my heart, reminding me how precarious Anthony's situation was.

'In 1938, my cousin was arrested for being a dissenter. I was so afraid for him. I didn't hear from him for months and went to the Gestapo headquarters, the Hotel Métropole in Berlin, and asked about him.'

He ran a finger along the scar on his cheek.

'They beat me with a bayonet, asking me about my beliefs, was I affiliated with any Jews or homosexuals or dissenters. I knew nothing but they accused me of promoting hatred towards the Nazis. I kept telling them I was a humble meteorologist.

'And that is what saved me. After six months, when my cousin came home, I visited him. He told me of things that had happened to him and to the other men. They made them get up at three in the morning. Breakfast was black coffee, and then they were marched off to do hard labour. All they had to eat was thin, watery cabbage soup. When they marched, the Nazis beat the people at the back for walking too slow, and beat people during the night for snoring. They were starved and lived and slept in dirt.

'The political prisoners wore two triangles on their arms, Jehovah's Witnesses wore a lilac triangle, homosexuals wore a pink triangle and the Jews wore a yellow triangle. They made him wear two triangles. He was a priest, nothing political, just a peaceful man.'

He spoke again, and this time his words were filled with dread. 'They hauled me away and demanded I become their meteorologist, or else they would hurt my cousin. I had no choice.'

The fire had dwindled to cold ashes. My head hurt. I looked over at Anthony, his face calm, his cheeks not as hollow. Then at Markus. The day took a hold on me, grabbing me by the neck. I felt like I was sinking.

'Help me carry Anthony to his room, and then I want you gone by the time I wake up,' I said firmly.

Markus wrapped his arms around Anthony's body, and

we struggled to keep him upright and support him. He slurred something incoherently. The situation felt heavy with tension, and all I wanted was some time alone to think of what to do next.

I woke before dawn, my sleep disturbed by the difficult conversations the day would bring. I hadn't closed my bedroom curtains, and morning light crept over the floor. The copper beech outside my window swayed lightly, its auburn leaves shimmering like glitter catching the morning sun. Normally, I loved watching the leaves' shadows on the floorboards, but as I lay in bed, the house pressed down on me, burying me alive.

Downstairs in the kitchen, Anthony sat reading a book. He had undergone a transformation. His hair was combed neatly, and his clothes appeared to fit him again. Even the scars on his hands seemed less noticeable. I felt a wave of relief wash over me as I noticed these details; yesterday, my distraction had prevented me from noticing them.

'He's gone, Kitty,' he said. 'He won't be bothering us any more. He won't be found.'

I cut him short. Now we were alone, I had to tell him I'd met Father Fitzpatrick.

'Anthony, I've something really important to tell you. Put your book down, and I'll make us tea.' Gathering my thoughts on how to tell him, I filled the kettle and placed the cups on the table, shifting the breadboard, the one Daddy had made. A lump of guilt formed, overwhelmed by how wrong we had been about him.

'On my way here, I met Father Fitzpatrick on the train.

He told me things – things about Daddy. Anthony, we were so wrong.'

As I told him what the priest had told me, Anthony sank deeper into his chair, his vitality seeming to dissipate.

'Father Fitzpatrick suggested to Daddy that he take us with him. He empathised with his plight. He extended a helping hand for him to escape our mother's clutches.'

I swallowed hard, the words almost choking me, my voice barely a whisper. 'Anthony, those were our suitcases you saw the night of the fire.'

His lips trembled and when he found his voice again, it was choked with grief. 'I had no clue, Kitty. I'm sorry for thinking Daddy would desert us like this, leaving us behind.'

'It's not your fault, Anthony. We can't blame ourselves for our ignorance. He also said that our mother's father abandoned her, and she was hurt; he said she was afraid to love because she thought she might get hurt again' – I paused – 'but I don't think that's an excuse to have been so cruel.'

He nodded slowly. 'But we have bigger problems. How much have you saved?'

'I'm making progress on the money but how can we pay off the blackmailer before June?' I asked, feeling the urgency in my voice. The question of whether the blackmailer would ever cease their threats hung in the air, unanswered.

With Anthony's health improving, there was the possibility of him working to bring in some money. Yet, as I thought about it, memories of the conversation I'd had with those two sisters outside the Permit Office came back to me – whispers of escapes through Northern Ireland, hiring fishermen for secretive crossings glimmered in my eye like a dim flickering candle.

The unexpected intrusion of the airman into our lives complicated matters further. If he were discovered here, our German heritage would undoubtedly cast us under suspicion, wrongly painting us as German sympathisers.

28

On Monday evening, as I watched Alice moving about the kitchen, my feet ached, reminding me of the long day at work. But it wasn't just the physical exhaustion. My mind seemed caught in a loop, obsessing over the German airman. Had he truly left? Would Anthony let him return? I knew I hadn't been forceful enough.

I was grateful when Alice's voice broke my thoughts.

'What a beautiful evening, Kitty,' she said. 'A testament to the simple pleasure of being alive.'

A fly danced in chaotic ballet around the pot, and Alice banished the unwelcome guest with a swift flick of the dishcloth.

'The bane of these sun-soaked days,' she sighed, then smiled. 'But let's not dwell on nuisances. I've a hearty soup simmering for us. Kitty, sit and share your day's news with me. How's Anthony? Is he well?'

Her voice was gentle, an acknowledgement of her concern.

'I'm just a bit worn out. And Anthony is well.'

A sudden sting in my eyes betrayed my attempt to seem composed.

Alice put down the knife. 'Kitty, you're crying.'

I wiped my cheek and forced a laugh. 'The onions have a way of prying tears out, don't they?'

She nodded, lifting the lid from the saucepan. Her glasses fogged up and she said, 'There's nothing quite like a wholesome soup with buttery bread.'

Lured by the aroma, Peter joined us from the sitting room and settled into his usual spot opposite the kitchen window. The willow-pattern bowls were filled with heart-warming, hearty soup. Accepting a bowl, I found myself battling an appetite dimmed by anxiety. I cut the bread for Peter into slender soldiers.

The soothing cadence of music from the radio floated from the living room. Alice hummed along, her body swaying lightly with the rhythm, her eyes closed.

'Every Sunday night, Maurice and I would dance,' she said, her voice soft in the memory. 'Peter would watch. Just the three of us, cocooned in our little world.'

Her gaze drifted, the light from her eyes dimming. 'He misses his father so much. Your presence is a solace, Kitty. I won't deny I was apprehensive when James reached out. But I'm grateful you came. And Peter cherishes your company too.'

Alice's words resonated deep within me, that I mattered to someone.

With our meal finished and the evening still young, we decided to step outside. The garden, bright with the fresh hues of summer, welcomed us warmly. We settled down to watch the sunset. As the fiery orb sank low, the treetops appeared ablaze.

When it set, I shivered from the sudden drop in temperature. Dark clouds began to roll in, and a chill wind stirred the leaves around us. A raindrop fell on my forehead, nature's gentle reminder that it was time to move.

'We'd better go inside,' Alice said. 'It'll be the death of us if we get drenched by the shower.'

She stood, rubbing her arms, and called to Peter as he ran his fingertips over the foxgloves at the end of the garden. A shiver coursed through me as I followed her into the house, not sure if it was fear or just the cold.

As soon as we were inside, I knew what decision I had to make. I had to go back to Kilkenny. Anthony's words resonated in my ears, insisting that Markus wouldn't be found.

The air was damp on my walk to work the following morning, and the scent of dew-soaked grass filled my nostrils. My mind raced with thoughts of Markus, that mysterious stranger who'd crash-landed into our lives. I felt a knot in the pit of my stomach, wondering if telling him to go had been a grave mistake.

I quickened my steps through the hospital corridors, my focus shifting entirely to the tasks that lay ahead. 'My apologies,' I stammered as I collided with a man. Then, at the sight of his face, I felt the colour drain from my cheeks.

'Kitty Flinn,' said Sam Daly. His voice, polished and measured, had a way of cutting through the fog of my thoughts. His dark hair and brown eyes were as unmistakable as they were unnerving.

'Sam,' I returned coldly, 'what brings you here?'

He glanced nervously over my shoulder, his eyes betraying him even as he tried to look nonchalant. 'I'm here to meet a friend.'

His words echoed in the corridor, hollow and unconvincing. I could almost smell the deceit wafting off him.

'By the way,' he said, his voice trying for casual but tinged with calculation, 'how is Anthony? What's he doing with himself these days?'

'None of your business,' I shot back with foreboding. Discussing anything about Anthony with Sam felt as safe as clutching a live grenade.

We traded a few terse words before I turned on my heels and left, but his unsettling presence trailed me like a stubborn fog. The day unfolded in a blur, tinged with the disquiet that Sam's appearance had sparked. It was an itch that refused to be scratched, a splinter in my mind.

With Markus entering, and hopefully gone, it felt as though I was navigating a minefield blindfolded. I resolved to tread carefully; secrets, like wild mushrooms, had a tendency to pop up where you least expected them.

When my workday finally drew to a close, I raced home, each footstep echoing the urgency pounding in my heart. I had to get back to Kilkenny.

29

As I approached James's cottage, my suspicions were confirmed when I saw a thin line of smoke billowing out of the chimney. The latch of the door clicked softly as I stepped inside, the familiar scent of peat smoke and worn leather greeting me like a warm embrace. A quiet and peaceful atmosphere enveloped the small room, disturbed only by the gentle crackle of the dying fire. Markus sat on an old wooden chair in the corner, his blond hair falling over his furrowed brow as he stared into the flames, lost in thought.

'Kitty,' he said and rose, a book falling from his lap. 'I'm sorry. Anthony said I could stay here.' The memory of James filled the cottage like a ghostly presence, and I couldn't help but think of how strange it was to have this man, this stranger, sitting in his place.

'Let me explain something to you. Please,' he said. There was a softness in his eyes, like beacons from a ship calling for help.

'You and your kind – Nazis,' I said. 'In London, I read the newspapers, saw the Pathé reels. How you treated

Jews, how you treated anyone that was different. Invading countries to make them German.' My words felt sour.

He sighed deeply, and the weight of his burden seemed to age him before my eyes.

'Kitty, I told you already that I am not one of them. I cannot tell you how much I despise that man and everything he has done. The atrocities committed during the war... they haunt me every day, like a dark cloud hanging over my soul.'

His voice trembled with anger and frustration. 'Men, women and innocent children losing their lives because of his twisted beliefs and blind ambition. Families torn apart, entire communities destroyed. It's unforgivable.'

I watched him, trying to gauge the depth of his emotions. If I were to let him continue to stay in James's house, I needed to trust him, and to trust that his hatred for Hitler was genuine. But as much as I wanted to believe him, my heart still guarded itself with caution, refusing to let go of the past.

'Markus, you have to understand,' I said quietly, 'the war has affected so many people – myself included. The pain it has caused can't be forgotten.'

'Kitty, I swear to you, on everything I hold dear, that you can trust me. I have made mistakes in my life, but I am determined to make amends for them. I will do anything I can to help you and your brother. You have my word.'

As we stood there, two strangers brought together by chance and circumstance, I felt the first stirrings of hope.

'Let me tell you about my life in Bavaria before the war,' Markus said, his voice softening as a hint of nostalgia coloured his words. 'My childhood was simple but happy. I grew up in a small village nestled between rolling green hills and dense forests. The air was always fresh and crisp, carrying the scent of pine and wildflowers.'

His words painted a picture in my mind of a world far removed from the one we now inhabited.

'During the summers, we would swim in the nearby river, the water so clear that you could see the pebbles at the bottom. And in the evenings we would gather around the fire, sharing stories and laughter with our friends and neighbours. Life was good, Kitty. It was peaceful and innocent.'

As he spoke, I saw a longing creep into his expression, as though he were reaching for something that had been lost forever. Then his voice wavered and he seemed to be revealing a hidden part of his heart that he had kept locked away until now.

'But beneath the surface of that idyllic life, there was also great pain,' he admitted, his eyes glistening with unshed tears. 'My wife and I struggled for years to conceive a child. We tried everything – doctors, prayers, old wives' tales – but nothing worked. We wanted a family more than anything in the world, and to be denied that... it felt like a cruel punishment. I would hear the laughter of children playing outside our window, and it was a constant reminder of what we could never have.'

The raw vulnerability in his voice resonated within me, stirring memories of my own losses and heartache. I found myself drawn to him, this man who had known both the beauty and the pain of life and was willing to bear his soul before me.

'Markus,' I whispered, 'I'm so sorry you had to endure that.'

'Thank you, Kitty,' he said, his voice just as quiet. 'But in a way, it was a blessing. It made me realise how precious life is, and how important it is to fight for the things that truly matter.'

As we sat there in the dim light of James's cottage, our shared experiences of loss and pain binding us together, I felt something shift within me. Perhaps Markus, too, could find redemption and solace amidst the chaos of this world. And perhaps together we could find a way through the darkness ahead.

'Kitty, there are more horrors that made me. In 1940, when we invaded Paris. I had to fire upon women and children as they attempted to escape the city. It was horrendous. I couldn't tell my wife I was killing children. The children we so desperately wanted.'

He sat up, his face etched with the horrors of his actions. 'It was then that I decided to do what I could. I fired, missing people on purpose. And I knew I had to leave Germany.'

I saw it in his eyes, the torment of the choices he had made during the war. It was a pain I knew all too well, as memories of my own past continued to haunt me.

'Markus,' I said softly, 'it's not your fault. You did what you could to protect those people. And now you're here, trying to find redemption and make amends.'

As I spoke, I felt a strange sensation stirring within me, a burgeoning emotional connection that both frightened and intrigued me. As much as I tried to resist it, there was something between us, an undeniable bond forged by our shared experiences of loss and pain.

My thoughts raced, struggling with the implications. I had been so certain of my need to protect myself and Anthony from any potential danger. But now, as I found myself drawn closer to this man who had suffered just as I had, I felt the walls around my heart begin to crumble.

'Kitty,' Markus said, his voice filled with emotion, 'I know you've both experienced great pain and loss in your lives. Hopefully you can move forward at some point and heal your loss.'

His words resonated within me, echoing my own deepest desires – to escape the shadows of my past and forge a brighter future for myself and Anthony. The weight of our conversation hung heavy in the air. In the silence that followed, it felt as though we were both contemplating the profound connection that had formed between us – a bond forged in the crucible of pain, yet tempered by the fragile hope of redemption.

I was tired, but maybe Anthony was in safe hands now.

I stood up. 'I must go. I've got to see Anthony before I go back to Naas.'

I gathered my coat and bag before tying my headscarf around my hair. The rain that had threatened earlier was now falling lightly. 'Soft day, thank God' James would have said.

I sighed, my heart still heavy with all the losses, but I had found a strange comfort in the words of a man I should not trust. Outside, the gate rattled, and I looked out into the yard. It was just the wind.

30

With a light touch, Alice drew closed the velvet curtains in the sitting room, erasing the view of a grey sky heavy with clouds.

'I know, Kitty, it's somewhat early to be drawing the curtains, but this evening has turned rather unpleasant, hasn't it? Best to keep the nasty weather out. Out of sight, out of mind, isn't that right?'

She glided her hands down the curtains where they met in the middle, cast a quick glance at her reflection in the mirror and fixed a few stray curlers in her silver hair. I busied myself adding bits of turf to the fire, before sinking into the armchair and tucking my legs under the wool blanket. Settling with my book in the comforting glow of the firelight, I mulled over how to tell Alice about Markus as I watched the peat spit and crackle under the intense heat.

Alice hummed as she knitted a jumper for Peter. The room was enveloped in a comforting silence, only punctuated by the rhythmic sound of her needles and the gentle rustle of my pages.

It was soon broken by two short raps at the front door. Alice peered over her spectacles and motioned towards the sound.

'Kitty, would you be a dear and get it? I'm in the middle of an important row. I'll just be a minute.'

The knocking, insistent and echoing, grew louder. Laying my book aside, I rose from the chair. As the door opened, the thunderous knocking was replaced by the imposing presence of Sam Daly and Frank Doolin. Their uniforms eliciting an involuntary shiver from me. Comdt Doolin was dressed in the emblematic green of the army and Sam wore the navy suit distinctive to what I now know was Special Branch. A gust of cold night air blew in and rivulets of rain ran down their overcoats, dripping onto the polished floor as they stepped in. Their expressions were stony.

Alice appeared beside me, her face creased in confusion. 'Gentlemen, how may I assist you?' she enquired.

With a stern and commanding gaze, Comdt Doolin looked at me. 'We've come concerning your brother, Anthony, Miss Flinn,' he declared with unsettling composure.

A frigid dread snaked its way up my spine. 'What does Anthony have to do with anything?' I stammered, my words heavy with trepidation. 'And why are you here, Sam?'

'Special Branch are assisting G2,' Sam replied, with a 'don't ask any more questions' look.

Alice stepped forward. 'Gentlemen, would you mind keeping quiet? My son is asleep upstairs.'

She motioned for them to follow her in. Their chilly, rain-soaked overcoats made the hallway seem smaller, almost suffocating. The house seemed to shrink around us. The rhythm of the clock was a drum roll.

Comdt Doolin spoke first. 'We have a warrant for Anthony Flinn's arrest. We have reason to believe he is a fifth columnist and working with the Germans.'

The accusation left me speechless and a wave of cold fear washed over me. Had they found out about Markus? My throat tightened and a sense of unease twisted in my stomach.

'There must be some misunderstanding,' I stammered, looking to Sam to contradict Comdt Doolin. 'What do you mean by that ridiculous statement?'

My eyes darted from Sam to the Comdt. Tears began to gather, unshed but threatening. Remembering Sam's compassion at James's funeral, I thought he had changed. Exposed now, was his true nature.

The room turned cold, echoing the storm outside.

Sam stepped forward, breaking the heavy silence. 'We have evidence that your brother has been working with a German spy,' he said quietly.

Had they discovered Markus?

Would I explain? I nervously chewed on my bottom lip as I considered whether or not to explain what happened. I knew if I did, my involvement would be brought into question and guilt and shame would weigh heavily on me. I didn't want any attention brought to myself.

Frank's gaze was piercing like a knife at my throat.

'The evidence at hand is considerable, Miss Flinn. Your brother has been observed in the company of known Germans who are Nazi sympathisers, attending covert gatherings. Do you know that he is in an organisation called Friends of Germany?'

I shook my head vehemently. 'No, he isn't! You're wrong about Anthony. He never leaves home.'

Comdt Doolin expelled a cloud of smoke in my direction, his blue eyes making a slow, deliberate journey across my form, scrutinising my eyes, my mouth, my neck, pausing indecently at my chest, and finally settling on my hands nervously kneading the fabric of my skirt.

'There was nobody home when I visited your family farm,' he said. 'So where do you think he is?'

'I don't know,' I replied, my voice barely above a whisper. My eyes pleaded with Sam, begging him to remember the bond of our friendship.

Comdt Doolin pushed his chair back. 'Daly, search the house.'

I sprang to my feet, protesting. 'You have no right to do that! Anthony isn't here. I'm not being detained, nor should Anthony be.'

'On the contrary, we can act as we deem fit. His association with the Germans violates the *Treason Against the State Act of 1939*. We are a dominion of the British Empire and so a threat to their security is an offence, and that means arrest.'

He dismissed me with a brusque gesture and motioned for Sam to follow him upstairs. 'Miss Flinn, I need you to wait here.'

Desperation made me clutch at Sam's overcoat. 'Sam,' I begged, 'what on earth is happening?'

He broke free and followed Doolin. I trailed them as they ascended the stairs with rapid steps.

Alice, her eyes brimming with fear, pushed past them and

stood outside Peter's bedroom door. 'Please leave. My boy must be terrified.'

Comdt Doolin went straight past her and pushed open my bedroom door.

'This is my home,' I objected, stepping in front of him. 'You have no right to invade it.'

His face was close to mine, too close. The stale aroma of his breath was nauseating.

'I am free to do as I please,' he hissed through gritted teeth. He flicked the switch, and the feeble light fluttered into life. He withdrew a torch from his coat, casting its beam around the room and beneath the bed, then began a slow, meticulous survey of the space. He paused to pick up a book from the bedside table. Sam rifled through my wardrobe, pushing aside my dresses, then closed it. He took in the room with a swift, practised glance.

'Where is your brother, Miss Flinn? I'm afraid I may resort to placing you under arrest,' Comdt Doolin declared with ominous certainty.

'That's impossible... you can't...' A wave of cold fear swept through me, leaving a tremor in my voice.

Sam stood beside my bed, his fingers wrapped around the old wooden box where I kept my possessions.

I snatched it from his grasp. The lid opened and its contents spilled onto the carpet. First to fall was a photograph of Daddy, its edges frayed and corners softened from frequent handling. The image, captured in better times, showed his warm smile, a stark contrast to the cold, harsh reality I now faced.

My diary followed, thumping heavily against the floor. Its leather cover weathered and creased.

Then a small tin can clinked open and coins rolled in various directions. My money, saved scrupulously over months, my lifeline, mine and Anthony's route to freedom.

And lastly, the phial of morphine. Sam's gaze hovered over everything, and in that moment, I felt naked, stripped of my defences, my inner world laid bare for him to see.

'Quite the collection we have here, Miss Flinn,' Comdt Doolin said, bending to retrieve the drug and the money. The smirk tugging at the corners of his mouth was almost as chilling as his words. He held the phial between the tips of his fingers, the liquid within shimmering – a secret dragged into the harsh light of truth. It disappeared into his coat pocket.

He held up the tin. 'And what might this be for?'

'My savings,' I gasped out.

Doolin's eyes narrowed. A palpable sense of dread choked the air.

He counted the money swiftly. A smirk crept across his face as, to my horror, he slipped my life savings in his pocket.

'You can't do that,' I said. 'That's my savings.' I stepped forward to catch his hand.

He grabbed my hand and leaned into my face, his stale breath hot on my skin. 'I can do what I like, Miss Flinn.' He leaned back, his gaze unmoving.

'I'd stay put if I were you, Miss Flinn. We'll be back shortly.'

Their footsteps echoed ominously down the stairs and I was alone once more, their departure marked by the final, resounding slam of the front door. I stood there, my heart pounding in my chest like a trapped rabbit.

My hands trembled, my breaths shallow and rapid as I

struggled to process the enormity of what had just occurred. My savings, the key to my dreams and escape, now rested in the pocket of a man.

I collapsed onto the bed, the weight of my shattered world pressing down on me. Countless extra shifts at the hospital, all for nothing. The money I'd scrimped and saved, gone. Anthony and I were both in danger of being arrested for a crime he hadn't committed. The door creaked open.

Alice's concerned voice snapped me from my trance. 'Kitty, you're pale as snow! Are you all right?'

Her words barely registered as I fought to suppress the tears stinging my eyes, a tide of fear and frustration. The gnawing dread in the pit of my stomach intensified. Anthony, accused of espionage… the thought was unbearable. Part of me yearned to recoil from Alice's comforting embrace, to retreat into my own turbulent thoughts. But I remained there, motionless, drowning in her concern as it enveloped me.

Abruptly, I sat up. 'Commandant Doolin said Anthony wasn't at home. So maybe he's at James's cottage with Markus,' I said, my voice quivering with a mix of hope and uncertainty. I also remembered the Comdt had said 'I' – so Sam had not been with him. So, he maybe didn't know about James's cottage.

Alice cocked her head sideways. 'Who's Markus?'

Avoiding her gaze, not wanting to lie, I shook my head. 'No one important right now,' I said quietly. I wanted to keep her out of this mess, not until I knew for sure what would happen next.

She kept holding my hand and smiled softly at me. 'You must let Anthony know immediately,' she said gently. 'Tomorrow, take the train to Kilkenny.'

Lying in bed that night, my thoughts and fear gnawed at me as I stared at the black ceiling. I willed the night to hurry to morning. Sam would eventually put the pieces together and tell the Comdt about James's cottage. I needed to get there before it was too late. I cursed Frank Doolin.

31

With every bend on the rail, I willed the train to go faster, the constant grating of metal on the tracks setting my teeth on edge but matching the tension in my stomach. I sprinted through the St John's graveyard, murmuring quiet apologies to the dead as I ran over their graves, and down the narrow path onto Michael Street.

As I had hoped, leaning against the crumbling flakes of paint on the whitewashed wall of Simon Brennan's house was a bicycle. Without a moment's hesitation, I swung my leg over the bike and pedalled furiously for the five-mile journey. The cold afternoon air ripped through my blouse while the wind tore my hairpins from their moorings, leaving me with a tangled mass of curls.

My thoughts focused solely on Anthony – what was going to happen to him? I prayed Sam hadn't told Comdt Doolin about James's cottage. At James's, the beech trees rustled as if whispering *hurry*. Dropping the bike, I ran through the yard and pushed the front door open.

'Anthony, are you here?'

The kitchen threw my words back at me with a hollow echo. Frantically, I scanned the room. Two empty mugs, two plates smeared with dried fried egg, and breadcrumbs on the tablecloth. I placed my hand on the teapot. It was warm.

There were maps, detailed and intricate, showing places in Ireland I had never been, and there was a notebook. My hands trembled as I leafed through it. Pages of photographs and details of the Irish landscape, of towns.

Inside was written:

Plan Grün. Operation Green.

The words 'Dienstgebrauch: Militär-Geographische über Irland' were stamped on the cover in a stern, black font, crisply outlined against the folder's mossy hue.

Official Use: Military-Geographical of Ireland.

The overall design was simple and non-ostentatious, but enough to set my heart racing and cloud my mind with disquieting thoughts.

I dropped it on the table, knocking the teapot onto the tiles.

'Well, well, if it isn't Kathleen Flinn.'

I spun around. Shards of ceramic scattered, coming to a halt at Doolin's feet.

'Commandant Doolin, what brings you here?'

He disregarded my question, stepping further into James's kitchen. With an air of nonchalance, he flicked his cigarette onto the tiles and crushed it under his boot, the ashes performing a brief pirouette before settling.

'So where's your brother?' he asked, methodically removing his black gloves, one finger at a time.

'He left a few weeks ago, gone to Northern Ireland,' I said, trying to maintain a steady voice.

Knowing I was lying, the hint of mockery in his eyes sent shivers down my spine. But it was not just Anthony I was concerned about, it was Markus with the accusations of Anthony's involvement with the German.

Doolin's gaze narrowed. He looked around James's kitchen. 'It looks very lived-in for a dead man.'

Before I could utter a word there was a shout from outside.

'Commandant Doolin, get out here now!' It was unmistakably Sam's voice.

Comdt Doolin dashed out into the yard, his coat fluttering behind him. It snagged on a nail, leaving a shred of fabric behind as he disappeared. I followed. Dusk was settling, and a bone-chilling coldness was creeping in.

I followed him out to the yard and the scene sent a shiver through me.

Sam, his face twisted in fury, had Anthony pinned against the wall, one hand pressed on his chest. The other held a bread knife close to Anthony's throat. 'Fucking traitor,' Sam spat with venom.

Standing a short distance away, in the middle of the yard, was Markus, his hands raised in a submissive gesture, a silent plea for reason.

'Jesus, Sam, what are you doing?' I pushed past Doolin. I reached out towards Sam, hoping to snatch his wrist.

Comdt Doolin's firm grip pulled me back.

'Miss Flinn, stay out of this,' Comdt Doolin growled, 'this doesn't concern you.'

Ignoring him, I wrestled free from his grasp and rushed towards Anthony.

'Stop, Sam,' I pleaded, my voice almost lost in the chaos that surrounded us.

Sam, now in a frenzy, knocked Anthony to the ground. Each brutal kick from Sam landed with sickening precision on Anthony's defenceless body. Blood began to trickle from Anthony's mouth, staining the dry earth beneath him. Sam continued to unleash his rage on Anthony. How could someone who had been my friend for so many years turn into such a monster?

Markus lunged towards Sam, and he tackled him, knocking the knife out of his hand.

I rushed to Anthony's side, cradling him in my arms as we watched the two men grapple on the ground. Fear clenched at my heart as I saw Markus struggling to keep Sam pinned down.

But before either of them could gain the upper hand, there was a loud bang, and everything went still. Doolin fired a warning shot into the air, bringing an abrupt end to the chaos.

Silence descended upon us as we all caught our breaths. The only sound was Anthony's laboured breathing as he lay weakly in my arms.

Comdt Doolin had secured Markus, his hands cuffed, the metallic glint of the handcuffs catching the sparse light in the shed. I caught sight of Comdt Doolin's revolver pressed against Markus's back.

'Markus Biegel, I am arresting you under the Emergency Powers Act, 1939.'

I turned my attention back to Anthony, tears stinging my eyes as I saw the extent of his injuries. His face was bruised and swollen, and there was blood coming from a gash on his forehead. He struggled weakly in my arms, trying to sit up.

Sam handcuffed Anthony. 'I'm arresting you under the Offences Against the State Act, for threatening to undermine the state's neutrality and security.'

As they read off the charges, Anthony's eyes widened.

'This is a mistake!' he protested, blood drooling down his chin. His handcuffs clinked as he struggled.

My heart raced as I heard the words being spoken. The tears continued to stream down my face at seeing Anthony's battered face.

The white of Anthony's shirt was now marred with crimson stains.

'I've done nothing to threaten the state's neutrality or security,' Anthony said.

Doolin shoved Markus into the car.

Standing, watching Anthony and Markus being taken away, I remained motionless, staring in to the void, until Bessie nudged my knee and licked my hand, bringing me back to the biting, cold reality.

Shock coursed through me at the brutal scene I had witnessed.

'What's going to happen to them?' I murmured, my voice barely audible as I ran my fingers through her soft coat. 'And to you, Bess? I can't take you to Naas with me.'

Behind me, the gates creaking hinge pierced the stillness,

pulling my thoughts to the present. The blackmailer seemed the least of my worries in the wake of this brutality.

Amidst the whirlwind of my thoughts an image of Father Fitzpatrick emerged. He had helped me before and he said he was a dog person. I felt a thin thread of hope that he might help.

32

Thankfully, Father Fitzpatrick agreed to look after Bessie. I told him Anthony was coming to Nass with me for a few days, but when he put his hand on mine, I tried quelling my shaking hand.

He asked, 'Kitty, are you feeling all right? You seem agitated.'

'I'm fine,' I replied. 'We are late for the train. Anthony is waiting for me.'

He nodded his head, satisfied with my answer.

The train ride back to Naas was harrowing as I struggled to process everything that had happened. The rhythmic clatter of the train on the tracks seemed to mock my turmoil, a stark contrast to the rage inside me.

The walk to Alice's house was a blur. When I reached her house, I saw she was drawing her bedroom curtains for bed. Fumbling with the front door keys, I slipped them into the lock, I hoped she wouldn't hear me. The last thing I wanted was to explain why I was distraught.

★

I lay in bed all night thinking about the events that had unfolded the previous day. After a night of restless sleep, I was greeted by the day with an unbearable heaviness in my heart. The morning light streamed in through the window, casting a pattern of shadows and light on the rustic wooden floor, a mosaic of my shattered peace. Outside, the world appeared untouched by my inner turmoil. Mr Casey's milk cart clanked rhythmically on its route, the glass bottles a melody of normalcy.

I rose slowly from my bed, my limbs as heavy as lead. I dressed and attempted to gather my thoughts. The mirror reflected a woman who had been through the wars – lines of worry etched deep, hair limp, stray stands pushed behind my ears.

Alice was in the kitchen with Peter, back turned to me, humming a soft tune. The inviting smell of fresh bread filled the room. I cleared my throat and her humming stopped. She turned, her warm eyes searching my face.

I swallowed hard, my heart pounding in my chest, and began. 'Alice, there's something you need to know. I'm so sorry, Markus claimed he was studying weather patterns between Ireland and England. He spoke against Hitler, yet his own actions...'

My voice trailed off. Taking a deep breath, I told her who Markus was, and our conversation.

'He said he had shot at families trying to flee, and hated himself for that. He said he shot wide on purpose. He had to escape and saw an opportunity over Ireland.'

Alice remained motionless, her skin as pale as the morning light.

'Anthony isn't a terrorist or involved with espionage or

anything like that,' I said, the words barely making it past my tight throat. I extended a hand, seeking reassurance, an anchor in the storm, and the tears flowed. 'I don't know where they have taken him. But that horrible man said Anthony was being arrested for some offence to do with terrorism.'

With a quick squeeze of my hand and a steely determination entering her gaze, Alice got up. 'Wait here, Kitty.'

Peter hadn't taken any notice of my distress. He sat at the table, his spoon poised over his boiled egg. The innocence in his summer-kissed face was a stark contrast to the harsh realities we were discussing.

'Peter, this is your favourite part of the day, isn't it?' I said.

There was no reaction, just pure bliss on his face as he salted his egg. I couldn't help but think his world was so much more tranquil, so much better than mine. I envied the simplicity of his life.

Alice came back in, her face flushed, her eyes blazing. Her voice was steady. 'I got in touch with my uncle Liam. He's a sergeant in the army. I explained Anthony's situation and he made a call. The German and your brother will be taken to the Curragh Military Camp. But, the bad news is that Anthony will be interned with the IRA men in Tin Town.' She inhaled deeply, as if steadying herself for the next news. 'Liam thinks they may have accused him of conspiring with the Germans for a possible invasion, and of being a member of the IRA. He said the IRA believes the Germans will help reclaim the six counties from Britain.'

I felt the blood drain from me. My grip on Alice's hand tightened as her words sank in. My heart pounded.

'But don't worry, Kitty, I vouched for you. I told him about everything you've done for us, for me and Peter.'

She passed me a slip of paper, her elegant handwriting spelling out an address.

McKee Barracks
Infirmary Road
Dublin

'Liam said to write to Commandant Doolin's office in Dublin. He might meet with you and listen. You might be able to convince him that it's all some mistake and explain about the airman.'

The cool morning air, fresh and light after the rain, hastened my stride as I made my way to work. Mr Casey returned my acknowledging nod. The mothers swept their doorsteps along Main Street. Did they share my worries? The O'Reilly children ran by, barefoot and carefree with their dog in tow, only stopping for breath on the bridge overlooking Millbrook Stream to lean on the wall and look at the river.

Rainwater had accelerated its flow, and twigs formed tiny eddies. Among the twigs, a field mouse was scrabbling in the water. Maybe one good turn would send good faith in my direction. Knowing how frightened it must be, and knowing I would be even later for work, I carefully descended the muddy bank and used a long branch to nudge the twiggy mess to the bank, allowing the mouse to scamper away to safety. I yearned for such an uncomplicated escape.

At the hospital doors, I stopped at the sight of Matron, arms folded, face like thunder. She put her hand on my arm.

'My office now,' she hissed, and I followed her. Inside, I smoothed my skirt, straightened my cardigan and prepared to sit, but she stopped me and held up a phial of morphine as though it were poison.

'Actually, Miss Flinn, don't bother sitting. Pack your things immediately. I am tempted to inform the authorities,' she said.

The room suddenly felt smaller, and the crucifixes on the walls appeared more pronounced. The painting of Jesus overlooking us filled me with remorse for my actions. A flurry of thoughts danced in my mind, all amounting to nothing.

'I'm sorry, Matron,' I said.

A chill washed over me. The phial was a symbol of my desperation, my panic, my complete lack of foresight. The walls closed in, and my breath hitched in my throat. It was as if I was being cornered by my own fear, my own shame.

I ran through a hundred desperate plans. Confession, seeking help, fleeing – nothing seemed to promise a safe escape. Every path seemed to lead to ruin, and time was running out. I was caught in a downward spiral of dread, each second ticking down to my inevitable exposure.

'Don't even attempt to justify yourself,' she said, flinging the door wide open. 'Go, and don't come back.'

I stood frozen, rooted to the spot, my mouth open.

'Go,' she shouted, echoing the finality of my situation.

Two new nurse's aides passing by averted their eyes at

the sight of the matron's fury, their curious glances swiftly turning into sympathy as I fled the office. As I ran down the cold, unforgiving steps of the hospital, anger mixed with shame coursed through my veins, raw and seething.

Dread at the thought of what I would tell Alice filled me. There was no way for me to get more money to pay the blackmailer, and Anthony had been arrested.

It was like the world was conspiring against me.

Back at the house, I joined Alice and Peter in the garden, where Peter sat on the grass among the yellow petals of the scattering roses. Alice was at the end of the garden on her hands and knees, pulling up weeds with determination and focus. As I walked towards her, the earth gave off a sweet smell. The irony didn't go amiss, juxtaposing what I had to tell Alice. Would Alice tell me to leave?

'What's wrong, Kitty? You look like you've seen a ghost.'

'No, Alice, I've just seen my future. And it's not good, even worse than before.'

I recounted the events of the morning to her, forcing each word out. Her expression hardened and her lips thinned. I felt my insides clenching as I pictured myself out on the street with a suitcase and nowhere to go.

With a sigh of resignation, Alice reached out, giving my hand a tight squeeze, and spoke with conviction.

'Kitty, I have an idea. You have to go to Commandant Doolin and plead Anthony's innocence. Don't overthink it. You have no other choice. A bus will be leaving soon. Kitty, believe in yourself. You can do this.'

She was correct. It was the only recourse. The colossal weight of the blackmailer that had loomed in my mind was diminished, a secondary concern; between G2 and the guards, I was stuck between a rock and a hard place. It was a gamble, a dice-roll in the treacherous game of survival. I had to try, for Anthony.

33

The crowd gathered in front of the waiting bus: men in worn tweed jackets and caps, women in practical frocks clutching tightly to their handbags, children eager for a trip to the capital held close by their mothers. My heart raced as I took my place among them and we boarded the bus.

The driver pulled out with a lurch, and I stumbled. He shouted back to the passengers.

'Apologies for that, I'll wait until you're all seated.' His voice reflected annoyance more than politeness.

There was only one seat left, next to a balding man in a grubby white shirt.

He nodded as I settled down. 'Lovely day,' he commented.

I agreed, staring out of the window at the sprawling green fields and yellow gorse, gradually replaced by whitethorn trees.

'Miss, I'm sorry, but I didn't get your name,' he said.

I wanted to reply that I hadn't told him it, but instead I simply said, 'Kitty.'

'Nice to meet you, Kitty,' he said, grinning widely to reveal a toothless smile. 'I'm Seamus, but you can call me Seamie. Everyone does.'

The name Seamus reopened the old wound of Seamus McGinty's betrayal when he left me in my vulnerable state of pregnancy. The name disoriented me for a moment, then unleashed a torrent of emotions. The hurt I once felt was now replaced with anger. Would I be here if I'd never got pregnant? All the emotions resurfaced; first, heartache, then anger when he'd abandoned me, and lastly grief at losing my baby in childbirth. Seamie was unaware of the storm his name unwittingly stirred. But now, faced with no other choice, I had to be strong. My thoughts were broken by a clucking chicken.

Sat opposite me was an earthy-looking woman, with a thick brown shawl wrapped around her. On her lap was a hessian sack moving furiously and squawking.

She looked at me and winked. 'It's a chicken for my sister's birthday dinner tomorrow. There's nothing quite like roast chicken,' she said, flashing a toothless smile. It was clear she wouldn't be doing much chewing.

Seamie shifted in his seat. Closing my eyes, I pretended to sleep. I wasn't in the mood for idle chit-chat.

'Do you want a piece? Chocolate always lifts the spirits,' he asked, offering me a small square. His hands were clean, a stark contrast to his shirt.

'Take a piece. It'll make you forget your worries. Just let it sit on your tongue for a moment, lean back and close your eyes.'

He demonstrated, smiling blissfully. 'It's heavenly.'

He opened his eyes again. 'I had hidden this from my

grandson, and now he's not here for me to share it with him.'

'I'm sorry.' I touched my hand to my mouth, struggling to find the right words.

He laughed heartily. 'No, not gone in that sense. He's moved to Liverpool. They've all moved to Liverpool. I advised them against it, but they didn't listen and left me behind.'

I accepted the chocolate square. As it melted, the sweet scent enveloped my senses like a blooming rose in a serene garden. For a fleeting moment, I closed my eyes and lost myself, forgetting the reason for my journey.

'It can be a bit bitter due to the sugar rationing, but it's still quite good, isn't it?' he asked, his eyes wide and sparkling. 'Are we off on a thrilling adventure? Starting a new job? Or perhaps meeting a gentleman?' He nudged me playfully in the side.

'No, just family,' I replied.

'I'm due to meet my sister,' he said, seemingly unaware of my discomfort. 'I'll be getting some peat for her. She's wheelchair-bound. Never married, quite the independent spirit. She doesn't like to bother her neighbours too much, so I offered to help her.'

'Collecting peat in Dublin?' I was intrigued.

'Yes, at Phoenix Park. It's plentiful. You'll see brown stacks reaching towards the sky. It isn't free, mind you. Nothing in life truly is, except for the air we breathe. It's a necessary resource, given the coal shortage.'

'That's commendable of you,' I said.

He absent-mindedly scratched his head. 'Family's worth any effort, don't you think? They're all you've got, after all.'

Smoothing out his thinning hair, he put on his flat cap. 'Where did you say you were headed?'

'To McKee Barracks,' I replied.

He leaned back and soon fell into a light sleep.

An hour later, the bus jerked to a stop. Seamie put his jacket on, hiding his grey shirt, making him seem more dignified and younger than my first impression. He gestured out the window.

'Follow those women with the pushchairs. They're off to collect peat, and the barracks aren't far off. There's a distinctive red-brick wall, and you can't miss the smell of horses.'

Nodding thanks, I stood there for a moment, observing the scene around me, watching people doing their normal mundane daily tasks. The road was busier with bicycles than on my last visit, perhaps because of fuel rationing. They criss-crossed the road, narrowly avoiding each other and the occasional delivery truck. Across the street, a woman in a mismatched brown coat and blue belt pushed a pram laden with black peat. Another woman with an empty pram moved in the opposite direction. They paused for a friendly chat, heads thrown back in laughter, hair tucked neatly into scarves. I crossed the road just as their conversation ended and they parted with a wave.

Finally, I reached McKee Barracks, which, with its red brickwork and matching roof tiles, reminded me of a picturesque art gallery. My expectation of soldiers on parade, rifles and helmets at the ready, as seen in the advertisements and the occasional newsreel, felt oddly misplaced. I approached a small wooden hut at the gate, its window fitted with white latticework. A soldier bearing the MP insignia stood to attention. His green uniform bore the distinct scent of fresh starch.

'Over there, those doors. Enquire at the reception for further directions.'

The barracks exuded a British feeling. They had left an indelible architectural imprint. Grasping the brass handle, I pushed the glass door open to reveal a marble-tiled room and approached the receptionist. Her blonde hair was cut fashionably short.

I asked to see Commandant Doolin and she sized me up, peering through her tortoiseshell-rimmed glasses. Her hair curled inwards, her rouge matching her red lipstick.

'Is he expecting you?' she asked.

'No,' I said. 'Tell him it's Kitty Flinn.'

She gave me the once-over, and I was only too aware of the difference between my cardigan and summer floral dress and her navy-blue blazer.

Then she reached for a black phone. 'Commandant Doolin, a Miss Flinn is here to see you.'

My heart pounded like a soldier's drum, echoing in the hollow barracks of my chest, reverberating against my ribs. Time seemed to slow, each ticking second feeling like an hour. The barrack walls held an age-old musk of varnished wood and drying paint, a smell that felt too heavy, too serious.

My palms became slick with nervous perspiration. I felt a distinct chill in my spine, a shiver of anticipation, uncertainty and fear. Every nerve ending prickled, and I clenched my handbag tighter, feeling the hard leather against my fingertips. It provided a strange, comforting solidity in this moment of suspense.

The secretary's gaze was sharp as she held the phone receiver, hawk-like, scrutinising every aspect of my being as I waited. I bit my lower lip and didn't try to meet her gaze. I found solace looking at the floor, at the worn, threadbare carpet that had seen countless soles.

With a curt nod, she returned the phone to its cradle.

'Follow me,' she commanded, rising from her desk. Her flat heels resonated on the floor as she came out to hold a door open for me. The hall was silent, and with each click, my heart beat harder. I pulled my coat around my cardigan as I followed her, her navy skirt unyielding, starched to remind me I was in a place of rules.

She led me into an office lined with desks, Bakelite headphones and typewriters. The room was dim, lit by a single bulb, and the small windows let in hardly any light. It was furnished with four wooden desks and austere high-backed chairs; it reminded me of Matron's office.

'Commandant Doolin will be with you shortly,' she said, gesturing towards the chairs. 'Please have a seat.'

I wished desperately to display a sense of calm, to be the picture of composed grace under her scrutiny. I took a seat, and to calm my anxious thoughts, to distract myself, I focused on the wooden poster on the opposite wall. It showcased the proclamation of the 1916 Rising. The seven signatories' names were prominently displayed: Plunkett, Ceannt, Connolly, Clarke, MacDiarmada, MacDonagh and Pearse. Just as I read the last name, a door to the left of the poster opened.

Comdt Doolin emerged into the hallway, beckoning me

with a nod. Leading me into an adjacent room, he pointed me to a leather sofa. As he struck a match and lit a cigarette, I glanced around. It was more like a living room than an office, with the furnishings and decor exuding a comforting warmth. Antiques and framed photographs were tastefully arranged, painting a narrative of personal history and sentiment.

My gaze wandered to the photos. A young boy in various stages of growth, his features mirroring Doolin's. A youthful man, his arms draped over the shoulders of older people, their faces etched with wisdom and age. Presumably, his parents or grandparents.

Smoke curled up from his cigarette as he extended his silver case towards me. I declined with a gentle shake of my head. I knew it was time to explain why I was there, but his uniform intimidated me.

I clasped my hands tight to steady my shaking hands. My voice trembled as I spoke, the air thick with tension.

'Commandant Doolin' – I inhaled deeply, ready to question a man in such authority – 'why did you give Matron the morphine you found in Alice's house? I lost my position. You must know that I'm not a threat, and that Anthony is not in the IRA; he has nothing to do with them.'

His eyes bore into mine, his face stoic and unreadable. The room was silent except for the sound of our breathing, drawn out and tense. I waited for something, anything, to break the silence.

'It is out of my control that your brother was arrested. Special Branch, led by Sam Daly, arrested him,' he said. 'I was looking for the parachutist. We have a duty to protect our citizens. So, your brother will be interned in the Curragh

Military camp in Tin Town, the IRA section, and Markus will be interned with the Germans.'

Before I could gather my thoughts, Comdt Doolin coughed, his mouth curving up into a cold smile.

'Miss Flinn, I want you to come and work for us,' he said. 'You would be employed by us as a translator.'

'Can I ask why me? Surely you have sufficient translators?'

He leaned back, his gaze steady. 'Well, we do and we don't. We believe your German is superior due to your mother's influence. Daly – Sam – informed us of your unique skills.'

He tapped his cigarette on the ashtray.

'And Kitty, if you don't mind the familiarity, think of this as a fresh start.'

I frowned. 'Forgive me, but I don't follow.'

He heaved a sigh, his forehead furrowing with stress. He leaned in closer, his expression softer than before.

'I tried to prevent Sam from giving the morphine to the hospital. However, he was unyielding. Please understand that this incident doesn't involve me. I regret the loss of your employment, Kitty.'

His lips curled into a semblance of a smile that never reached his eyes, as he noticed me looking at the photograph with older people on his desk.

'Family is everything, Miss Flinn, isn't it? My parents. I was lucky they found me and gave me a good home.'

'Were you lost?' I asked, intrigued by his remark.

'That's none of your business, Miss Flinn.'

His eyes darkened slightly as he issued instructions in a stern, clipped tone.

'My driver will fetch you at seven-hundred hours on

Monday morning. Stand by your home, and remember, Miss Flinn, do not be late.'

He ushered me out with a decisive gesture. He held the door ajar, the final rays of the setting sun creating a silhouette of his figure.

Had he always seen me as a potential recruit? But that question was soon replaced by anger. Sam had turned deceitful, but this hurt more and angered me more, because it felt like a betrayal. He was rotten to the core like a shiny sweet apple that once bitten, revealed the rancidity and black decay inside.

34

On Monday morning, I washed and dressed, made my bed and flattened the eiderdown, wondering how my hands stayed still. Picking up my hat, I had a cursory glance in the mirror, nodding in approval of my choice of lime green skirt and cream blouse to blend in with the military personnel.

My stomach twisted and turned as I waited at the corner of Basin Street. The cold air cleared my head but did little to still the tempest in my heart. I had to find a way to save Anthony. I couldn't let him be swallowed by the horrors of the Curragh. Failure was not an option.

I took an icy breath, my resolve hardening.

Soon, a rumble pierced the air and a black car came to a stop beside me. A young man not much older than me rolled down the window and said in a broad Dublin accent, 'Miss Flinn, I assume? I'm Private D'Arcy.'

He got out and opened the back door for me. The car glistened intimidatingly, and I got in and slid my hand under my skirt to avoid getting it creased.

We moved through the plains of the Curragh, and like an

artist's swift brush across a canvas, the landscape became verdant green, a never-ending plain meeting the sky at the horizon. We passed a saluting MP and entered the camp itself.

Alice was right, it was like a small town. There were rows of red-brick buildings, similar to McKee Barracks, but the Curragh covered an expanse like I had never seen before, flanked by a tall red-brick tower.

D'Arcy looked at me in the rear-view mirror. 'That's where my wife works. She's a nurse in the hospital over there.'

I followed his gaze to a beautiful Victorian building with four painted arches over the windows that glinted in the morning sun, then I stared out at the camp, not knowing what lay ahead of me. It was as busy as midday on a bustling market day in town, and it was just eight o'clock.

D'Arcy slowed the car and stubbed out his cigarette in the car ashtray.

'Welcome to Curragh, you'll be working in MacDonagh,' he said, 'it's one of the seven barracks here. Aside from this, we have only internment camps and the golf club.

'Then there's also Tin Town, where the bloody IRA are. Apologies, miss. But after the Civil War in '22, many of them refused to accept the Irish Free State. There's several hundred of them here, and they're living in terrible conditions, living like rats. Nothing more than they deserve. They are not far from the British and German camps.'

I followed his gaze to rows of small white huts with corrugated roofs. But he drove on before I could get a good look at them.

'There are only about twenty-six Brits and forty Germans,

with just a handful of men to each hut. But the IRA huts are overcrowded, with around twenty-eight men in each.'

When the car stopped, I stepped out and the cold wind whipped through the air, cutting into my cheeks as I made my way onto the Curragh for the first time. Rows of identical huts stretched out before me, their weather-beaten exteriors offering little comfort or warmth to those who called them home. They were encircled by a towering, barbed wire fence.

Before D'Arcy drove away, he said out the open window, 'Not long ago these men were firing at each other in the skies, and now they're simply separated by this corrugated boundary.'

I observed the activity in both camps – men strolling and seemingly gardening.

I could feel the tension in the air, a palpable unease that clung to the camp like a heavy fog. Soldiers marched past, their boots striking the earth in unison, while the prisoners watched on with hollow eyes.

'Kitty Flinn?' a voice called, pulling me from my thoughts. Sam Daly stood in front of MacDonagh, his face blank of emotion, like he was trying to hide himself. His curls were flattened into submission, thick and glistening with Brylcreem, cut short at the back and sides. He eyed me up and down, his gaze cold and detached.

'Sam, I wasn't expecting you here. I thought this was military!' my voice was tinged with bitterness like a blade dipped in poison. Struggling to conceal my anger at the role he played in Anthony's arrest bubbled beneath the surface. Reminding myself I needed to keep control of my emotions not to jeopardise my chances of seeing Anthony, I shelved my anger for the moment.

'I'm here on business. Commandant Doolin sent me to meet you,' he said, his brown eyes avoiding mine. Could remorse have finally seeped into his conscience for the role he played? And the brutal treatment he'd dealt Anthony, maybe that was gnawing at him too? At least he was now bringing me closer to Anthony.

'Follow me. You're just here to translate German letters,' he said.

The air vibrated with the thud of boots from all directions, and the sharp, pungent smell of horse urine hung in the air.

I fell into step behind him and we arrived at the barracks Private D'Arcy called MacDonagh. A wave of apprehension gripped me, tightening around my chest. Entering a long hall that shone from wax wood polish, the cloying scent overwhelmed my senses, causing me to take shallow breaths. We turned down another hallway and into a large room filled with soldiers. Everyone was standing still like statues while the commanding officer issued instructions in a loud voice against a backdrop of whirring electrical machines that made it hard to hear.

Sam knocked on a door, entered without waiting for a reply, and held the door open for me. I glanced at the brass name plate as we entered. Colonel MacNally.

A square-shouldered man sat behind an equally square desk with all the hallmarks of neatness demanded by a man in charge, an authority that everyone else was answerable to. Standing by his desk was Commandant Doolin.

I stood to attention like a soldier. My confidence waned under my nervousness.

'Colonel MacNally, this is Kathleen Flinn,' Sam announced. 'She has signed up to help us with German translations.'

MacNally folded his hands on his rosewood desk and scrutinised me, his eyes travelling from my red hat to my brown shoes. He lifted his cigar and sucked slowly, his pale grey eyes narrowing. He blew smoke in my direction, the plume settling around the lamp on his desk. He placed his hands flat on the desk as if in thought and then snapped a file shut, dropping the brown folder into the wire basket.

Sam continued, 'And, sir, we have more internees. A German and an IRA lad, and he's a bloody communist as well.'

The colonel stared at me as he inhaled deeply and released the breath through his nostrils. My stomach lurched at Sam's mention of German and his accusation that Anthony was an Irish communist and IRA member.

'They will both be in the military hospital for a few more days to recover from their wounds,' Sam said. 'When the Irish prisoner is better, we'll transfer him to Tin Town with the rest of the scum.'

Colonel MacNally blew a long thin line of smoke. 'I hope he's under armed guard. We don't want him escaping like the other lads,' he grumbled, the edges of his words sharpened by the distinct pop of the burning tobacco. His gaze, steady and unwavering, met mine. 'We can't afford another IRA escape.'

A knot of worry twisted in my chest. Every fibre of my body shuddered thinking that Anthony would be sent to Tin Town. I wanted to scream and ask about the severity of my brother's injuries, but the words got stuck in my throat.

The colonel kept looking at me. He spoke in a quiet yet intimidating voice that seemed to reverberate around the office. 'Are you a German teacher?'

'No. My mother was German, but she grew up in Kilkenny. She was just a child when she came here. It was from her that I learned German.'

MacNally's impatience was mounting; his face deepening into an alarming shade of crimson. He gestured emphatically and I felt he was like a dog ready to pounce on me. But instead, he turned to Comdt Doolin. 'Do we really need another translator? Haven't we got enough personnel? I thought many men responded to your call for German speakers.'

'They did, sir. However, Miss Flinn possesses a unique skill. She understands the Bavarian dialect, which none of our soldiers do. I met her mother when we investigated the German colony. She was one of the two hundred people here who had links with Germany. Mrs Flinn spoke of her childhood in Bavaria until her mother's death when she was seven and her father sent her to be brought up with relatives. Her father stayed in Germany. She told me she passed the language on to her children – a son and a daughter.' His gaze locked directly with mine.

In England, I'd heard stories about the plight of Germans. Every last one, regardless of their established lives, businesses or distance from their German roots, had been rounded up and sent to internment camps. The British authorities demonstrated an unrelenting indifference towards these people's circumstances.

Thoughts started to whirl in my mind. When did Comdt Doolin and my mother meet? What could she have shared with him about our family, our past? The overwhelming urge to find out more about his meeting with my mother took hold of me, distracting me from my primary focus – Anthony.

'Miss Flinn, did you hear me? We are to go to my office now,' Doolin announced.

His words snapped me out of my thoughts. Quickly, I gathered my composure and followed him across the hall, my shoes clicking on the polished wooden floor. We stepped into a smaller room, crammed with four large wooden desks that lined the walls, each with a black telephone, an ashtray and a wire tray overflowing with paperwork. The walls were painted a deep-green hue, giving off an air of authority and formality. On one desk near the centre of the room, there was an older Bakelite typewriter, and I imagined its keys chattering away as secretaries churned out document after document.

Doolin introduced me to a woman in uniform. 'This is Miss Browne, my secretary.'

Miss Browne, a lady of sharp features yet gentle countenance, exuded efficiency. Her neatly pinned hair was a stark contrast to the curls that framed her face with an unexpected charm. Her posture was as straight as a ruler.

She greeted me with a warm, affable smile, the kind that puts people instantly at ease. She put her hand out. 'Call me Mona.'

I smiled back, but she turned away and leaned towards Doolin, whispering something into his ear. He nodded and took a brown folder from her.

She nodded and smiled at me again before she left the room. Doolin placed the brown folder on a desk, covering it with sheets of writing paper, but not before I managed to glimpse the words TOP SECRET embossed on its cover.

Sam came in, and with a swift nod, Doolin gestured for

him to join him. The two men huddled over the desk, their heads close together, flipping through pages and scrutinising photographs, their expressions veiled with concentration.

I stood in the centre of the room, racked with uncertainty. The two men, unperturbed by my nervousness, remained engrossed. As I watched them silently read the documents, all I wanted was to take a drink from the glass on the desk.

'Miss Flinn, take a seat,' Doolin finally instructed, pointing at a modest desk imprisoned by a pair of metal cabinets. Above it was a sprawling map of Europe. Two regions were written in the same bold lettering – Ireland and Great Britain – and Germany was boldly underlined in crimson.

Sam's expression shifted into a troubled frown, his fingers delicately massaging the bridge of his nose as though to keep a headache at bay. As he leaned on the table, he unwittingly toppled the folder, papers and photographs spilling over the wooden floor, skidding beneath the desks and sprawling across the rug. He quickly retrieved everything and left the room, but I saw some of the papers before he did so.

Dienstgebrauch: Militär-Geographische über Irland.
Official Use: Military-Geographical of Ireland.
Plan Grün.

Operation Green. An icy realisation dawned: I had seen something like this at James's house when Markus and Anthony had been arrested. *Wetterberichte.* Weather reports.

Commandant Doolin finally addressed me. 'Miss Flinn, your primary task will be to translate and transcribe the internees' letters and any responses they receive. They'll be subject to further scrutiny in Dublin. Despite our non-alliance with the British, we cannot compromise our neutrality by letting the Germans send potentially damaging intelligence. You may encounter letters to loved ones, mothers, fathers, paramours, all in the disguise of hidden espionage. Your task is to read and translate, and if you see something untoward, underline it.'

His expression suddenly contorted with pain, and he pulled out a drawer and scattered its contents onto the rosewood desk: a stapler, an inkpot, and a handful of pencils.

'Bloody hell, Miss Flinn, I need a remedy for this accursed indigestion. I'm going to the medical hall. Wait here.'

There was a document left on his desk, and I couldn't help myself. I walked over and turned it over. A photograph, dated 30 September 1940. A couple posed against a cliff's edge overlooking a beach, the scene disrupted by looming mountains. Scribbled on the image: *Kilkee, Co. Clare*. Were they German spies?

My heart pounded and I sat back down at my desk, looking out the window, trying to make sense of it. Germans emerged from their huts, some in blue-grey uniforms, others in white shirts and baggy trousers. One thing remained clear: I had to find out how ill Anthony was and prevent him from being sent to Tin Town.

After a few minutes, Mona came in.

She cleared her throat. 'Kitty, here are some letters for you to translate. We scrutinise all the post they send and letters they receive. We suspect they might be sending or receiving messages from the Abwehr, the German intelligence, so we check all mail.

'Don't look so alarmed, you won't be expected to do anything except transcribe the letters and use this stamp to mark them as read.' She held up a black stamp by its wooden handle.

I read the black stamp backwards: EXAMINER 1. Was I going to be the first person to read the words of Nazis?

'German intelligence?' I shuddered as I said it.

'Yes, but also tell us if you see anything unusual. They will undergo another review in Dublin.'

She looked out the window. 'Have you seen the Germans yet? They're rather handsome, and so well dressed. Not like the grubby English.'

She clapped her hands together, and looked around the office. 'Anyway, I've work to do. No time for idle chit-chat.'

Opening the folder, I wondered about the men who had written these letters. Would their mail contain secrets? I shuddered at the thought that these letters were the penned thoughts of killers. I picked up a brown envelope, my eyes tracing the foreign address:

Peter Müller
Rosenweg 70a
45678 München

I put it aside and read another:

Jen Palacios
Berliner Allee 23
40224 Düsseldorf

I counted twenty letters.

Mein lieber Hans, Ich bin so erleichtert, dass du lebst und es dir gut geht.
My dear Hans, I am so relieved you are alive and well.

These weren't hardened messages of war, but letters woven with love and concern. The words of affection to their sons reminded me of my father. I put the letters back in their envelopes as I finished with them, stamping each with EXAMINER 1.

The Hurricane had to make an emergency landing. I thought we were in south Wales, but it was a place called Wexford in Ireland. We were shot down by a Heinkel.

The letter continued with a detailed description of the camp, then devolved into the strange musings of a bored man.

My darling Gertrude, I am well, and we have good food. The guards treat us with respect. We are going to the cinema next week in Naas, and hope to get parole for shopping in Dublin.

Was there a secret message hidden here? I didn't think so.

The door opened and Doolin entered, holding a glass filled with a milky liquid. He carefully wiped its underside before placing it down on his desk. He didn't speak, rubbed his chest, and grunted something inaudible. When he glanced over at me, I quickly averted my eyes and returned to my work.

The day was taking an emotional toll on me, leaving me to wonder about this course of action.

I finished translating the final letter and placed it back in its envelope. The afternoon light filtered in through the window, casting long shadows across the room.

Mona, who had been diligently tapping away at her typewriter, stopped and stood, her body stretching like a cat after a long nap. She glanced down at her wristwatch. 'I think it's time for tea, I'll pop over to Sandes Home for some tea,' she declared in a tone that suggested it was more a statement to herself than an invitation. With that, she slipped on a green cardigan that had seen better days, and quietly left the room without another word.

Doolin, meanwhile, had risen from his chair, his movements deliberate as he gathered a stack of papers, the contents of which were hidden from my view. 'Miss Flinn,' he said, his voice carrying a note of formality as he handed me a new pile of letters. 'I have a meeting with Colonel MacNally. Please see to these letters while we are gone. All of them.' His instructions were clear, his tone leaving no room for discussion.

I waited for a while, expecting Mona to return with the tea, but the room remained empty, save for the persistent tick of the clock. Resigned, I continued with my translations, my mind occasionally drifting to Mona's absence.

The afternoon passed in a blur of words and phrases, punctuated by the occasional pause to decipher some particularly challenging handwriting.

The hours seemed to merge as I worked through the pile

of letters. The only sound in the room was the rustle of paper and the scratch of my pen against the pages, and the stamp.

Each letter was a snapshot of someone's life, a glimpse into their hopes, fears and dreams. Their words, filled with hope and love, were a stark contrast to the reality of the world outside.

Just before five o'clock, the office door opened and in entered a young soldier with a baby face that looked so smooth despite being untouched by a razor. His pale skin was speckled with freckles across his nose and cheeks. His boots gleamed in the stream of evening sun and his uniform looked rigid, as if just unwrapped. He removed his cap, revealing short brown hair, and nodded politely.

'I was told to come here for the letters you translated. I've to bring them to Dublin,' he said in a voice so meek I had to strain to hear it. He took the stack and put it into his bag, leaving without another word. How strange it was that someone so young should have such an important job.

I grabbed another envelope from the pile. It was simply a letter from a mother to her captured son. She wrote about how relieved she was that he was safe and well taken care of in the camp – nothing out of the ordinary, but the soothing words of comfort still brought tears to my eyes. There were three types of people in this war: those enduring it on the front lines, those interned far from their homes, and those living in anticipation, waiting anxiously for their loved ones to return.

Anthony was in the hospital only yards from me, and I couldn't see him. I had to at least try. My gaze drifted towards the window, watching as the last remnants of daylight disappeared, swallowed by the night.

A plan started to form. I cast my mind back to the layout of Naas Hospital, the winding corridors, the sterile smell, the harried nurses rushing to and fro. Could I get lost among them without arousing suspicion? Would the guards mistake me for a nurse?

35

The following morning, I fixed my red scarf over my hair for my long cycle from Alice's house, over the plains of the Curragh. The luxury of the car had only been for the first day. The misty drizzle lifted, leaving behind a low soft fog on the furze, like tufts of white angel wings clinging to the bushes, hiding their yellow flowers like they were wrapped in a soft blanket of cotton wool. Ignoring the cold air flowing over my hands on the handlebars, I passed the sentry box, the MP lifting his head as I cycled on to the main gate.

There was the same normality of town life in the centre of the camp, children walking to school, some followed by their mothers pushing prams, but mostly they ran together or held hands with an older child. Organ music drifted through the air from the Methodist church. Glancing at my watch, I saw that it was nearly eight o'clock and so I hurried on my way. Doctors and nurses in the distinct green uniforms of military medics ascended the steps of the hospital, beginning their day.

I slowed my pace to look at the nurses and dismounted from my High Nelly. Could I simply slip into the hospital, blending with the nurses, maybe find one of their uniforms? The thought lingered until the clinking of milk bottles brought me back to the present. Pallins Dairy Guaranteed Pure Newly Bottled Milk was written in white paint on the side on the milk van, the milkman nodding hello as he passed with a familiarity as if I had always been part of this place. I paused and turned to look back at the hospital, and thought maybe it would not be too difficult.

Pushing the bicycle as I observed the camp, I noted how different its sounds were to those of the hospital in Naas. The thud of army boots caused the air around me to vibrate. There was a cacophony of horses, trucks, and men shouting orders from all sides.

Finally stepping into the corridors of MacDonagh, I welcomed the quietness. The office was still with the low morning sun streaming across the floor. Neat piles of letters had been sorted by size and shape on my desk. As I studied the names and addresses, some penned in elegant cursive writing, some scrawled abruptly as if in protest being held against their will, I wondered if they would become familiar to me in time.

Suddenly a voice, tight and sharp, echoed through the room. 'Miss Flinn, you're finally here.'

Doolin's entrance startled me, sending a jolt of anxiety coursing through me as his sharp blue eyes studied me. A thin line of smoke billowed from his mouth as he rolled his cigarette from one side to another, bits of ash littering the floor.

'Miss Flinn, come here and look at this.'

He stood aside for me to join him at the window.

'That's the two camps. One for the British airmen and the other for the German airmen,' he said, pointing across the road to the ones Private D'Arcy had told me about. On closer inspection, the camps became clearer. The corrugated iron fence was flanked on either side by wooden huts, B Camp painted on one and G Camp on the other. The barbed-wire fence, stretching as high as a two-storey house, surrounded the two compounds, with a narrow walkway and more corrugated fencing separating them, like no-man's land. I counted twenty huts in the German compound, and six in the British compound. I tried to imagine what the men whose letters I had been reading looked like.

The German flag whipped in the wind, like a black, red and gold serpent uncoiling in the breeze. Three men leaned against one of the wooden huts, leisurely smoking pipes. They wore blue shirts and baggy trousers. Six men walked behind the wire fence, their boots scuffing off the ground. They wore navy uniforms, neatly buttoned, and white caps. Two men kneeled at the side of the hut, white shirtsleeves rolled up, holding small trowels.

My eyes were drawn towards the towering watchtower. The grim vigilance was unwavering. Guards marched along the rippled corridor of corrugated iron, their boots echoing the hard reality – escape was impossible.

'And up there near the golf club is Tin Town, where your brother will be going,' Doolin said, pointing. 'He'll join the other five hundred or so IRA lads, the dissenters and German sympathisers.'

The disdain in his voice stirred my protective instincts.

'He's not involved with any of them,' I shot back, my

voice thick with indignation. 'Anthony has nothing to do with them. His only guilt lies in the ideals of communism, that all men should be equal. He's never been involved in sabotage or dissent, he simply believes there should be a world where your background doesn't dictate your future. That's a far cry from being lumped together with dissenters and German sympathisers.'

He ignored my protest and adopted the tone of a teacher explaining complex principles to a beginner. 'Essentially, we're responsible for keeping these men here and preventing their escape back to Germany. Any slip-ups could land us in a diplomatic conflict, which we don't want. Within these parameters, we're expected to make their stay as internees as comfortable as possible. I remind myself that I have to be nice to them, that both groups are at war.'

Staring over at the German camp, I saw that two men were deeply engrossed in a game of chess. Their focus was unbroken until one man looked up in my direction. Startled, I quickly moved out of view. He had bronzed skin and neatly slicked-back hair. Mona was right, the Germans were handsome.

Doolin stood there for a few minutes watching the men behind the wire, only turning away when the phone rang, and I returned to my task.

'Miss Flinn, I'm off to fetch the newspapers and letters for the internees,' he said as he hung up the phone and slipped on the green coat that the higher ranks of the military wore.

Once the reverberations of his boots had subsided in the corridor, I darted towards the filing cabinet, noting a lingering ring stain from a glass. Maybe I could find some information about Anthony, and what hospital ward he was in.

Opening the top drawer of the filing cabinet, my fingers traced over the rows of alphabetically arranged files. There were two labels: G – GERMAN, B – BRITISH. I pulled open the drawer beneath, which held the same two categories.

I tugged at the bottom drawer. Locked. I gave it another pull, jangling its contents. I yanked harder, and the drawer reluctantly opened. This one was arranged differently, with maps and rows of numbers.

A sudden engine roar outside startled me, drawing my gaze to the window. Three soldiers were marching towards the British camp, their stark uniforms cutting through the expanse of the camp, followed by Commandant Doolin. I grabbed the first document I saw, slammed the drawer shut and slipped back to my seat. It was a crude map of woods, deeply shaded in pencil.

And there, at the centre, a simple sketch of our house labelled 'KATHLEEN FLINN'. A surge of shock washed over me. They'd been watching me.

I hastily shoved the paper into my handbag, my hands trembling, adrenaline racing through my veins. Commandant Doolin said he had met my mother. The date on the drawing was February 1941 – two months after her death. Why was my name on it?

Doolin walked in, eyes scanning the office, and dropped a new bundle of envelopes on my desk. 'Miss Flinn, these letters from the German internees are ready for posting. The post office is the red-brick building at the corner, across from the church,' he said, leaving no room for me to question and adding, with a sneer, 'I'm going to meet with the Special Branch about your brother.'

Berating myself for not having the courage to question

him about the map, I waited for him to drive away before I got my headscarf and left the building. The winds coming across the flat, treeless Curragh were strong.

On the walk, I quickly read the envelopes. Each one was stamped with EXAMINER followed by a number. Two were addressed to England – Christopher Mayhew and Marcella Verity – and two were addressed to Germany.

I tied my headscarf. A thin cloud covered the sky. Near the post office, the camp got busier. Ten soldiers marched, wearing a different uniform to Sam's. They wore short black boots with their trousers tucked into them and held rifles across their chest. They trotted down the road towards the golf club. Two trucks passed with their tarpaulins tied back, filled with fresh-faced recruits sitting in full view. One or two proffered a whistle in my direction. I lowered my eyes to the footpath – I had no interest in young men hardly out of their teens.

Walking with hurried steps, I passed the married living quarters. Thin streams of smoke filtered from the chimney stacks, the homes made of same red brick as the barracks, like poppies in a field, lined up with military precision. At the Methodist church, as I waited at the crossroads, a blue bread van tooted, heading back to the bakery after its early morning deliveries.

At the post office, I joined the queue behind two women, the younger gently rocking a pram as she looked anxiously into it, pulling back a brown blanket and feeling her baby's head. Two young girls held on to the side, and a young boy stood plastered to the folds of his mother's coat. The girls were dressed in identical blue dresses, their hair in plaits, one of them with yellow bows, the other with red. The boy's short pants were the same material as the girls' dresses. They looked no more than three years old. Triplets! The mother looked about my age, and her pale face spoke of the stress of having four children. She wore a beautiful red tartan coat with matching shoes – probably a coat she'd bought before motherhood took over.

As I handed the letters to the balding post clerk, he regarded me over the rim of the round spectacles sitting on the bridge of his nose.

'New here, are you?' he asked as he slid the envelopes across the counter, looking at the top address as he did.

I nodded. 'I'm in MacDonagh, in the office.'

'That's ten and halfpence,' he muttered, his pen scratching on a slip of paper. He looked up at me. 'These are for your records to go in the ledger.' He placed the letters on the left side of the counter alongside other envelopes stamped with EXAMINER and a number.

Outside the office, I glanced at my watch and walked towards the German camp. A chicken roamed, pecking the stones. The chess players were gone but in their place was an internee in a brown checked shirt who was leaning on a shovel, smoking a cigarette. As I watched, he took the cigarette from his mouth and looked at the tip, deep in thought. He blew rings skyward. He was small, with blond clipped hair. He flicked the butt into a pile of dirt and bent to check the rows of vegetables, pulling a few weeds. Life looked so normal. The men were tending to chores outside their own huts, but the towering, corrugated fence starkly divided the reality of their lives as prisoners from those on the outside.

In silence, I took in the camp around me. On impulse,

I turned on my heels, making my way back towards the military hospital. Reaching the bottom step, I paused briefly, telling myself that I was a nurse, not a translator sneaking into the hospital to look for her brother, who was under arrest. Sometimes it's better to think less.

I hastened up the steps into the daunting hospital, each footfall echoing off the stern grey and red walls. The smell of antiseptic hung heavy in the air, a potent reminder of Naas. Concentrating on slowing my breath, to stave off my nerves, I maintained an air of confidence, carrying my head high as though I had a right to be there. Every room I examined was a mirror image of the last, an unending picture of stern-looking nurses and unwell soldiers.

Just as I was about to give up and turn back, I spotted a solitary soldier standing guard outside a room. He was lean, his face shrouded by the brim of his cap. His features were etched with boredom and his attention seemed to be elsewhere. Taking a deep breath, I strolled slowly past him, stealing a clandestine glance through the slightly open door.

The room was empty, the beds neat with sheets flattened tight, waiting for a patient.

Moving on, I stopped at a trolley cluttered with empty tea cups and plates speckled with the remnants of breakfast. Needing time to think, I casually began to tidy the trolley, scraping the leftovers onto a single plate. My thoughts raced, hatching a plan. Now I had an idea where my brother was, I would return again, maybe when the soldiers changed, and sneak in. Time was not on our side. I couldn't let him out of the hospital; it was our only hope. As to what we'd do after that, I had no idea.

I hurried towards the hospital exit, my heart pounding,

when I was suddenly stopped by an elderly doctor. His hunched figure stood out among the young nurses, a stethoscope hanging loosely from his neck. Behind thick spectacles, his enlarged eyes strained to focus on me. He seemed to be searching for something in my face, his wrinkled brow furrowed with concern.

'Nurse, fetch me some sheets from the storeroom,' he said, his hand waving vaguely in the direction.

My heart raced as I quickly glanced around. Then, spotting some sheets on a nearby trolley, I grabbed a few.

'Here you go, Doctor,' I said, handing them over while trying to steady my trembling hands.

'Thank you, Nurse. Lovely weather we're having, isn't it?' he continued, launching into idle chatter.

I nodded, my voice tight. 'Yes, it's pleasant all right,' I said, praying he would stop asking me questions.

He took off his spectacles, and cleaned them with a large white hanky. Seizing this opportunity, I excused myself and hastened back to the office.

Upon entering, Doolin looked up from his desk, a questioning icy stare on his face.

'Where have you been?' he asked, his icy eyes narrowing.

Forcing a casual tone, I replied, 'After I posted the letters, I just took a walk around the camp. It's such a nice day, isn't it?'

'Miss Flinn, you're here for one purpose – to translate German letters. Nothing more.' His tone was sharp, cutting the air like a knife. 'You are not to go wandering around the camp.'

I dropped my eyes to the paperwork on my desk. The air

in the small office felt suddenly stifling, the stale scent of tobacco clinging to my throat.

The silence was suffocating. The only sound was the shuffling of papers on Doolin's desk. I missed the busy noise of the hospital, the never-ending clicking of trolley wheels and the incessant chatter of Ethyl and Harriet.

Finally, after what seemed an eternity, he pushed back his chair and left the office without another word, the door clicking sharply shut behind him. I let out a shaky exhale, my lungs burning as I drew in fresh air. His warning lingered like a black cloud, threatening to unleash its fury if I stepped out of line.

But time was not on my side – Anthony would be transferred to Tin Town in a few days.

The church bell chimed five times and I gathered my coat and bag, preparing to leave MacDonagh and head home. My thoughts were still consumed by Anthony and my determination to try to see him again tomorrow, despite Doolin's warning ringing in my ears.

As I walked down McSwiney Road towards the Water Tower, my mind drifted back to the hospital. Passing by the post office once more, I turned towards the hospital and quickened my pace. The streets were quiet at this hour, the soldiers already gone to Sandes Home for their tea.

My heart raced and my palms grew clammy as I approached the steps of the hospital. Stepping into the sterile hallway, I passed by rooms that only had empty beds inside them, while others had patients with solemn expressions etched on their faces. I walked directly to the room I had seen the soldier guarding earlier, anticipation and nervousness building with each step. Within seconds I saw the soldier at the end of the corridor and kept him within my peripheral vision. He drew a pack of cigarettes from his pocket, examined it and squashed it in his hand, muttering a curse. He glanced into the room before closing the door and turning towards the hospital entrance, rolling back his shoulders as he left the building.

Stepping cautiously towards the door, my heart pounded relentlessly. I gently eased the door open, wincing as it creaked slightly. I was greeted by a sight that stole my breath. There, almost unrecognisable, lay Anthony, swathed in harsh white bandages that emphasised the pallor of his skin. His chest rose and fell in a faint rhythm, but he was otherwise alarmingly still. His cheeks protruded sharply. I rearranged his blanket, lifted his head and adjusted the pillow.

His eyelids quivered.

'Kitty,' he murmured, his voice grating as sandpaper.

I reached for the glass jug on the bedside table, pouring the last of its contents into an empty teacup, fearing that an eagle-eyed nurse would later wonder how he had found the strength to pour himself water.

I slipped my hand beneath his head, raising it slightly and holding the teacup to his dry lips. 'Drink this,' I encouraged him. When he was finished, I wiped the inside of the teacup dry, before placing it back where I found it.

'Why are you here? You might get arrested too,' he managed to utter, his voice tinged with worry.

'I've agreed to translate a few documents. Well, letters, really. Those that the Germans are writing to their families. I needed to be near you.'

His face creased, as if speaking hurt. 'Surely they have translators, Kitty. Why you?'

'I'm utterly at a loss. I really don't know, Anthony. It's all rather peculiar. Doolin told a Colonel MacNally I had volunteered.'

A silence fell between us, the tranquillity in the room almost ironic.

'Anthony, don't talk, just listen. They want to send you to Tin Town when you're better. I've heard the beds are infested with fleas, that is if you get a bed. There could be twenty-six to a hut, no hot water – no water at all.'

He blanched even more, his face nearly translucent now. Then he squeezed my hand, and the tension fell from my shoulders. We had a secret way of holding hands, something we'd invented when we were younger and had to be silent in the evenings when Mother was in one of her rages.

'And I found a map of our house,' I said. 'It had my name written on it.'

The clattering of a trolley outside brought me back. I urgently had to leave before the soldier returned. I squeezed his hand again.

'I really have to go, Anthony. Even if you feel better, don't show it. I suspect that if they think you can walk and stay conscious, they'll turf you into Tin Town.'

I slipped quickly out the door, praying again to Saint Cajetan as if we were old friends.

Later, I pulled the door closed at Alice's and breathed in the familiar smell of lavender and leather polish. The radio hummed in the background.

'Kitty, is that you? I've just made some tea, come and join me.'

Alice handed me a cup and saucer as I sat down, and my tears began to flow.

'I saw Anthony, Alice, in the hospital. He wouldn't be there if I hadn't left him alone in the house. Maybe if I had worked with Doolin and G2 when he first asked me to, Anthony wouldn't have been arrested.'

I still couldn't understand why Frank Doolin wanted me to work for him. Reading the letters didn't seem that difficult of a task.

The cushion next to me was depressed with weight and I felt my hand being rubbed. Peter sat beside me, concern in his eyes. He rubbed my hand the way Alice rubbed his when he was upset. The low evening sun fell across the sitting room, and sweat gathered on the back of my neck. The sitting room window was closed and I found it hard to breathe.

He held out a drawing and gave it to me.

'Peter, that's lovely,' I said.

It was a pencil sketch of a girl in the garden, crude lines criss-crossing a square house, the sun high in the sky. His attempt at a butterfly would only be known by me, but it was beautiful. He pointed at the girl, then at me.

My heart melted. 'For me?' I put my hand on my chest. 'Thank you, Peter.'

I could feel the warmth of Alice's smile.

'I told you, you've made such a difference to him. He's calmer and more content. He spent the last few days perfecting this.'

I was almost lost for words.

'Thank you so much, Peter. I'll put it in my diary.'

'He learned the style from some of my art books. He can copy anything. It's amazing that once he learns a skill, he has it for life.'

A ghost of a smile hovered around Peter's lips, then disappeared as he lowered his head to look again at the picture he had drawn.

36

The next morning, I left early, slipping out of the house before Alice got up. As I cycled across the plains of the Curragh, the cool morning wind was fresh against my face. Passing the empty sentry box, I cycled down Pearse Way and turned up McSwiney Road as soldiers clambered into an army truck.

At MacDonagh, I took a moment to pause and survey the British and German camps. Pulling my cardigan tight in the crisp morning air, I was glad that in a few hours the sun would break through the clouds and burn away the haze.

One of the English pilots came into my line of sight.

'Hitler!' he shouted, and a black Labrador ran towards him, its tail wagging furiously, and dropped a ball at his feet. Painted on to its side was a red swastika. The man bent down and gently rubbed behind the dog's ears.

Over in the German camp, it was a hive of activity. One figure in particular caught my eye – a man fully decked out in his military uniform, a peaked cap sitting snugly on his head and polished boots mirroring the weak sunlight. He held a clipboard in his firm grasp, standing rigid in front of the first hut. His voice, loud and commanding, shouted names. 'Lieutenant Konrad, Webber!' he began, each internee responding to their name with a disciplined click of their heels of acknowledgement.

The roll call concluded with Markus Biegel. I watched Markus carefully. He looked well under the circumstances, his skin glowed and any signs of the recent struggle with Doolin was minimal in contrast to what Anthony had endured.

On impulse, I raised my hand in the hope he might see, but he turned and joined his comrades as they lined up to go into the huts.

Glancing at my watch, I saw it was eight o'clock and hurried inside, my shoes echoing in the hallway. Sam turned to me as I entered the office. He was leaving a file on my desk.

'Sam, I wasn't expecting you,' I said. At the sight of him, anger simmered through me, threatening to explode like steam straining against a valve about to explode. But I had to be civil for Anthony's sake. In this place, I was powerless.

'Kitty, I've got to ask your brother some more questions. He's still in the hospital.'

I sighed with relief and Sam continued to speak. 'I left some cards on your desk for Doolin. Tell him the printers in Naas said he was a few short.'

He had placed small green booklets on my desk, and I picked one up.

I hereby give my word of honour that I will return to my quarters in the Curragh Camp by _____, that while on parole I will not make or endeavour to make any arrangement whatever to seek or accept any assistance with a view to escape, for myself or my fellow internees, that I will not engage in any military or any activities contrary to the interests of Ireland and that I will not go outside the permitted area.

'What are those?' I asked, momentarily forgetting my anger.

'They are parole cards,' he explained. 'The internees go out every day for a few hours and they sign the parole form. They give their word of honour not to escape.'

'Why?' I asked. 'I thought it was a soldier's duty to try to escape.'

Sam sighed. 'Their governments have ordered them not to. It's to do with the strategic position of our seaports, on the west and east of our coast. You don't really need to know this, but understand that both Germany and Britain want access to our ports, so their governments have been ordered not to upset us. It works in our favour really; they want to keep us happy so they can have our ports.'

For a moment, a flicker of the old Sam emerged, the boy who once was our friend.

The door creaked open, Doolin entered and instantly the mood changed. With one quick brusque movement, he threw a German newspaper onto my desk, the pages fluttering as it landed. He picked up the parole cards and deftly counted them.

'The printer said he was a few short,' Sam said.

Doolin responded with a grunt and rubbed his chest.

'Miss Flinn, take the German newspapers to the

Germans,' he said. 'Jesus, they have a great feckin life here,' he muttered. 'And Sam, would you bring the parole cards to the camps on your way out?'

He went to his desk and straightened the row of six pencils, all the same length with identical sharpened tips. Beside them lay the notebook he'd had at Alice's house that night.

'And your brother... we have to decide what to do with him. We are waiting to hear from Dublin when to transfer him or what other charges we can bring against him.'

'Other charges?' I asked, but he didn't answer.

He returned to his paperwork, and after a minute, he looked up. 'Are you still here, Miss Flinn?'

They surely didn't know he was homosexual. Would he be sent to Arbour Hill Prison or Kilmainham Gaol in Dublin?

Sam coughed, held the door open, and motioned with his head for me to follow him. I grabbed the newspapers, clutching them tight, and followed him. He looked up briefly at the watchtower – the guard, a silhouette against the morning sky.

Sam pushed the gate open for me, holding it back, allowing me to go first. In front of a hut, Sam paused, his eyes tracing the neat rows of scallions and cabbages in the garden, their green shoots a stark contrast against the brown soil. I pulled the gate closed behind us, the metallic clink of the bolt echoing slightly as it slid into place.

The Germans, now out of their stiff uniforms, were dressed in light, airy clothing. Their trousers and shirts, in matching shades, were impeccably tailored, giving them an air of casual elegance. Some even sported ties that added a touch of formality. They looked strikingly dapper, their appearance a sharp departure from the drabness of military life. It was easy to imagine how their refined looks might turn the heads of local women, drawn to their foreign allure and polished demeanour.

The men retreated into the hut, laughing and chatting. I was becoming immune to the language, something I never thought would happen.

Sam broke my thoughts. 'Be aware that you may be asked to go with them to the dances.'

'Dances?' I said, 'with who?'

He looked across at the Germans.

'Them?' I said, unable to hide my shock.

He shifted, and laughed at my question. Again, the old Sam reappeared, and ostensibly I couldn't separate the two.

'Yes, dances. We follow them, for their own protection. People hate the British here, but a lot hate the Germans just as much. We must go with them.'

Sam left me wondering what a strange place I had found myself in.

37

The following day, just as I set my cup of tea down on its saucer, there was a gentle tap on the open office door. Markus stood in the doorway, holding a bunch of letters. He wasn't dressed in his military uniform but wore a cream shirt, sleeves rolled up, and tan pleated trousers with a black belt.

'Kitty, I was told to bring these letters to you.'

He looked around the office, taking in the maps and the clocks with the different times. He swayed a little and I noticed he looked paler than the day before, the colour drained from his face like the last light of dusk.

I yearned to get up and embrace him, but he was the enemy.

'Markus it is so good to see you,' I said, my voice laden with concern. 'I was worried when I heard you were in hospital.'

'I'm fine, really. It is good here,' he insisted. 'We are warm, and the huts are well furnished. We even have running hot water.' He laughed, but his eyes became serious, his pallor telling a different story. 'And Anthony, any news of him?'

'He's in the hospital,' I said, feeling the sting of tears. I held them back as I recounted how I had sneaked into the hospital to see him.

His hand wrapped tightly around mine and he spoke with urgency. 'Kitty, you will have to try again,' he insisted, grasping my hand. His face was pale with concern. 'He is a good man, and there are tales of how the men in Tin Town are mistreated...' His voice trailed off, unable to continue. 'Men like Anthony, and his kind would have no chance.'

An image of the blackmailer's letter flashed in my mind, but it paled into insignificance. If Anthony didn't have his life, what difference would it make?

Trying to grasp the positive of the situation, I thought about how the blackmailer had no clue we were here, that for the moment we were safe from him.

'Are you all right?' Markus asked.

'My head. It just feels a little light.'

He picked up the tin jug on the desk and poured me some water, and I quietly drank it, composing myself.

'Markus, I must make it appear as if everything is normal, and continue my duties. All I can hope is to get to the hospital again at some point.'

I began to shift through the letters, gauging the task ahead of me. Some of them were two or three pages long, others just a few lines.

The men were writing to their mothers, describing their day-to-day lives here, and how they could go cycling across the Curragh, go the horse races, or the dances in Newbridge.

'Do they think we are plotting to escape in the dead of

the night?' Markus said with a laugh. 'And to where would we go? The men tell me there's nothing but open fields around here. All they do is go to the races, or to the local pub to dance –' he raised his eyebrows – 'it is not the worst place to be.'

'That's true,' I said.

'Maybe you could come with us,' he suggested slyly, with a glint in his eye.

Sam did say the Germans have to be followed for their own safety.

The German camp was fully awake now. Inaudible shouts from the men, dogs barking, and the sound of trucks filtered in from outside. I looked out across at the camps. It wasn't yet nine o'clock and the Germans were up and about in their casual clothes, some in the garden, some playing chess. In contrast, there were no signs of life in the British camp. Not one hut door was open, and all the curtains were still closed.

'You can help me,' I said, gesturing to the letters on my desk. 'I would be glad of the company.'

Markus nodded, smiled and took one of the letters. He, unfolded it to lay it flat on his knees, then took his spectacles from his shirt pocket. At first, he read silently, only his lips moving as his eyes moved from word to word; then he started reading aloud. The cadence was lyrical, ending sentences with an upward kick.

Markus cleared his throat. 'And now in English.'

My dear mother. We go swimming in the afternoons. It's not as nice as the lakes at home but when I slip into the lake here, the water slips over my skin like cool silk. And

when I lie on my back and look up at the clear blue sky,
there are no clouds, just me and nature.

They were the words of a lover of nature. The handwriting
was beautiful, the author had used a soft-nib ink pen. The
words swept across the pages, the script like an artist's
brush, as if painting a picture. But maybe not; was this letter
secretly describing something more insidious?

Markus took his time folding the letter and putting it
back in its envelope before placing it on the desk.

'I miss my wife, Kitty. I miss when we would sit on our
deck watching the changing of the season. You can sense the
change in the air before the leaves of summer turn, and then
you have the wonderful cacophony of colours of autumn.
The air becomes thinner, less dense. Summers in Germany
can be very hot, and the autumn cool.'

We sat silent for a moment.

Markus started to read another letter, and I tried to
reconcile the man before me with the things I knew about
the war, his country and Hitler, and the bombs, and what
Anthony had told me about him. And here we were in the
Irish countryside, talking about horse racing, swimming
and dancing.

There still wasn't anything suspicious in the letters,
unless 'bland food' was a code word, and it felt wrong to be
reading about other people's private lives. They were full of
compassion and love, ever praising their new home.

Dear Mother,
I am well and healthy. I can't believe how good it
is here and that I made the right choice of crash landing

here. Luckily there was a break in the clouds so I saw Ireland painted on the cliffs. After being interned in Belgium by the British, I knew the conditions would be bad if I was captured by them. So, I took a chance landing here, and what good fortune it was. The food is good, albeit a bit bland.

Did the military think that the complaints about bland food might be a secret message because there were so many? I'd have loved their food. They ate like kings: three meals a day, one of which was a good dinner with meat and two veg. I thought of my soggy mashed parsnip sandwich as the tower bell tolled one o'clock.

I carefully opened a letter, its creased edges revealing the passage of time and the distance it had travelled. Connecting me to my German heritage, the words began to weave their story as my eyes scanned the lines. There was no hatred here, no animosity, only the quiet desperation of men trapped in a situation beyond their control. Each line pulled me deeper into a world that I didn't truly understand.

My family, I hope you are safe and well. Time here passes slowly, each day blending into the next. I have made some friends among the other prisoners, though we are cautious with our trust. We share stories of home, longing for the day when we can return to those we love.

I paused, the depth of emotion catching me off guard. This was not the enemy I had always imagined, faceless and cold, but a man who longed for his family and the comfort of familiar surroundings. A pang of empathy stirred within me, an unexpected connection to a stranger whose life had crossed paths with mine in the most unlikely of ways.

Despite my uncertainty, I knew I could not turn away from these letters. Their stories deserved to be heard, their voices acknowledged amidst the chaos and destruction of a war that had torn us all apart. And perhaps, in some small way, I could find a measure of understanding and healing here.

'*Wir sind alle Menschen*,' the letter continued. 'We are all human, caught in the storm of history's making. I pray for peace, so that we may find our way home once more.'

I felt something shift within me. A shared humanity bound us together, transcending the barriers of language and nationality. And though I had never met these men, I knew that their stories had left a mark on my soul – one that would remain.

I unfolded more letters. The words spilled across the page, a tapestry of longing and pain woven by a soul caught in the crossfire of war. It was as if the ink bled through time, staining the present with the echoes of a past that refused to be silenced. Stories came to life before me, the shadows of memories dancing upon the walls of my heart. There was love lost and dreams dashed, the crushing weight of a world crumbling beneath our feet. And yet, there was also an undercurrent of hope that cut through the despair, a flickering flame in the darkness: 'Sometimes, when the night is still, I can almost hear your voice on the wind,' one prisoner wrote.

'If we are finished for the day, I'll leave,' Markus said, and bowed his head as if in thanks. He looked over the desk, leaned in and tidied the letters into neat piles.

I smiled. 'Thank you for your help, Markus,' I said, and meant it. 'The company was nice.'

★

The gentle orange hue of the evening sun danced off the puddles on the main street of Naas as I strolled down the near-empty street, thinking about the Germans and their dance. Suddenly a head of mousy brown hair caught my attention. 'Ethyl!' I called, lifting my hand.

Her pale face lit up in a bright smile, her freckles a constellation across her cheeks. She quickened her steps towards me, her eyes narrowing with curiosity.

'Kitty! What a surprise! Why did you leave the hospital?'

A shiver ran through me, the sharp memory of my abrupt dismissal still fresh. I grimaced and said tersely, 'I just left.' I was glad that the news of my sacking hadn't spread.

Her eyebrows furrowed in puzzlement and I felt guilty. 'A better opportunity came up, better pay. Couldn't turn it down.'

'But you were passionate about the hospital!' she exclaimed, surprise colouring her voice. 'You never mentioned leaving.'

I found my gaze fixated on my shoes.

'They let me go, Ethyl,' I confessed, my voice barely a whisper. 'I didn't have a chance to say goodbye.'

'Oh, Kitty, I'm so sorry.'

'It's fine,' I said, pushing an artificial cheeriness into my voice. 'The new job even involves a dance.'

Her eyes grew wide with intrigue. 'A dance? With who?'

'The German airmen in the Curragh. They crash-landed here and are prisoners of war of sorts, but they're allowed to leave. They're required to sign a document promising they won't escape.'

Ethyl shook her head. 'That's extraordinary, I saw a few in Lawlors one night.'

I couldn't suppress a smile.

'Strange, isn't it? Anyway, why don't you come to the dance?'

I knew she'd like nothing more.

There was a moment of silence before Ethyl's face broke into a wide grin. We arranged to meet at the dance hall later.

Later, Comdt Doolin questioned my motives behind offering to go to the dance with the Germans.

'Miss Flinn, it is a responsibility that the British airmen do not mix with the Germans. They will arrive first at the dance, then they are the first to leave when the dance is over,' he explained, his voice carrying an undercurrent of stern caution.

He eyed me suspiciously.

'A break, Commander, is all I want. Nothing more.'

That was the truth – a night with Ethyl was the break I needed, to drown out any guilt I felt over Anthony lying in the hospital. Maybe tomorrow I would have some inspiration.

While I waited at the camp gate for the Germans, I picked a few bits of lint from my skirt and smoothed it down. With the clothes rationing, no one would bat an eyelid at my well-worn outfit.

First to emerge was Markus. He tipped a well-worn fedora to me. His face bore the flush of a hasty shave and his suit, though neat, was clearly well-used, with the trousers a tad wide at the hem and the waistcoat fitting snugly over his shirt.

'Kitty, apologies for our tardiness.'

'No trouble at all, Markus,' I replied, observing the other

Germans as they emerged. Some wore double-breasted suits, their shoulders padded to give a square shape, while others had single-breasted blazers, all carefully paired with wide-legged trousers. Their ties, a mix of bold stripes and solid colours, lent individuality to their uniform look.

Markus nodded to two young Germans. 'These two young men are Karl and Otto.'

'A pleasure,' Karl said, bowing his head slightly. His black hair was slicked back, framing his smoky eyes; he was ready to set a young girl's heart on fire. He looked extremely dapper in an expensive looking navy suit, its double-breasted design crisply tailored.

Markus saw me looking at the suit and leaned towards me to whisper, 'They were allowed to get measured in Newbridge for suits – it's the first time many of these boys have worn proper suits.'

Otto didn't have his friend's good looks, with his long, narrow face and thin nose, but at over six foot tall and with an infectious smile, he carried himself with a confidence that would attract a lot of attention.

We set off, the Germans cycling two by two, their bicycles clinking, a jovial symphony that echoed in the crisp night air. Outside the dance hall, they started leaning their High Nellys against the wall of the bar, and I remembered something Sam had told me.

'Markus,' I said, 'get them to leave their bicycles in the ditch. The RAF men leave theirs against the wall. We don't need a reason for a fight tonight.'

They did so, then Karl flattened his hair, looked at his reflection in the window, straightened his blue vest under his jacket, fixed his tie and said, 'I do look handsome.'

Otto playfully punched him on the arm. 'Looking to catch the eye of a young Irish girl, are you?'

A grin spread across Karl's face. 'You never know what will happen.'

Local women in their finest summer dresses and men in their cleanest shirts danced in the middle of the floor to a set reel, their shoes tapping the wooden floor in rhythm. As we walked in, the bodhrán player stopped beating and the fiddler put his bow on his knees. Suspicious eyes followed the Germans as they walked to the bar.

There were introductions, and Karl slapped a pound note on the wooden counter. 'Viskey,' he said, then turned and grinned at the farmers standing next to him. 'And viskey for my good friends here!'

The local men in flat caps smiled and slapped Karl on the back, delighted with the free whiskey. They lifted their glasses and threw back the drink in one gulp.

'Music!' a local man shouted, and within seconds it started again. The floors creaked as women and men took to a set dance. As soon as the fiddler started, Otto and Karl put down their glasses and clapped in time with the fiddlers, and then took to the floor themselves.

Across the whirlwind of faces and colours, I spotted Ethyl. She was watching the two Germans dance, a mixture of fascination and disbelief painting her freckled face. Every now and then she'd break into a light chuckle, her laughter blending seamlessly with the tunes of the fiddlers. It was evident that the unusual spectacle of the German airmen partaking in this Irish revelry intrigued not only Ethyl, but others as well.

Our eyes met and she lifted her glass a bit higher, a

silent nod of acknowledgement. Her smile was infectious, radiant against the warm glow of the dance hall, as if to say, 'Isn't this something?' I returned the gesture, my own smile tugging at my lips.

The music fell silent once more; glasses froze in mid-air. Ten RAF men had made an entrance, their eyes fixed on the Germans dancing with the local girls.

'Bloody Nazi lover,' one bellowed over the fading music.

The crowd, however, chose to ignore him, resuming their revelry and dance.

Markus tapped his foot to the music; his gaze narrowed, taking in the sight of Karl, Otto and the other young Germans as they twirled the local girls around the dance floor, their differences momentarily erased by the joyous rhythm and harmony. The floorboards vibrated with the synchronised landing of three men and three women, twisting and swapping arms to 'The Siege of Ennis'. Fiddlers played with a fervour that echoed the crowd's energy and others clapped in rhythm, the melody sweeping through the room like a swirling river.

I leaned across the table towards him, careful not to spill the beer. 'Fancy a dance, Markus?' I asked, raising my voice to be heard over the roar of the party.

He shifted uncomfortably in his seat, then smiled and shook his head. 'I can't dance,' he confessed, 'but my wife intends to teach me once I return home.'

He glanced around the room before leaning closer, lowering his voice to a whisper. 'Kitty, I have never held another woman. It sounds silly, I know. It's not that I fear I'd be betraying her, it's just that I miss her so much. I came so close to losing her once.'

He took a deep breath. The clamour of the bar dimmed as he began to speak, the lightness in his tone belying the weight of his words. He ran his fingers along the rim of his glass, his eyes far away. Then his gaze met mine, and I saw the pain in his eyes, raw and unguarded.

'It was a miscarriage. Our little one, we never even had the chance to hold him. You cannot understand... I felt so helpless, Kitty. I wanted so much to save them, to protect them. I nearly lost her. My wife, my beautiful wife. She's my world, you know? I wouldn't survive without her. I'd be nothing.'

He looked past me, towards the joyful chaos of the dance floor. 'When we lost our child, I realised how much pain such a loss could bring. That's why I couldn't bring myself to fire at those families leaving Paris.'

The man who sat across from me was no longer just a German soldier; he was a grieving father, a devoted husband. I wanted to share my story, but this was not the time or place. We were both prisoners of our pasts, trapped in grief for children we never had.

The tension in the air thickened as an English voice, laced with venom, rang out across the room: 'Bloody Nazis!'

Markus's face drained of colour. 'That's Captain Zenick. His parents are from Poland. I believe it's time for us to leave. He despises Germans.'

Getting to his feet with an air of resignation, he quickly donned his overcoat. His eyes darted towards his men, silently communicating the urgency of the situation. They began to gather their belongings.

Just then, the heavy wooden door of the bar creaked

open, admitting two more RAF servicemen. They were both strikingly tall, over six feet, their leather bomber jackets lending them an intimidating air. The entire atmosphere of the room shifted ominously.

I gestured hastily to Otto and Karl to join us. 'We must leave, and we must leave now,' I said. 'The situation is becoming precarious.'

I grabbed my coat and handbag from the back of my chair and tried to catch Ethyl's eye, but she was deeply engrossed in conversation with one of the RAF pilots, oblivious to the tension enveloping the room.

As we navigated our way past the RAF men stationed at the bar, I could feel their eyes boring into us. The jovial strains of the fiddle that had filled the room moments ago were now gone. The atmosphere was taut, as if the entire room were collectively holding its breath, watching us tread cautiously past. It was as though time itself had stilled, capturing us all in this fragile, suspended moment.

Outside, the stars in the night sky were like glittering diamonds on black velvet. We gathered our bicycles from the ditch. Karl and Otto stood beside Markus, laughing.

'They were letting the air out of the English tyres,' he said shaking his head, and a smile spread across his face.

I swung a leg over my saddle. 'Come away, don't be so childish.'

The moon guided us back to the camp. The odd bird chirped in the warm night. Soon we gathered speed, freewheeling wherever the flat road had a decline, following the path of silver moonlight.

But it wasn't long before jeering and shouting filled the air behind us.

Otto laughed. 'The RAF men mustn't have been too happy with their flat tyres.'

I shot him an angry glance. 'Pedal harder!' I urged, not wanting a confrontation. We all stood up on our bikes, cycling hard up the hill. I looked behind me and saw Markus was struggling. Even in the dim light I could see his face puffed in exertion.

I slowed to wait for him. 'Markus, pedal harder!'

Captain Zenick shouted 'Nazi!' at Markus as he rode past me, his front wheel touching Markus's back wheel. Suddenly, Markus was thrown over the handlebars of his bike and onto the hillside, crashing into the bushes and stones.

I hastily hopped off my bike and rushed over. Otto and Karl were already trying to pull Zenick away from Markus, but he held on to his hair and then kicked him in the head. Another RAF man shouted at Zenick to drop him, but he ignored him, continuing to spew venomous words while kicking and spitting at poor Markus.

When Zenick finally stopped and stepped back, Karl and Otto carried Markus back onto the road and laid him on the ground. One of the RAF men crouched down and pressed his hand to the pulse point on his neck.

'Miss Flinn, I'm Captain Mayhew. Get help, quickly!'

His voice was sharp with urgency. His gloved hand pressed a clean handkerchief to Markus's forehead, and it quickly stained with a spreading patch of crimson.

I pedalled into the inky night as fast as I could. It was only a ten-minute ride to the hospital, but it felt like a painful eternity. The cool night air bit into my face as I navigated through the quiet streets of the Curragh, my heart pounding.

Abandoning my bike at the steps of the hospital, I ran up two at a time. The moment I crossed the hospital threshold, the change was immediate. Sterile air, tinged with the scent of antiseptic, a far cry from the earthy aroma of the night air outside. A sense of despair washed over me. A haunting stillness pervaded the dimly lit corridors. Patients lay asleep in their beds, their slow breathing the only sign of life in this eerie, seemingly abandoned sanctuary.

Driven by desperation, I scoured the hospital and finally stumbled upon a nurse who seemed almost as startled to see me as I was relieved to find her. Gasping for breath, I quickly told her what happened.

Her air of complacency set me on edge.

'You'll have to wait. It's a busy night,' she said, barely lifting her eyes from the medical charts she clutched in her hands. Her tone was mundane, as if we were discussing something as trivial as the weather. The hospital was far from busy. On her desk was a teacup, steam gently rising from it. Next to it lay a freshly lit cigarette, its smoke curling upwards, resting on the edge of a plate with two untouched rich tea biscuits.

She stood with a languid posture, the weary look in her green eyes seemed more dismissive than compassionate.

'This is an emergency! A man is seriously injured!' I shouted, my voice reverberating.

'All right, all right! Stay here, I'll get Dr Sheehan,' she said and hurried off, cursing me under her breath.

Soon a doctor appeared, and his eyes, though youthful, were serious. 'Wait here,' he said, pointing to a chair and leaving me to grapple with my escalating fear and guilt.

I sat alone in the corridor, the doctor's voice seeping

through a closed door as he spoke into a telephone. Each second that ticked by felt like an eternity stretching out before me. My thoughts raced back to Markus, vulnerable and injured. Attacked again.

Finally, the doctor reappeared. 'Comdt Doolin has informed me that one of his men is on the way and will drive you home to Naas,' he stated in a matter-of-fact way.

I stood up. 'And what about the injured German?'

'There's an ambulance gone already.'

Any flicker of hope I'd harboured about staying and visiting Anthony dissipated when a soldier walked into the corridor, the same young man who had collected the letters the other day.

'A car's waiting outside for you, miss,' he said, his eyes briefly meeting mine before respectfully nodding towards the door. The distant wail of the ambulance siren punctuated his words, the chilling sound echoing through the quiet night as it raced towards Markus.

As I walked along McSwiney Road the next morning, a twinge of guilt shadowed my thoughts that I planned to use Markus's hospitalisation to my advantage and see Anthony. I knew the hospital's routine well. The changeover from the night shift to the day staff happened at eight, and I hoped that I could use this brief window to slip into the hospital unnoticed.

The sun broke through the clouds, its rays streaming across the sky. I was almost at the top of the steps when a grey-haired doctor ran past me two steps at a time, and held the door open for me as I reached the top step.

'After you,' he said. His white shirt was a little too large for him. 'Are you visiting someone?'

'Yes, I'm here to see one of the German internees. He had an accident last night.'

He seemed to be pointing to a large white statue of the Virgin Mary, her head bent downwards like she was apologising for letting people get sick. For a moment I thought he was going to say *Ask her*. Instead he said, 'Turn left at the end. Follow her.' He was pointing to a nurse in a green cape.

I pushed open a succession of doors, offering hurried apologies as startled patients looked up from their breakfast. I had given up hope of finding Markus until I pushed the last door open. He was lying on a narrow bed, his head bandaged, a speck of dried blood above his left eye. His eyes were closed, his hands resting over the folded top of the blanket.

Quietly, I dipped a white flannel into the tin bowl of water on the table beside him and gently dabbed his cracked lips. His eyes twitched under his eyelids but didn't open. A droplet of water trickled down his chin, and as I wiped it away, his chin quivered. That was a good sign. His breathing was slow but steady.

A chaplain walked by, chatting to a small, plump girl pushing a trolley of clattering teacups, serving tea. He offered a smile and a quick sign of the cross. Tea and a blessing. I stood and bowed my head at him.

A nurse came over, lifted Markus's hand and looked at the clock on the wall, counting the beats. She picked up the chart at the end of the bed, and the chaplain smiled and nodded at me.

She said, 'I don't think he is going to wake up just now, Miss...'

'Flinn,' I said.

She smiled. She thought I was his girlfriend.

'The cut looks small, but he's concussed and hasn't woken since we brought him in. He'll be asleep for another few hours.'

I quietly slipped out of the room, blending in with a group of passing nurses. Their lively chatter about their mundane duties was the perfect camouflage, enabling me to navigate the hospital's labyrinthine corridors.

There was no one outside Anthony's door and I pushed the door open.

'Anthony,' I whispered, cautiously closing the door behind me.

'Kitty!' His surprise quickly melted into a smile. 'You're a sight for sore eyes.'

He lay in bed, looking pale and tired. His voice held a thread of cheerfulness, but it couldn't hide the fear lingering in his eyes.

I was bitter at the injustice of it all. Anthony was innocent, a pawn caught up in the machinations of a war he didn't ask for, and his fate remained uncertain. Yet the RAF men who had played an active part in this chaos would surely walk free. Their futures held the promise of family reunions and a return to normalcy, while my brother was facing the threat of Tin Town and more uncertainty. It wasn't right, it wasn't fair.

38

Back in the office, my thoughts wandered to the girls in Dublin who had said fishermen would take passengers across the sea for a price. I picked up a fresh pile of German letters. I guessed the Germans knew someone was reading their words. Were they honest when they wrote about how well they were treated, and how much they liked it?

A shadow fell across the desk. It was Sam holding a mug of tea. He wasn't dressed in his usual navy suit but wore a white shirt, his sleeves rolled up, and tan pleated baggy trousers with a black belt.

'You gave me a fright,' I said. 'I didn't hear you come in.'

He picked up a letter. 'Anything interesting?' He put it down and took a sip of tea.

I stretched my foot out and accidentally knocked against something – a black briefcase. He moved the letters and wire tray aside, placing the case on my desk with a sense of urgency. With a swift movement, he flicked the clasp open, producing a sharp click that echoed in the quiet room.

'Kitty, don't bother with those letters,' he said abruptly, his voice firm.

He inhaled deeply, his expression growing serious. 'Listen to me, Kitty, this is very important. Don't utter a word to anyone about this. It's really important.'

I leaned back in my chair, my curiosity piqued. What could he possibly have to say that was so vital? Just a week ago, he had been beating up my brother, once his best friend, and now he was confiding in me. His duplicity was staggering.

'I've got the cards for the RAF. We're planning to send them up north. I need your help. Mona has taken a half-day; her child is ill, or something,' he explained, his tone laced with a mix of impatience and urgency.

I took the paperwork he handed to me and began to scan through the list of names and accompanying photographs. One name immediately caught my eye – Markus Biegel.

'Why are you letting Markus go?' I asked, unable to mask my surprise.

Before answering, he walked over to the window, peering out as if to ensure we were not overheard. The morning light spilled into the room, casting long shadows that seemed to accentuate the gravity of the situation. His next words stunned me.

'Kitty, we knew he was at your home with your brother. I was waiting to see if any other IRA men turned up. That's who Frank and I were going to arrest – well, detain. Markus had been sending accurate weather reports to the British, and false ones to Germany. He was working as a double agent.'

He paused for a moment, his face emotionless.

'MI5 contacted us when they lost contact with him. They thought he might be dead, or exposed. We scoured the countryside. When we found the crashed Heinkel on Tramore Beach in Waterford, we found only two bodies, and a parachute was missing. It took weeks, but eventually we located him at your farm.'

The implications swirled around me. My thoughts raced.

'MI5?' I whispered, the syllables tasting foreign on my tongue. 'And Anthony? What about him? Why did you arrest him?'

'Kitty, it was for his own good. G2 contacted me when they found him with Anthony. G2 have no interest in the IRA. They work with MI5.'

Sam slowly walked to the window. His face gave nothing away. Outside it was quiet, the soldiers were all inside having their tea.

'Type those up tonight. A group of airmen will be released soon. We had to convince Markus that we were not working with Germany. Those damned IRA were helping the Germans, giving them information, photos and maps. The fools think that if they help Germany invade the north, they'll get the six counties back and have a united Ireland.'

The maps I had seen on my first day. The photographs of the seaside.

'Then why did you let Markus get beaten up?'

'It was a set-up. We didn't think it would be so serious, we just needed to get him into the hospital for his own safety. Zenick was ordered to give him a gentle beating, but he got carried away.'

His shoulders tensed the way they always did when he was stressed. I sat back down and turned my chair to face him. I still remembered the sunny evenings when Anthony, Sam and I had played hide and seek in the woods.

'Could Anthony go as well? You were once blood brothers, remember?'

Sam scoffed at that, mocking me. He put on his coat and pulled up the collar. 'Jesus, Kitty, we were children. Anthony chose a different life.'

Sanctimonious shit.

He didn't say anything else, he just walked out the door, slamming it behind him. I put any thoughts to the back of my mind and started work. It didn't take long to put the papers in alphabetical order, but I wasn't a quick typist.

Making a hasty decision, at two o'clock I left the office. I ran up the steps into the hospital. Had Markus confided his secrets to Anthony?

When I entered his room, Markus was awake and sitting up. His face was flushed, but not in a bad way.

'Kitty, I'm glad you're here. I was practising getting up and about.'

'You're looking better,' I said, and meant it.

I refilled his glass of water, then used the pen and paper beside him to write: *Lieutenant Daly told me the truth. I am typing your new identity card. They will have a uniform ready for you soon.*

'It's fine, Kitty, no one here is a threat,' he said. He leaned back and closed his eyes, let out a long sigh, then began again, his voice a mix of regret and determination. 'I became a double agent because I couldn't bear the thought of supporting Hitler's regime any longer. I told you I saw the destruction first-hand. Innocent lives lost, families torn apart.'

He took a sip of water. 'I was so frightened that I wouldn't see my wife again. Her golden hair, her eyes blue as sapphires.' He closed his eyes as if taking her in, then lay back again and smiled.

'I'll see my Henrietta. I haven't told you, but she is going to get to France. She will meet the resistance there and get passage to England.'

The door handle twisted. Markus sat up straighter as Sam came in, holding a bundle of clothes and a large brown fur-trimmed flying jacket. He put them on the bed.

'These should fit you, Markus, but I've no shoes so you'll have to get some of your own. We're probably going tomorrow night, but we need to wait until the British lads up north are ready to meet you. You're to stay in the hospital.'

He walked to the window, pulled the curtain back and looked around the camp. His eyes flicked to me, and he immediately pulled them back to Markus.

'We're not sending you back to your hut. It would be too hard to get you out again. Miss Flinn, will you go to the office and get the rest of Markus's files?'

I nodded and stood up to leave. Outside, the rain was falling in heavy droplets, tapping against the windowpanes like impatient fingers. I wrapped my arms around myself, feeling a chill that had nothing to do with the damp air.

39

When I entered Doolin's office, Mona's cheeks flushed red. Her hand rose to her chest. I was surprised to find her here, after Sam had said she'd taken a half-day.

'Oh, Kitty, I'm…' She was flustered. 'Doolin, you know how he is. I made an awful mistake in the letter to the colonel, and I told him I had finished it.'

She glanced at the clock behind me and put on a blue cloche hat and matching coat.

'I came in to fix it. I missed the second post, but I'll post it on my way home to catch the first one tomorrow. I must go, Kitty. If Lieutenant Daly sent you, you'll find the files on the table.'

After she left, I was drawn to Comdt Doolin's rosewood desk. A fountain pen lay on the left, a telephone on the right. The lingering smell of his cigarettes was the only discernible sign he had ever been present. Running my fingers over the smooth leather insert, I thought how his desk reflected him: meticulous and neat.

My fingers curled around the cool brass drawer handle,

and I pulled it open to discover an unexpected sight. Crushed cigarette boxes, paper clips and loose tobacco covered a light, straw-coloured writing pad, several sheets of carbon paper and what looked like half a sandwich. The scent of fish paste filled the air as I sifted through the drawer. The writing paper bore black swirls, rows and rows of incoherent doodles, hastily scribbled on each page.

A noise in the corridor made me drop the pad, and a yellowed sheet of paper slipped out.

Bessborough Mother & Baby Home
BIRTH CERTIFICATE
Name: FRANK DOOLIN
Mother: Unknown
Father: Unknown
DOB: April 15, 1906

Frank was adopted. That was what he had meant by his parents finding him.

Then I spotted my money tin, the one he and Sam had taken from me. I opened it nervously, praying the money was all there. Would they notice a few notes missing? They were mine to begin with.

I stashed the notes in my coat pocket, making sure to close the flap. They wouldn't be seen; more importantly, I wouldn't lose them. Hastily, I returned everything to the drawer.

The door handle rattled and I grabbed a file, thinking wildly about what I would say to Doolin. But it was Sam. He was silent for a moment, his face showing strain.

'Kitty, leave that. There's a change of plan. The RAF

men are leaving tonight, and Markus is going with them. However, he's received some bad news. He's extremely upset, but he needs to leave.'

He inhaled sharply. 'Will you go to him? Be ready this evening. He trusts you. Women often handle these situations better than men. I've seen how gently you treat him. He needs a friend.'

'What happened?' I asked.

But Sam was already at the door, hand on the knob, shoulders tensed, his back to me.

'War,' he said, 'the cruelty of war. Just go to him and get him ready.'

And then he was gone.

As soon as I left the building, I realised I had left my bag on the desk and turned back. The door was slightly ajar; Sam and Comdt Doolin were inside. I stood outside quietly. I couldn't fully hear them, but was sure I heard the word 'Flinn'.

Doolin then spoke loudly, and my heart stopped.

'That bastard Anthony Flinn will be hanged for sedition.'

Hanged. This couldn't be happening.

'Lieutenant Daly, did you hear me? That Flinn will dangle from the neck. I'd send him to the guillotine if I could. Let him dangle and suffer the way my father did in Spain when those murdering communist bastards tried to take Guernica from Franco. He only went over to see if he could talk sense into those foolish lads that joined Eoin O'Duffy in the International Brigade. My uncle's two sons went over and all he wanted to do was save them. But they all ended up dead.'

Peering through the crack in the door, I could see that Doolin was stood in front of Sam. His breathing was hard, and his eyes bulged.

'My mother never got to bury him. We told her he'd been buried in a little Spanish church. The truth was, he'd been beaten and mutilated. Imagine, he fought for his country only to die like a dog in a foreign land. If only more people had listened to Eoin O'Duffy instead of berating him. He was a great man.

'Do you know, Sam, I was very lucky to be adopted by kind, loving, good Catholics. They loved me like I was their own flesh and blood. And then, just like that, they were gone. And then I found her, my real mother.'

He spat on the floor.

'She didn't want me. She had no regard for me. She said she had two children and no room for anyone else. She said she was glad she abandoned me. And I left her there in Kilkenny, but I didn't forget. When we had the German colony under investigation, I found out she'd been in the home for unwed mothers in 1909. It was easy for me to get my mother's name from the nuns, so when I saw her maiden name on the birth certificate, I couldn't believe it was the one and the same.'

In my mother's diary, that was what she had meant: *Dec 1939: I met him.* It was Doolin. It was Frank Doolin she had written about. I stormed into the room, eyes wide with shock, no longer able to contain myself.

'You can't hang Anthony!' The words left my mouth before I could grasp their full weight. 'You never needed me to translate! You only wanted to get to me and Anthony because of my mother.'

Doolin's blue eyes were now dark, full of loathing. He grabbed my arm.

'A whore, that's what she was,' he hissed, his voice laced with disgust. He threw his cigarette down, grinding it into the ground, crushing it under his foot. 'A German whore.'

And he spat in my face. His face flamed; his eyes darkened the same way my mother's used to when she was in one of her rages. The air was sucked from the room.

'Frank, your mother? Your real mother? Who was she?'

'God, can't you figure that out?' He spat the words. *German.*

'Then... that would mean you're my half-brother. And Anthony, he's your half-brother too.' Then another realisation hit me like a towering wave in a tsunami: 'The blackmail letter. You knew so much about us. It was you.'

He just laughed. My stomach churned. I was going to vomit.

'Your brother will hang. You will watch him hang and suffer.'

Doolin pushed me aside and walked out the door. Numb from his words, I willed myself to go after him, to make him change his mind. If he was anything like his mother – *our* mother – he had no empathy, but I had to try. I had to get to Anthony.

40

In the midst of chaos, my feet took me up the steps of the hospital and through the blurred whirl of trolleys and orderlies. I was barely aware of my surroundings.

Markus stood in his doorway, his tall frame casting a shadow that stretched across the floor. His sandy hair was dishevelled and his stormy blue eyes were clouded with an intensity that sent a shiver down my spine.

'Kitty,' he rasped out, his face a hollow canvas of loss, 'my Henrietta is gone. I am but a shell now.' He sat down on his bed.

I rushed to his side. This was the bad news Sam had meant.

'How? What happened?'

'A bomb in Munich. She's dead.'

'It might be a ruse, Markus. Perhaps the Germans found out about your assistance and are spreading lies to wound you.'

He gently took my hand and placed it over his heart.

'My heart beats differently, Kitty. I can sense her absence. She awaits me.'

Before I could say more, his fingers slowly unfurled to reveal a small white tablet. He swallowed it before I could react.

'Markus, no!' I screamed, but it was too late.

His words were already beginning to slur as he said, 'Kitty, thank you.' I watched, helpless, as his breathing slowed and he surrendered to a long-awaited sleep.

I cried, choked with grief. I shook him, my heart sinking as the reality of his decision became starkly apparent. His death was almost peaceful, a startling contrast to the chaos raging within me. He was gone.

The room was eerily quiet, save for my ragged breathing. I adjusted the blanket over Markus, my fingers lingering over his already cooling skin. I turned the photo of his beloved Henrietta to face him, hoping that in his eternal sleep he would find some solace.

Torn between grief and the urgency of Anthony's impending fate, I took the RAF uniform meant for Markus and I left the room. I had to get to Anthony before Doolin did. My plan seemed absurd, but it was the only shred of hope I had.

I sprinted down the hospital corridor and burst through the front doors, my mind whirling. Grief, fear and determination tangled within me. As I peered around the corner, I saw the soldier on guard look at his watch, yawn and stretch his neck. He looked up and down the corridor, then took out a cigarette and lit it as he walked up the corridor. I hastily slipped into Anthony's room, nudging the door open to make as little noise as possible.

'Anthony! Get up now.'

He stirred, woken from sleep, grumbling something inaudible. 'What are you doing here, Kitty?' he mumbled, rubbing his eyes as he sat up.

'There's no time to explain. Just trust me. Put this on.' I tossed him the RAF uniform. 'No questions, Anthony. We need to leave. Now. Can you walk?'

His eyes widened slightly, but he nodded, quickly shedding his hospital gown and pulling on the uniform. As he dressed, I turned away, pressing my ear against the cool wood of the door, listening for approaching footsteps.

Once Anthony had fully dressed, I slowly opened the door, peering into the dim hallway, and motioned for him to follow me. He winced as he put weight on his leg. We stepped into the hallway and moved slowly, ensuring each step was as quiet as the previous one. Our shoes padded softly on the carpeted floor as we made our way towards the exit.

Outside, I could hear the faint murmur of voices and muffled laughter – the soldier and the nurses. Anthony gripped my arm tightly, his fingers cold against my skin.

'Ready?' I asked in a whisper. He gave me a curt nod.

And then we were out, stepping into the night, the hospital fading behind us as we hurried into the shadowy embrace of the camp. I realised I had no idea where the RAF men were leaving from.

The often boisterous camp was shrouded in an eerie calm. Only the faint bleating of the sheep dotting the distant plains of the Curragh punctuated the silence. Night had come abruptly, pulling a velvet blanket of darkness over the day, thickening the air with an impending storm's humidity and a palpable sense of unrest. Maybe it was the imminent departure of the RAF men, or perhaps it was something more.

In the obscurity, my senses were ignited, heightened. The rush of adrenaline coursing through my veins took me back to the daring games of hide and seek we played as children, my heart beating in sync with the relentless ticking of the clock, my breaths shallow and hurried. I forced myself to close my eyes and count to ten, willing my lungs to draw in the night air slowly and deliberately.

The outline of the barracks was just visible under the starless sky. It seemed deserted, save for the occasional rustle of a bush or the muted hoot of an owl. Silently, we weaved our way towards the British camp, Anthony's hand tightly clutching mine, a nostalgic echo of our shared childhood when we'd seek refuge from our mother's gaze. The looming guard tower appeared deserted.

A dog, its coat a dull grey in the scarce moonlight, lay curled beside the first barracks. Its ears twitched as our footsteps neared and its head popped up, nostrils flaring. I froze in my tracks, locking eyes with it. A faint wag of its tail eased my racing heart, and I gestured for Anthony to hold back. The guard, evidently disturbed by our presence, emerged to flick his half-smoked cigarette onto the gravel, the ember briefly illuminating his surly face. A growl from the dog was met with a contemptuous spit, before the guard retreated into the sanctuary of the watchtower.

I quickly turned to Anthony and gasped at his bare feet. 'You're shoeless, Anthony!'

He looked down in mild surprise. 'But you said…'

'Never mind,' I interrupted, waves of frustration washing over me.

As we stealthily crept past the dog, it raised its head to sniff Anthony. Seemingly satisfied, it settled back on its paws, its watchful eyes tracking our retreat from the compound. My hand tightened around Anthony's as I paused to regain my composure.

'What I am about to tell you might not make sense, but we have no time. Markus is gone, and this RAF uniform you're wearing was meant for him. Doolin plans to hang you.'

His hand jerked in surprise. 'How did he...'

'There's no time for explanations. We have to get out of here. I can't lose you too. My heart won't bear any more loss.'

'Kitty, you're crying,' he said, his voice strained. 'I can't leave you behind. You stayed for me. You'll be in deep trouble if they discover I'm gone.'

I brushed my tears away with the back of my hand, my vision blurred. 'And it would be worse if they hanged you. Once this war is over, I'll make my way to London. But for now, you need to leave.'

He stood rooted to the spot.

'Anthony,' I said more urgently, gripping his hand. 'Markus was meant to escape with the RAF. He was a double agent. Now you have to take his place.'

I opened his hand and pushed in a small bundle of banknotes. 'You're going to need this.'

Out of the corner of my eye, I spotted Sam sprinting towards the hospital. Instantly, I pushed Anthony into the shadows. 'Keep low and out of sight,' I warned him.

Without waiting for a response, I took off after Sam, my

breath coming out in gasps, lungs burning with the strain. I managed to reach him at the hospital steps.

'Sam,' I began, my thoughts racing as fast as my words. 'I was with Markus. He was very upset and I managed to calm him. You should let him rest.'

Ignoring me, he started up the steps, just as a gust of wind howled around us. 'Seems like a storm's brewing,' he commented, looking up at the black clouds.

A sharp scent of smoke wafted through the air, growing denser with each passing moment. Suddenly, a monstrous flame erupted from one of the camps. The shrill wails of sirens filled the air as fire engines rushed past us. Was this a German attack?

'Sam, go. I'll get Markus,' I offered.

Sam remained motionless, his gaze fixed on the billowing smoke swallowing the camp, a dark and ominous fog rising from its heart. A nauseating, acrid stench permeated the air and I covered my mouth and nose with my cardigan.

'Go, Sam.'

He finally tore his gaze away from the fire and nodded. He turned to race towards the chaos, gunshots punctuating his departure.

'Wait! Where should we meet?' I yelled over the din.

Sam spun around, shouting back, 'At the British camp gate! The guard's been informed!'

As soon as Sam was out of sight, I rushed back to Anthony. The dog's frenzied barking added to the escalating chaos.

'What's going on?' Anthony shouted.

'I'm not certain, but we need to reach the British camp gate. The RAF are departing from there.'

We crawled silently through the darkness, frantic soldiers

racing past us. As we drew nearer to the gate, Doolin came into view, lips compressed into a thin line. Sam was beside him.

Doolin barked at Sam: 'The lads in Tin Town are staging an escape! Get Markus to the lorry, it's ready. The Brits will be leaving shortly.'

An enormous new explosion ripped through the night, casting monstrous fire skyward. Fierce orange and black flames spewed out from Tin Town's huts, the smoke swelling into the night, engulfed by the clouds. The flames flickered ominously against the camp buildings while a cacophony of engine roars, panicked voices and frenzied barking filled the night.

Doolin sprinted towards the chaos. As soldiers rushed past us, a gust of wind fanned the flames, spreading the fire like butter on hot toast. IRA men charged through the camp, striking the guards with broken planks and iron rods. Firefighters struggled to unroll their hoses, battling to pump water. In the melee, one of the Tin Town lads struck a fireman with a plank, and he swiftly retaliated. Their shouting was lost amidst the noise.

As the fire spread uncontrollably, the wooden huts surrendered to the flames without resistance, spurred on by a gusty southern wind. Suddenly, a hailstorm of bullets filled the air overhead.

Choking smoke stung my eyes, tears streaking down my face. Tin Town was ablaze. Guards atop watchtowers began shooting into the camp. Those within Tin Town were frantically clearing any huts not yet burning, tossing clothes, books, shoes into the growing inferno. The smoke, as black as a spectral shroud, sent a chill down my spine.

Rain started to fall, its droplets merging with the mud on our shoes, our arms, our hands.

'Just follow me,' I told Anthony. 'Stay close, head down.'

Men, hundreds of them, darted around, dodging bullets. Soldiers barked orders at men fleeing from Tin Town. Bullets whizzed past, barely missing my head. Pressing ourselves against a wall, Anthony and I melted into the shadows as four soldiers marched past us, rifles trained towards the fire. Their uniforms were hastily buttoned, their boots untied. Their eyes were wide with fear and anxiety.

Anthony squeezed my hand and whispered, 'We need to go, Kitty. They're as scared as we are. Who knows what the IRA lads will do?'

With our hearts pounding, we hesitated. Could we risk it?

A sudden easterly wind cleared our view towards the British camp. A lorry was stationed by the gate, its back filled with soldiers.

'Hurry, Anthony! The Brits are boarding the lorry. We must get there now!' I urged him.

Dodging between the racing soldiers, we ran as a fire engine tore past us, its siren wailing. The camp was a blur in the smoke and rain. Orders were shouted, bullets ricocheted, and screams filled the air. Amidst the chaos, I heard Doolin's distinctive voice.

Miraculously, we found ourselves at the British camp. The lorry driver had hopped out to secure something on the side. I could see six or seven men in the back, all in British uniforms.

'Quick, it's still there!' I said, but placed a hand on Anthony's sleeve instead of urging him on. 'Can I ask you something? Did Markus mean something to you?'

He blanched, shook his head and avoided my gaze. He squeezed my hands and said, 'No, Kitty. It was never Markus.'

The lorry revved. 'We have to run, Anthony!'

The lorry was starting to move when Captain Mayhew spotted us. He squinted at Anthony, whose RAF jacket was flapping in the wind as he ran, then banged on the lorry to stop. He extended his hand for Anthony to grasp. As he tried to pull himself up, his hand slipped and he tumbled onto the gravel. I ran to him, screaming for him to get up, and he rose, blood streaming from his lip. Mayhew reached out his hand again. This time, Anthony managed to grip it firmly and was hoisted onto the lorry. But before Anthony could get his legs aboard, Sam appeared from nowhere, lunged for his ankle and yanked him back.

For what seemed like an eternity, Sam and Anthony stood face to face. I tried to speak, but the acrid smoke left my mouth dry and speechless.

In a break of the clouds, the moonlight fell on their tear-streaked faces, their eyes locked in a wordless conversation. They shared a brief hug before Sam pushed him away and shoved him back onto the lorry. As Doolin's voice echoed in the distance, Sam banged on the lorry, signalling it to depart. I watched in stunned silence as it disappeared from the camp.

Turning, I met Sam's gaze. He wiped his cheeks and softly said, 'Kitty, he'll be safe now. Don't worry.'

I glanced at my trembling hands then back at Sam's brown eyes, seeing a lie finally laid bare, like an open wound.

★

I busied myself packing my possessions.

The echo of footsteps on the floorboards reverberated through the room, but I knew they were not Doolin's. It's curious how one becomes an expert in distinguishing subtle differences in gait.

I glanced at Sam, noting his soft, melancholy brown eyes, mourning a reality that could never materialise. I found myself reminiscing about the summer Anthony and Sam had pledged their undying friendship, symbolised in a blood pact.

'I knew he was battling his inner demons when he travelled to Spain,' Sam admitted, his countenance softening. In his features, I recognised my childhood companion. He cast a sideways look in my direction, his eyes narrowing against the bright shards of sunlight illuminating his face. After a moment's pause, he enveloped me in a gentle hug.

'Kitty, I never intended to hurt you. I suspected something amiss when Doolin mentioned your volunteering. It was merely coincidence that we discovered Markus at your house.'

He clasped my hands in his and pulled me into a hug.

Abruptly, the door was wrenched open. Doolin loomed in the doorway, his eyes narrowing suspiciously. 'Quite cosy, aren't we?' he snarled.

His suspicions were aroused, but he was unable to pinpoint the cause. His face was a ghastly pallor that brought out the permanent blemishes. I was repulsed by the knowledge of our kinship; perhaps, one day, I would reveal it to Anthony.

My anger towards him for his attempted execution of my brother was strangely absent. When I threatened to expose him to Colonel MacNally, he spat in my face, seething at his failure to prevent Anthony's escape.

'Just get the fuck out of here,' he growled.

As I prepared to depart, Sam took my hand, slipping something into it.

'Take this. It's enough to help you start afresh.'

In my hand lay £20.

41

I'd walked into this small world of Alice's with my brown suitcase, and seven months later I was still here. Often, we forget that home is not just a mark on a map, any more than a river is just a river: it's the centre of the compass, and where we let that arrow direct us is within our control.

The doorbell rang, and Peter looked up. He had been jittery ever since Sam and Doolin searched the house. I still couldn't believe I had never suspected that Anthony and Sam were anything more than friends.

'Kitty, there's someone here for you.' Alice's voice was light.

I looked up from my book.

Father Fitzpatrick stepped into the garden, and with him Sister Assumpta. I stood up, as we had been taught to at St Margaret's when a nun entered the room. She wore the same black habit with a rope as a belt, the ends dangling at her knees, but her headdress was slightly different, not as wide, fitting more neatly on her head. Her smile was the same, kind and soft. Her eyes wrinkled and gleamed when she saw me.

'Kitty, how are you?' Father Fitzpatrick took my hand and held it tight, not letting me pull away, then he embraced me. 'I am so sorry I didn't help you and Anthony. But Claire – Sister Assumpta – has something to tell you, and someone for you.'

She was standing there with a child in her arms.

I stopped breathing. Everything around me stopped: the birds stopped singing, Alice's lips were moving, but I couldn't hear anything. Sister Assumpta moved towards me and lifted the baby's white bonnet up from her face. She had a blue ribbon in her strawberry-blonde hair.

'Look! It's your mammy,' Sister Assumpta said.

'How?' I whispered, my eyes on the child.

'She didn't die. The nuns did this all the time, telling poor mothers their babies hadn't lived, and then sent the children away, sometimes as far as America. It made me sick, but I kept her away when prospective parents came. The home was evacuated shortly after you left. The babies were being sent away for emergency care. So I took Sophie.'

'Sophie,' I repeated, her name balancing delicately on my lips. She was called Sophie.

'I said I had someone to take her, and I arranged the paperwork.'

She stopped, her eyes watering. 'I didn't lie, because that someone was me. I was afraid of the home she might end up in. I wasn't immune to the horrible stories of where children ended up. The homes were not always nice. Your father, he was a good man and he'd meant so much to me at one time. I couldn't let his granddaughter go away with strangers who might be cruel to her.'

I held Sophie. Her warmth felt familiar, even though

this was my first time holding her. She smelled as fresh as washed cotton in a spring breeze. She moved from Sister Assumpta's arms into mine, fitting effortlessly into place. With one hand on her back, I stroked her hair with the other. Her warm soft breath tickled my neck.

Her heartbeat against my chest, synchronising with mine. I inhaled, the knot untwisting in my stomach. I felt whole, complete, the missing jigsaw piece found where I'd least expected it.

'I promise you won't regret this,' I vowed. 'She will have a good life, full of love. No matter what may come.'

Sister Assumpta smiled. 'I know she will. You have endured much hardship, but your resilience has not faltered. Trust in your heart, and you will find the way.'

I hugged my daughter again, whispering a prayer of thanks. With her in my arms, the future seemed bright with possibility. I would always protect this precious gift I had been given. My darling girl was home, and our life together was just beginning.

Alice stepped forward then, placing a hand on my shoulder.

'You and the little one are welcome to stay here as long as you need,' she said kindly. I nodded, gratitude welling up in me for this woman who had become like the mother I'd never really had. I gazed down at my daughter, her little fingers playing with the buttons on my dress. She was a miracle, my precious girl, and I would move heaven and earth to give her the childhood I never had. No more running or hiding. The time had come to heal, to put broken pieces back together.

I met Alice's eyes again and smiled through my tears.

'We will make it work, the three of us. I'll find a way to provide for her. She will have everything I did not. This I vow to you both.'

The future was uncertain, but we would face it as a family. My daughter gave me the strength to hope again. And our lives would be filled with joy.

I held my daughter close as we all sat in the garden for a while. The late afternoon sun cast a warm glow over her cherubic face. She babbled happily, oblivious to the tumultuous events that had led to this quiet moment.

Looking into her clear blue eyes, I saw endless possibilities stretched out before us. We would make this a home filled with laughter and light. No more darkness or fear – those days were behind me. I would give her everything she needed to thrive.

My voice was thick with emotion as I said, 'You will grow up strong and clever, my darling. I'll teach you to cook and sew, to tend the earth and care for animals. We'll read books curled up by the fire, and I'll tell you stories of your grandfather.'

I kissed her downy head, breathing in that sweet baby scent.

The road ahead would not be easy, but we had each other. My daughter gave me purpose. She was the light guiding me through the shadows into a hopeful future.

I turned to Alice, overcome with gratitude. She had taken me in when I was lost, given me shelter and friendship without judgement. Now she was offering me a lifeline so I could raise my child in safety and peace.

'Thank you,' I said, my voice cracking. 'For everything you've done for us. I don't deserve such kindness.'

Alice enveloped me in a warm embrace. 'Of course you do,' she said firmly. 'Everyone deserves a second chance, and I'll not have you hiding away in shame.'

I looked at Father Fitzpatrick and Sister Assumpta. She had protected my daughter against all odds, and he had guided me with wisdom and compassion through my darkest hours.

'I don't know how to repay you both for this gift,' I said.

Father Fitzpatrick smiled gently. 'Seeing you reunited with your wee one is payment enough. Make a good life for her.'

I turned my face up to the sun, feeling its golden rays wash over me. The future was uncertain, but I had been given the chance to walk a different path. My daughter cooed in my arms, and my heart overflowed. We would face whatever came together.

The longest journey can be the journey inwards. I finally felt complete, my mother's shackles gone. I didn't need to be in London to find peace. It didn't matter where I was; it was within myself that I needed to find acceptance and move on.

Poor Anthony – secrets can shame us, close us off, and often what we bury drags us down, stopping us from flying. I closed my eyes with Sophie lying on my chest, and hoped Anthony could find his own missing piece of the jigsaw.

I took a deep breath, the ball of air in my stomach gone, the hole filled in. Alice smiled, put her hand on mine, and handed me her wedding band.

'What is this?' I turned the glinting gold band around.

'You're like a daughter to me. James treated you as one of his own, and he would want this. And Peter is so happy with you. A war is on. We can say your husband died in the war, that your child had been staying with her grandparents.'

Looking at my daughter as she playfully blew raspberry kisses at me, I found myself contemplating: if my mother hadn't forced me to flee, if Doolin hadn't pursued Anthony and me with such venom, would I be here, cradling this bundle of love in my arms? Glancing at Alice, I gave a solemn nod.

It's strange, isn't it? Sometimes, we have to tread treacherous paths only to find ourselves completing a fulfilling circle in the end.

After dinner, with Sophie in my arms, I went back in to the garden and looked up at the night sky, glittering with stars. People say a new star is born when someone dies. Was my father there, and James, and Markus?

If we remain in the past, we become prisoners, burdened by mistakes and regrets, often bound by anger or remorse. If we are bound to the future and worry about things that have yet to pass, we can become anxious that we might fail.

Time constellates itself in three parts. The past, the present and the future.

The only time we have is now.

I looked into Sophie's blue eyes; I'd never felt anything like this before. I saw my reflection, and the reflection of my emotions, my fears, my hopes and dreams for my daughter. I saw love.

Acknowledgements

Kitty's War is a novel that intertwines fiction with historical fact and delves into the unique circumstances of the two hundred and sixty Germans interned at the Curragh in County Kildare during the Second World War. Their well-treatment, atypical of internment camps in Europe, offers a compelling contrast.

I am deeply thankful to the Irish Arts Council and Kilkenny Arts Office for their crucial financial support. This backing was essential for my extensive research for the novel.

And to the Cathal Brugha Military Archives in Dublin, where I read many G2 Military Intelligence documents. One such paper suggested that German complaints about Irish food were secret messages to the Abwehr!

I extend my sincere gratitude to Words Ireland for their mentorship with Henrietta McKervey. Also, thanks to Michael Rowley for sharing his extensive knowledge of the German internees and the camp tour, and to James Durney, historical consultant, for his invaluable historical resources.

Thanks also to Kevin Murphy at Kildare Local Studies in Kildare County Library and Kilkenny County Library, who I am sure raised an eyebrow over the numerous books I borrowed on the rise of the Nazis.

And to acknowledge all the women who were forced into mother and baby homes, and their harsh, unforgiving treatment. Yet, in all the darkness of the mother and baby home era, I found one story of a midwife nurse, Julia Goulding, who selflessly tried to help the girls.

A special mention to John, whose steadfast support and patience were vital during my writing process and research trips – including to the Curragh and the Military Archives in Dublin, and even to Belfast to see where the city had been blitzed in 1941 and where we managed to take in a Coronas concert.

About the Author

EIMEAR LAWLOR was born in County Cavan and now lives in the medieval city of Kilkenny with her husband John and two sons. She met John in London while she was studying for a BSc. Unfortunately, her middle child, Ciara, who was the inspiration for her writing career, passed away in 2016. Eimear had worked as a teacher for a few years and became a stay-at-home mum after the birth of Ciara when Eimear was diagnosed with Multiple Sclerosis. When Ciara was twelve, she told Eimear to do something with her life other than drinking coffee with her friends. She did the NUI Maynooth Creative Writing course in 2014. Her writing has been on the *Ryan Tubridy Show*, and the *Ray D'Arcy Show* on RTÉ Radio 1 and her short stories have been published in two anthologies.